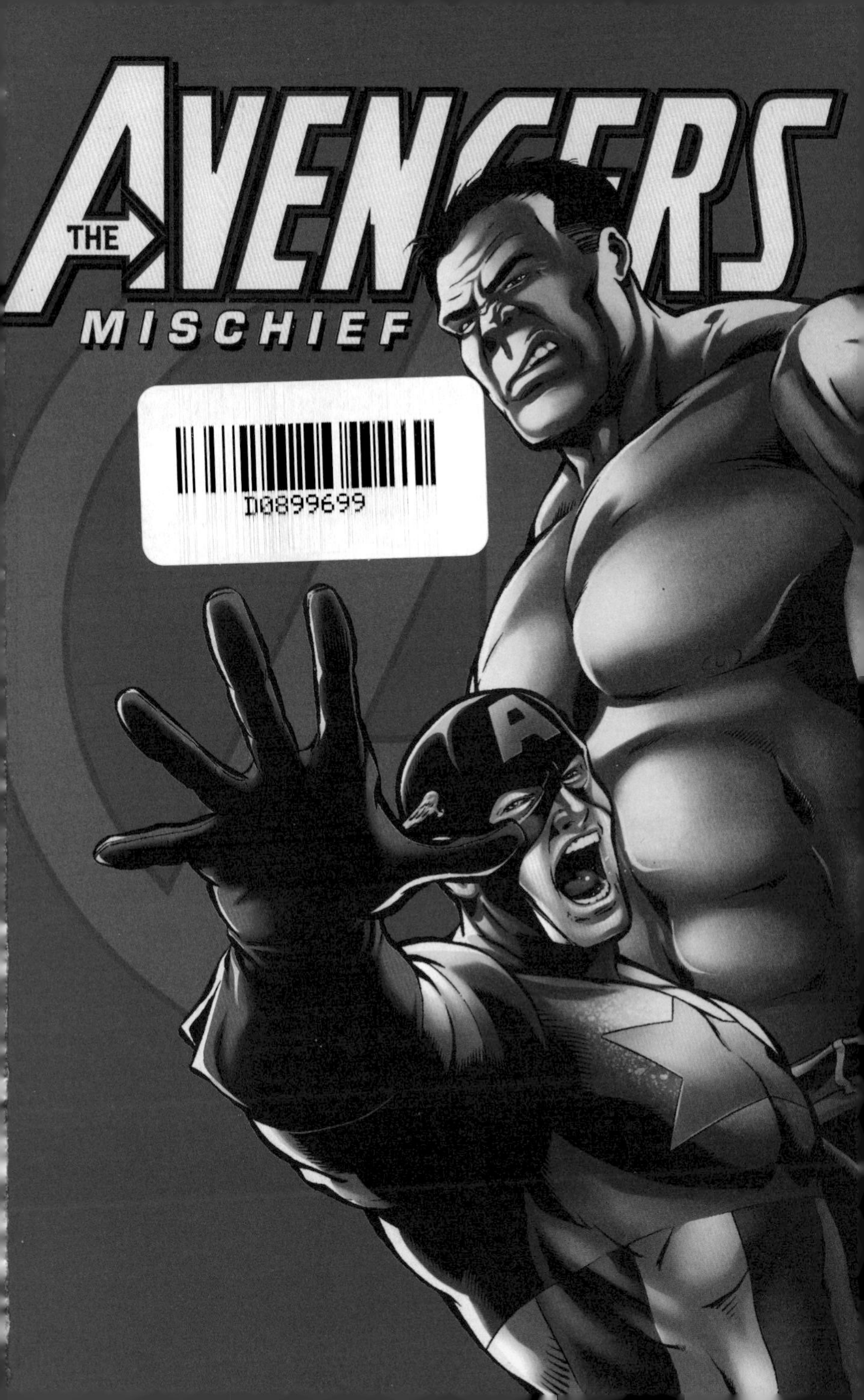
THE AVENGERS
MISCHIEF

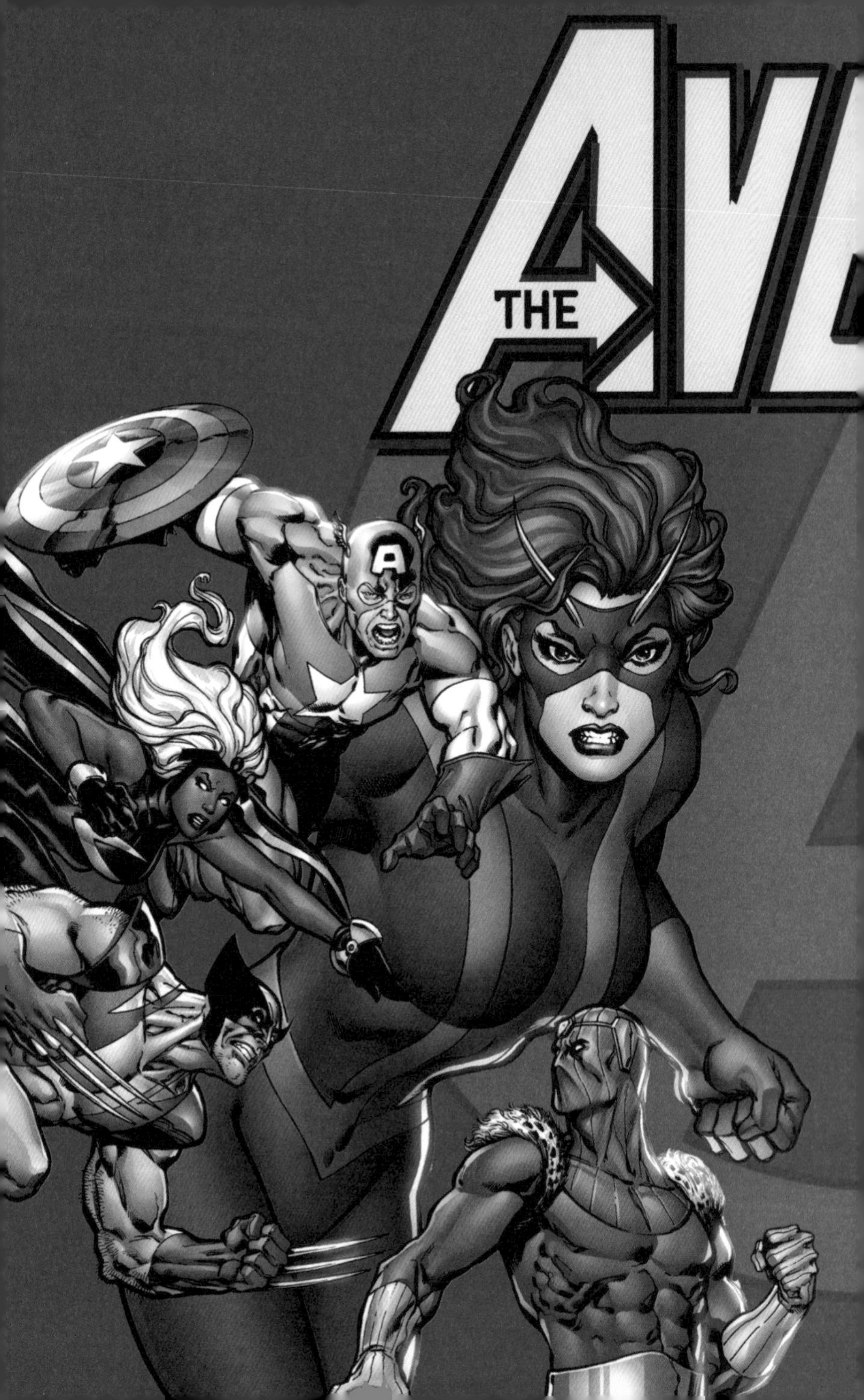
THE AV

ENGERS

MISCHIEF

Writer: Tony Bedard
Pencils: Shannon Gallant

Inks: **John Stanisci, Cory Hamscher & Norman Lee**
Colors: **Gotham Studios & Impacto Studio's Adriano Lucas**
Letters: **Dave Sharpe**
Cover Art: **Sean Chen, Sandu Florea & Guru eFx**
Assistant Editor: **Nathan Cosby**
Editor: **Mark Paniccia**

Captain America created by **Joe Simon & Jack Kirby**

Collection Editor: **Jennifer Grünwald**
Assistant Editor: **Michael Short**
Associate Editor: **Mark D. Beazley**
Senior Editor, Special Projects: **Jeff Youngquist**
Senior Vice President of Sales: **David Gabriel**
Production: **Jerron Quality Color**
Vice President of Creative: **Tom Marvelli**

Editor in Chief: **Joe Quesada**
Publisher: **Dan Buckley**

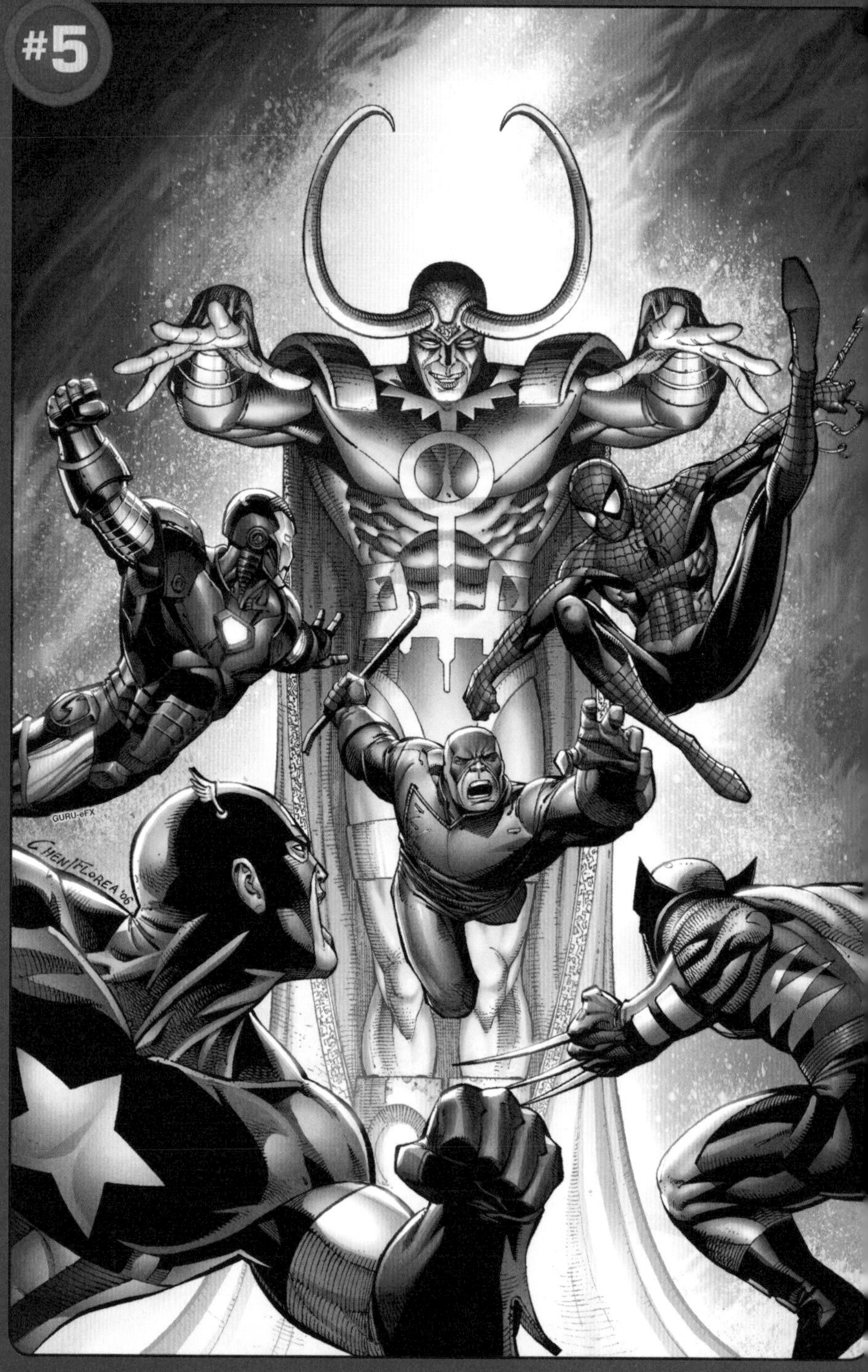
#5
GURU-eFX
CHEN/FLOREA '06

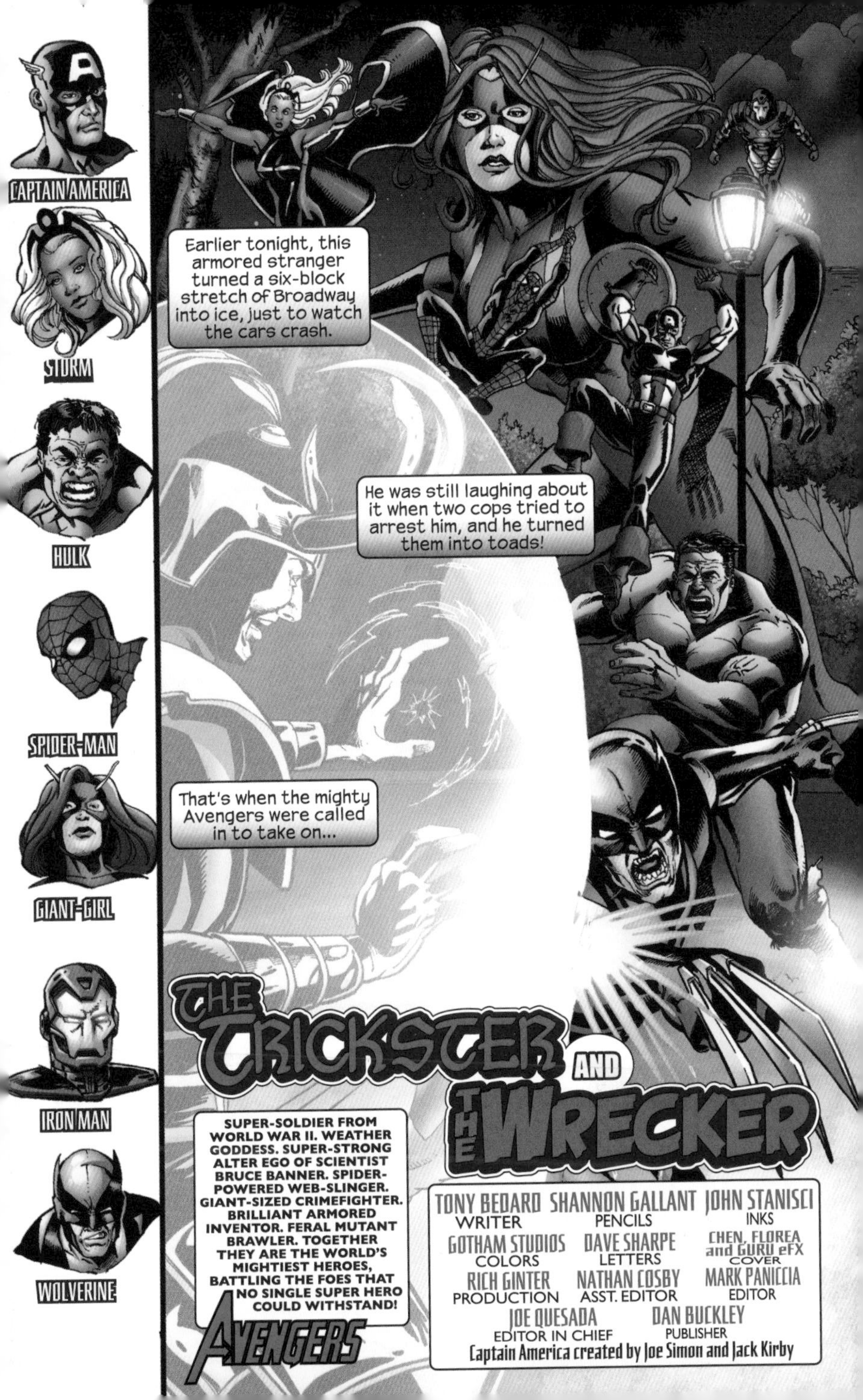

CAPTAIN AMERICA
STORM
HULK
SPIDER-MAN
GIANT-GIRL
IRON MAN
WOLVERINE
Earlier tonight, this armored stranger turned a six-block stretch of Broadway into ice, just to watch the cars crash.
He was still laughing about it when two cops tried to arrest him, and he turned them into toads!
That's when the mighty Avengers were called in to take on...
THE TRICKSTER AND THE WRECKER
SUPER-SOLDIER FROM WORLD WAR II. WEATHER GODDESS. SUPER-STRONG ALTER EGO OF SCIENTIST BRUCE BANNER. SPIDER-POWERED WEB-SLINGER. GIANT-SIZED CRIMEFIGHTER. BRILLIANT ARMORED INVENTOR. FERAL MUTANT BRAWLER. TOGETHER THEY ARE THE WORLD'S MIGHTIEST HEROES, BATTLING THE FOES THAT NO SINGLE SUPER HERO COULD WITHSTAND!
AVENGERS
TONY BEDARD WRITER
SHANNON GALLANT PENCILS
JOHN STANISCI INKS
GOTHAM STUDIOS COLORS
DAVE SHARPE LETTERS
CHEN, FLOREA and GURU eFX COVER
RICH GINTER PRODUCTION
NATHAN COSBY ASST. EDITOR
MARK PANICCIA EDITOR
JOE QUESADA EDITOR IN CHIEF
DAN BUCKLEY PUBLISHER
Captain America created by Joe Simon and Jack Kirby

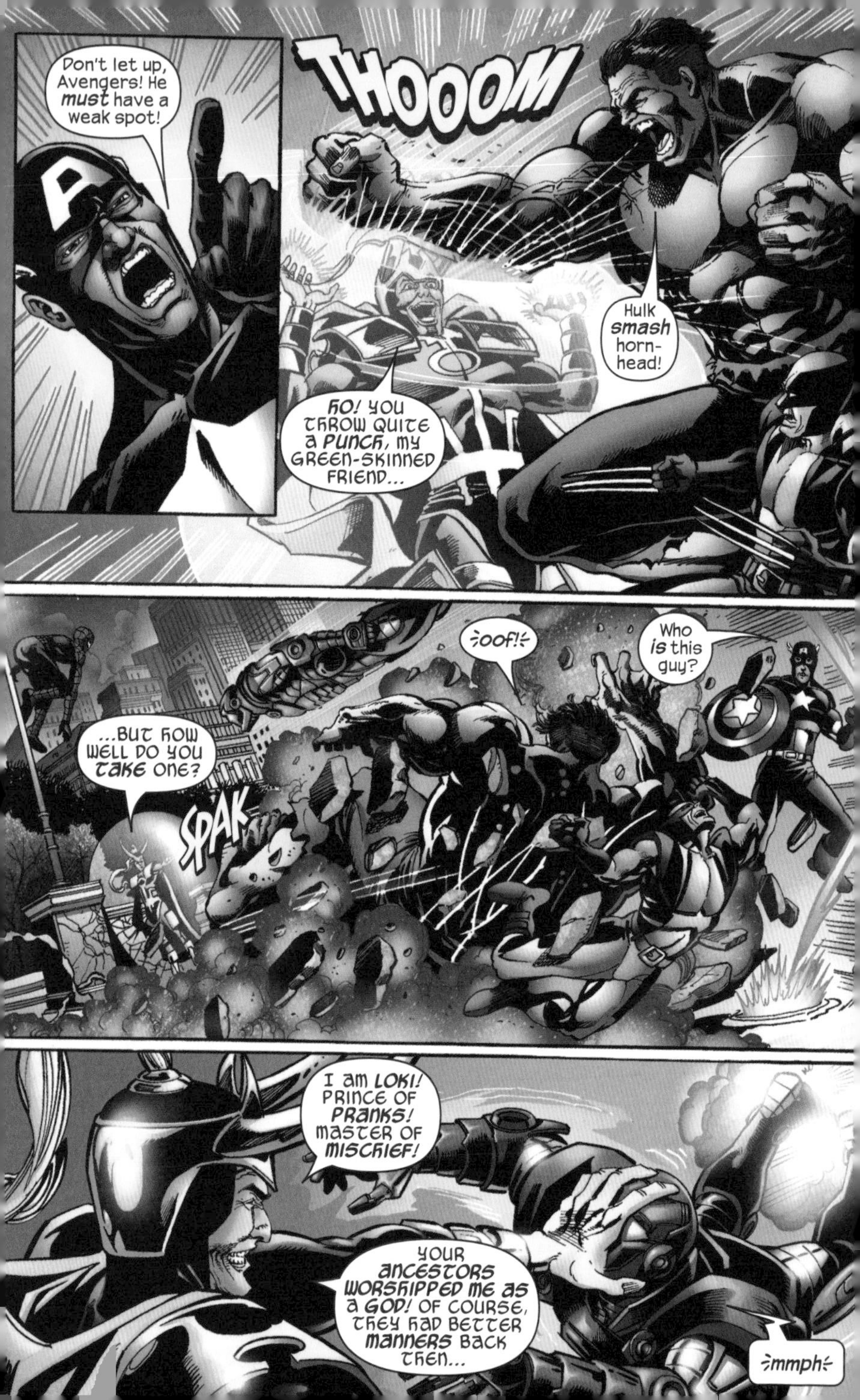
Don't let up, Avengers! He must have a weak spot!
THOOOM
Hulk smash horn-head!
HO! YOU THROW QUITE A PUNCH, MY GREEN-SKINNED FRIEND...
...BUT HOW WELL DO YOU TAKE ONE?
SPAK
oof!
Who is this guy?
I AM LOKI! PRINCE OF PRANKS! MASTER OF MISCHIEF!
YOUR ANCESTORS WORSHIPPED ME AS A GOD! OF COURSE, THEY HAD BETTER MANNERS BACK THEN...
mmph

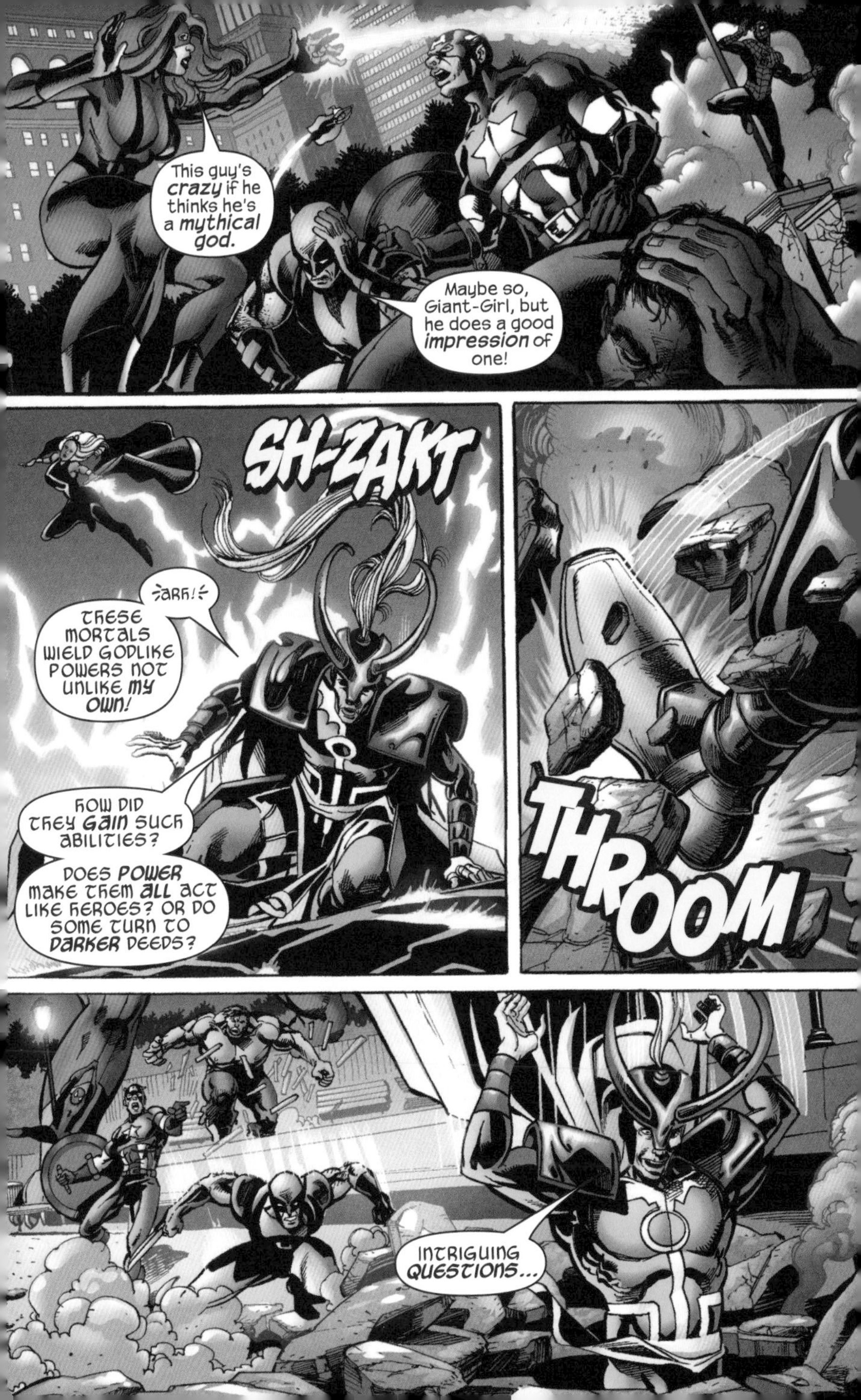
This guy's crazy if he thinks he's a mythical god.
Maybe so, Giant-Girl, but he does a good impression of one!
SH-ZAKT
ARH!
THESE MORTALS WIELD GODLIKE POWERS NOT UNLIKE MY OWN!
HOW DID THEY GAIN SUCH ABILITIES?
DOES POWER MAKE THEM ALL ACT LIKE HEROES? OR DO SOME TURN TO DARKER DEEDS?
THROOM
INTRIGUING QUESTIONS...

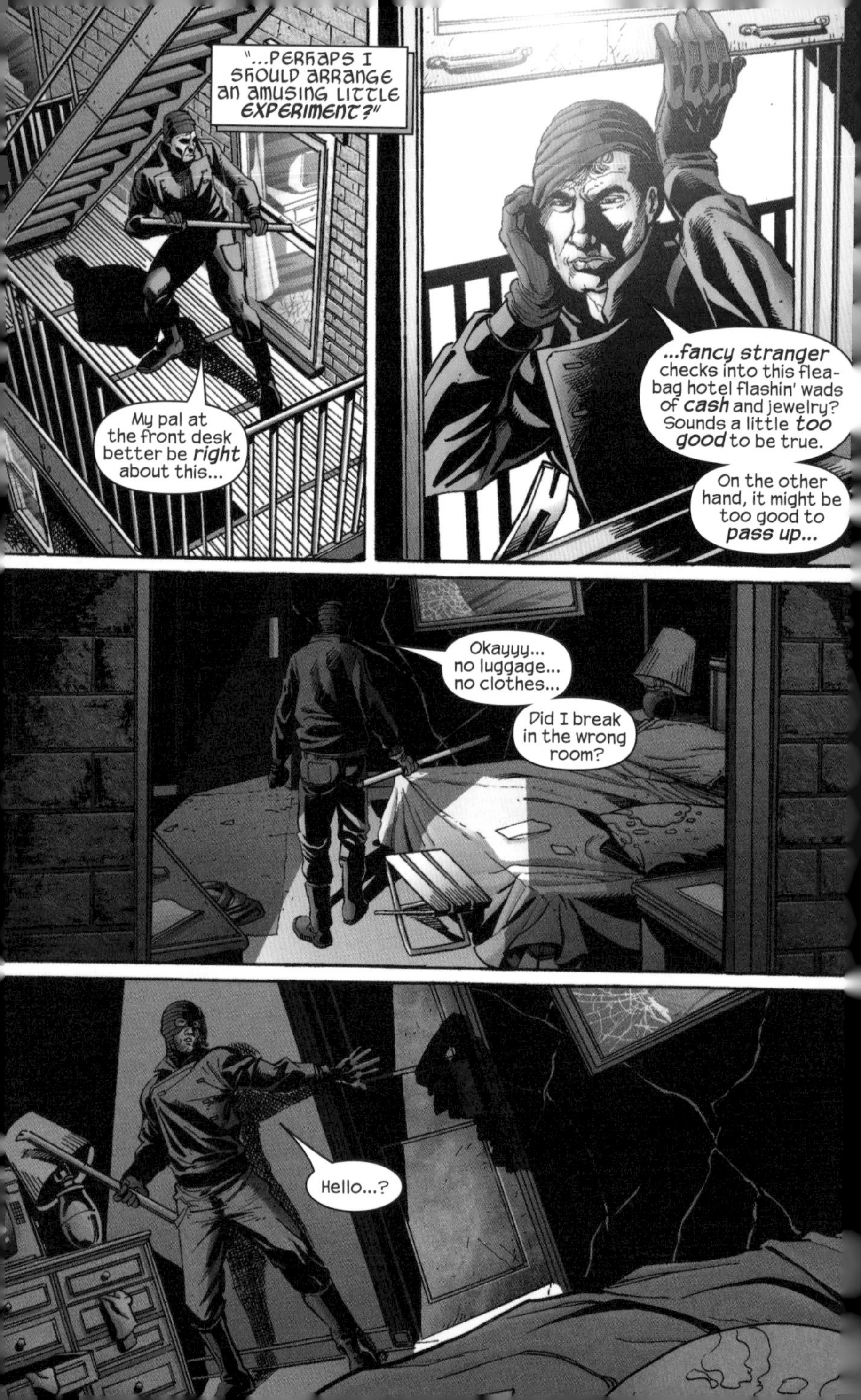
"...PERHAPS I SHOULD ARRANGE AN AMUSING LITTLE EXPERIMENT?"
My pal at the front desk better be right about this...
...fancy stranger checks into this flea-bag hotel flashin' wads of cash and jewelry? Sounds a little too good to be true.
On the other hand, it might be too good to pass up...
Okayyy... no luggage... no clothes...
Did I break in the wrong room?
Hello...?

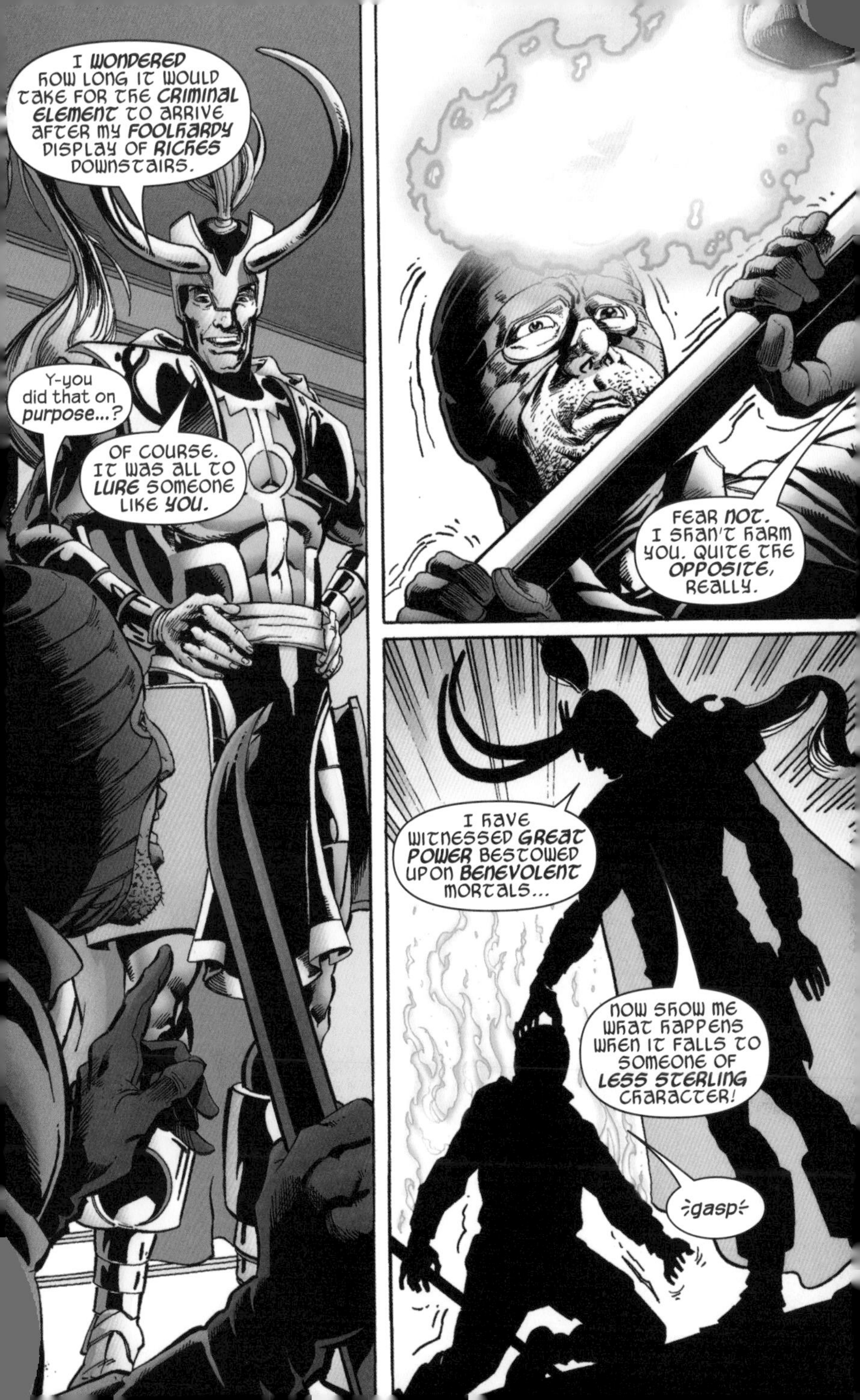

I WONDERED HOW LONG IT WOULD TAKE FOR THE CRIMINAL ELEMENT TO ARRIVE AFTER MY FOOLHARDY DISPLAY OF RICHES DOWNSTAIRS.
Y-you did that on purpose...?
OF COURSE. IT WAS ALL TO LURE SOMEONE LIKE YOU.
FEAR NOT. I SHAN'T HARM YOU. QUITE THE OPPOSITE, REALLY.
I HAVE WITNESSED GREAT POWER BESTOWED UPON BENEVOLENT MORTALS...
NOW SHOW ME WHAT HAPPENS WHEN IT FALLS TO SOMEONE OF LESS STERLING CHARACTER!
gasp

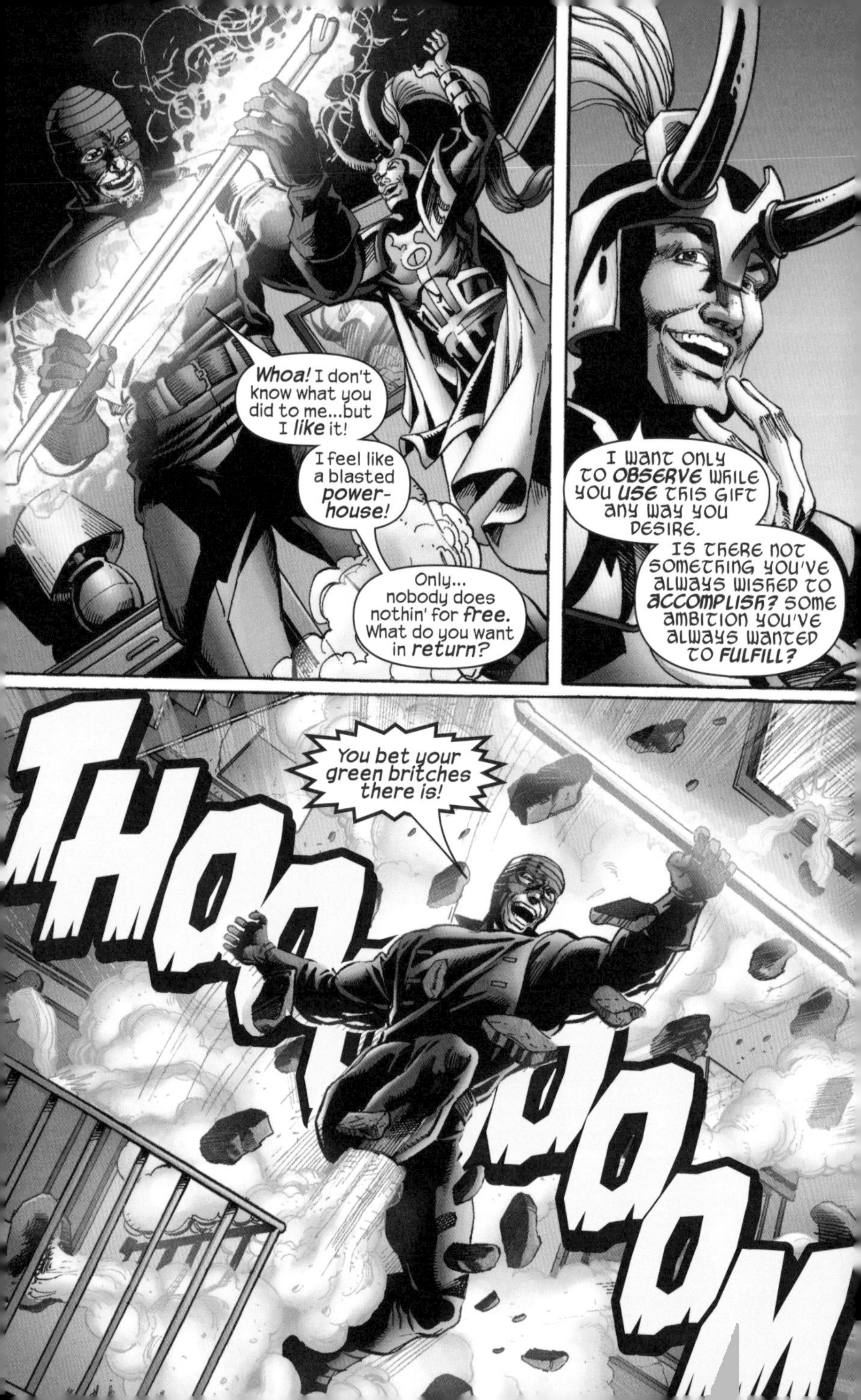
Whoa! I don't know what you did to me...but I like it!
I feel like a blasted power-house!
Only... nobody does nothin' for free. What do you want in return?
I want only to observe while you use this gift any way you desire.
Is there not something you've always wished to accomplish? Some ambition you've always wanted to fulfill?
You bet your green britches there is!
THOOOOOM

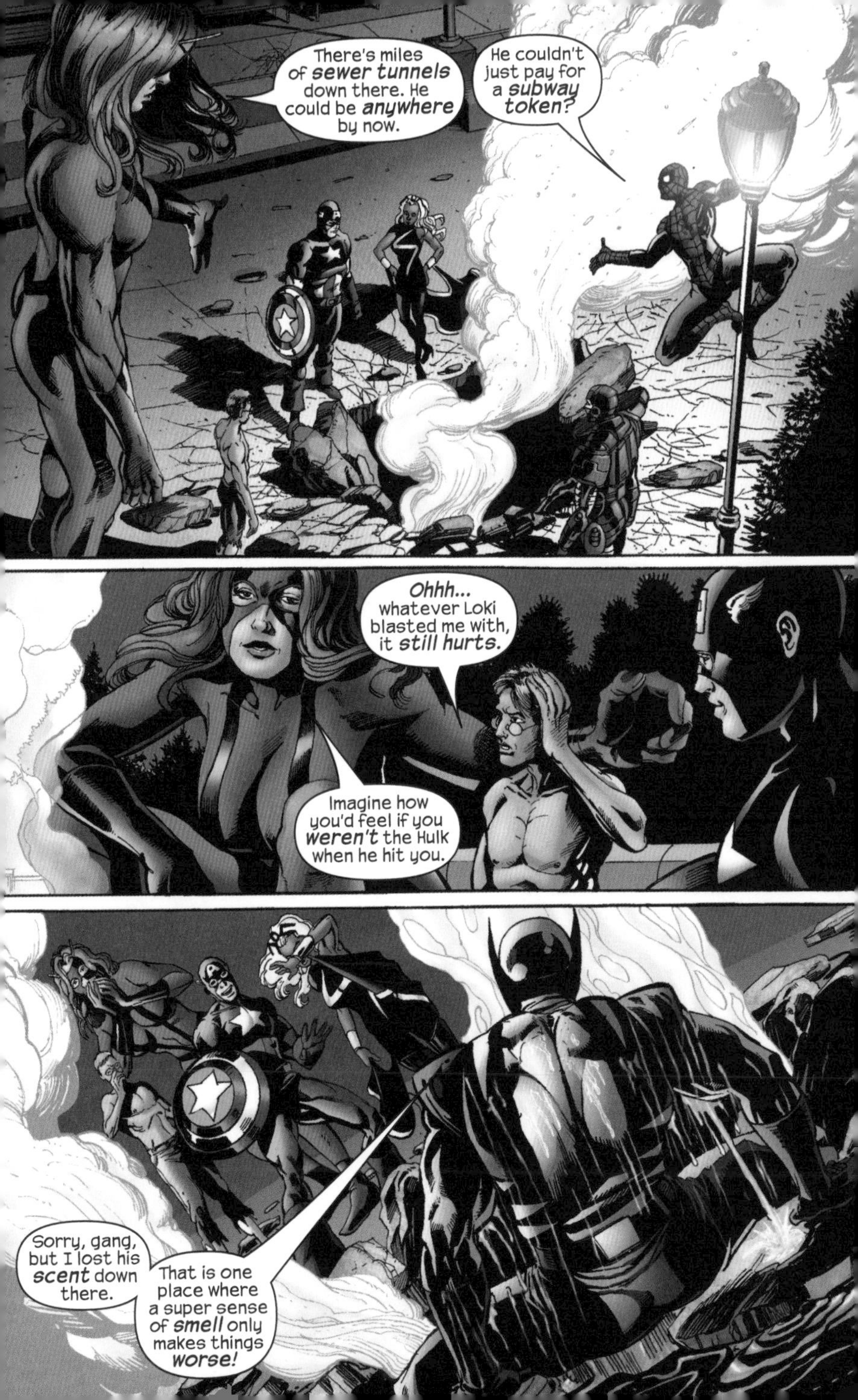
There's miles of sewer tunnels down there. He could be anywhere by now.
He couldn't just pay for a subway token?
Ohhh... whatever Loki blasted me with, it still hurts.
Imagine how you'd feel if you weren't the Hulk when he hit you.
Sorry, gang, but I lost his scent down there.
That is one place where a super sense of smell only makes things worse!

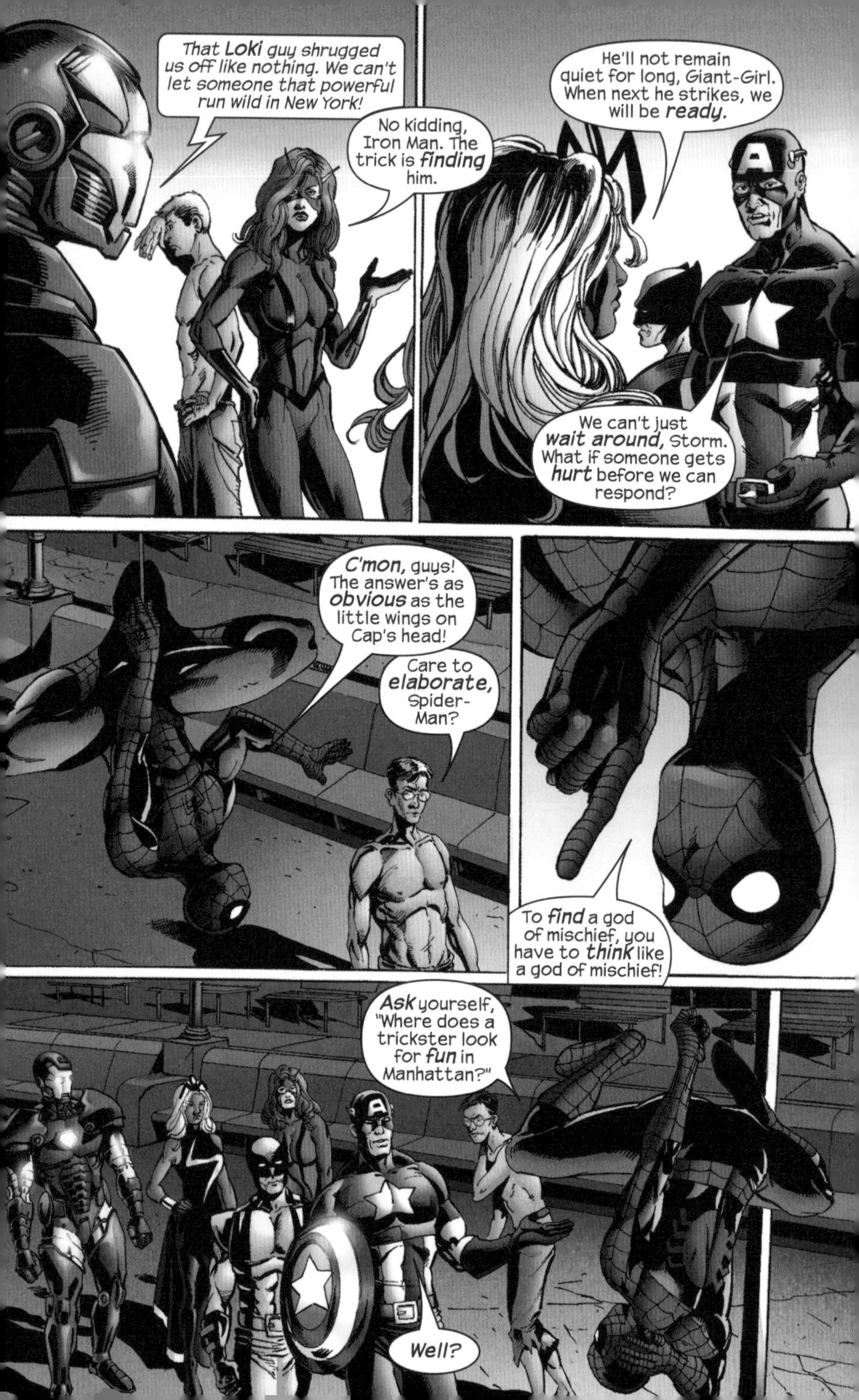
That LOKI guy shrugged us off like nothing. We can't let someone that powerful run wild in New York!
No kidding, Iron Man. The trick is finding him.
He'll not remain quiet for long, Giant-Girl. When next he strikes, we will be ready.
We can't just wait around, Storm. What if someone gets hurt before we can respond?
C'mon, guys! The answer's as obvious as the little wings on Cap's head!
Care to elaborate, Spider-Man?
To find a god of mischief, you have to think like a god of mischief!
Ask yourself, "Where does a trickster look for fun in Manhattan?"
Well?

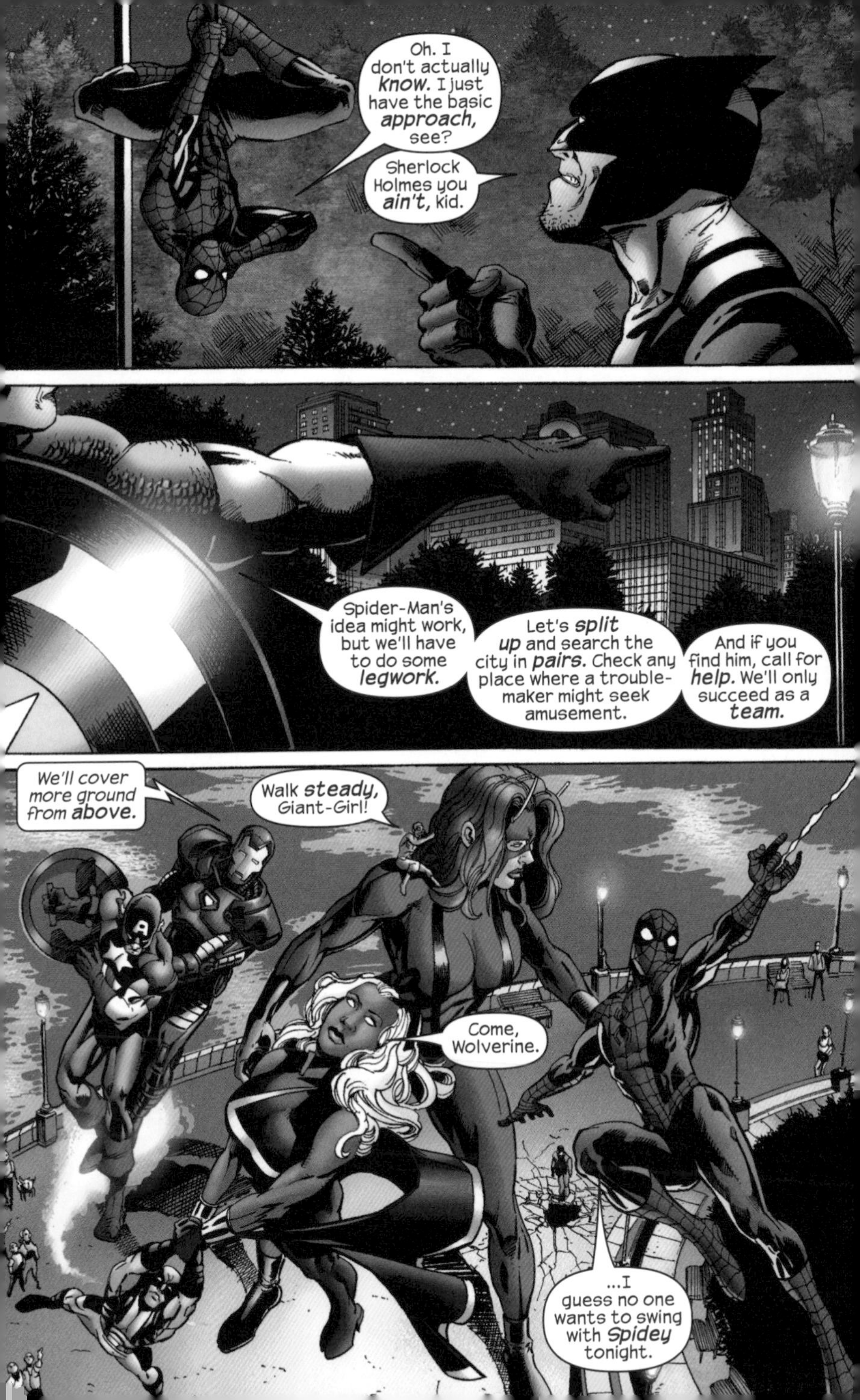
Oh. I don't actually know. I just have the basic approach, see?
Sherlock Holmes you ain't, kid.
Spider-Man's idea might work, but we'll have to do some legwork.
Let's split up and search the city in pairs. Check any place where a trouble-maker might seek amusement.
And if you find him, call for help. We'll only succeed as a team.
We'll cover more ground from above.
Walk steady, Giant-Girl!
Come, Wolverine.
...I guess no one wants to swing with Spidey tonight.

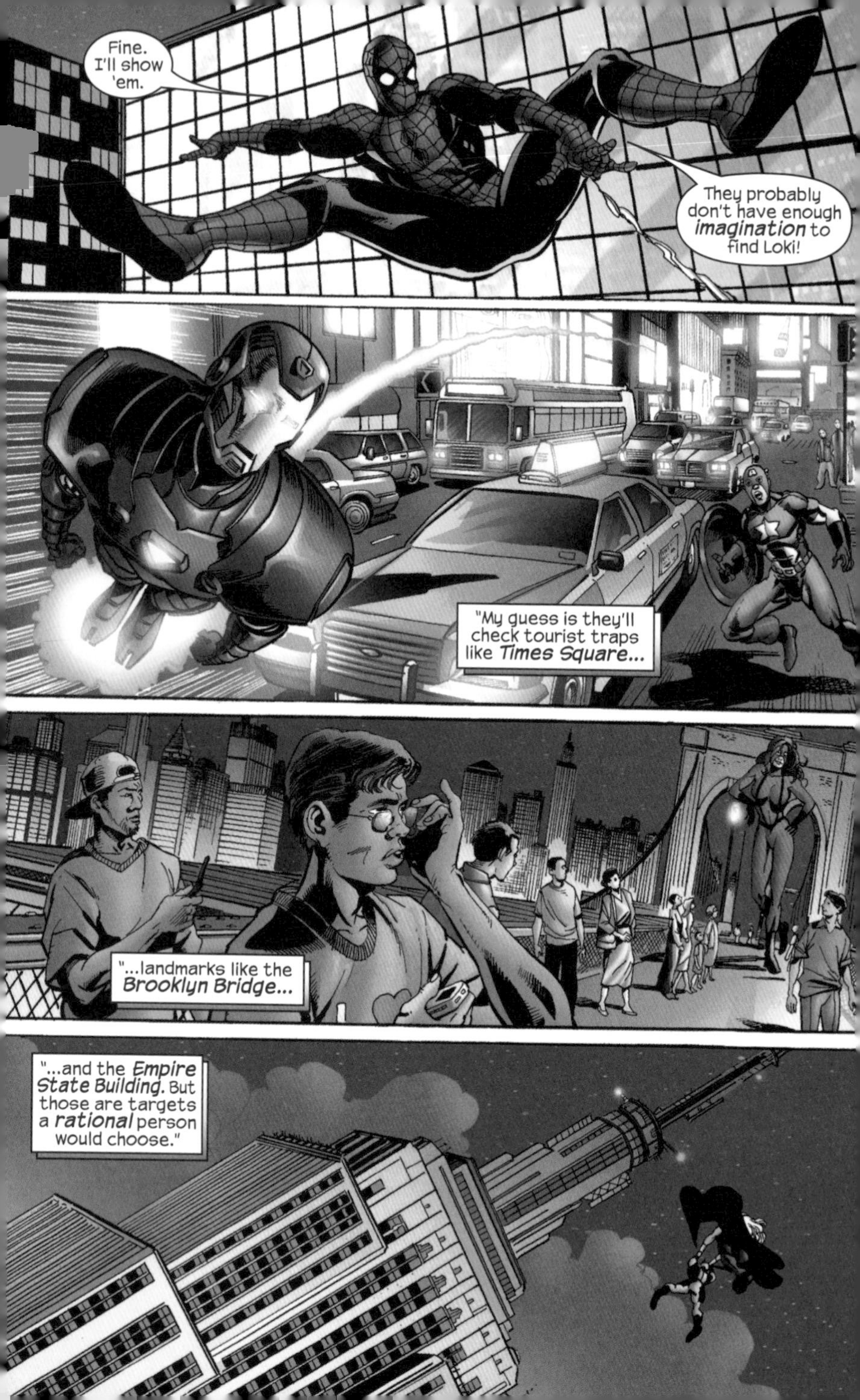
Fine. I'll show 'em.
They probably don't have enough *imagination* to find Loki!
"My guess is they'll check tourist traps like *Times Square*...
"...landmarks like the *Brooklyn Bridge*...
"...and the *Empire State Building*. But those are targets a *rational* person would choose."

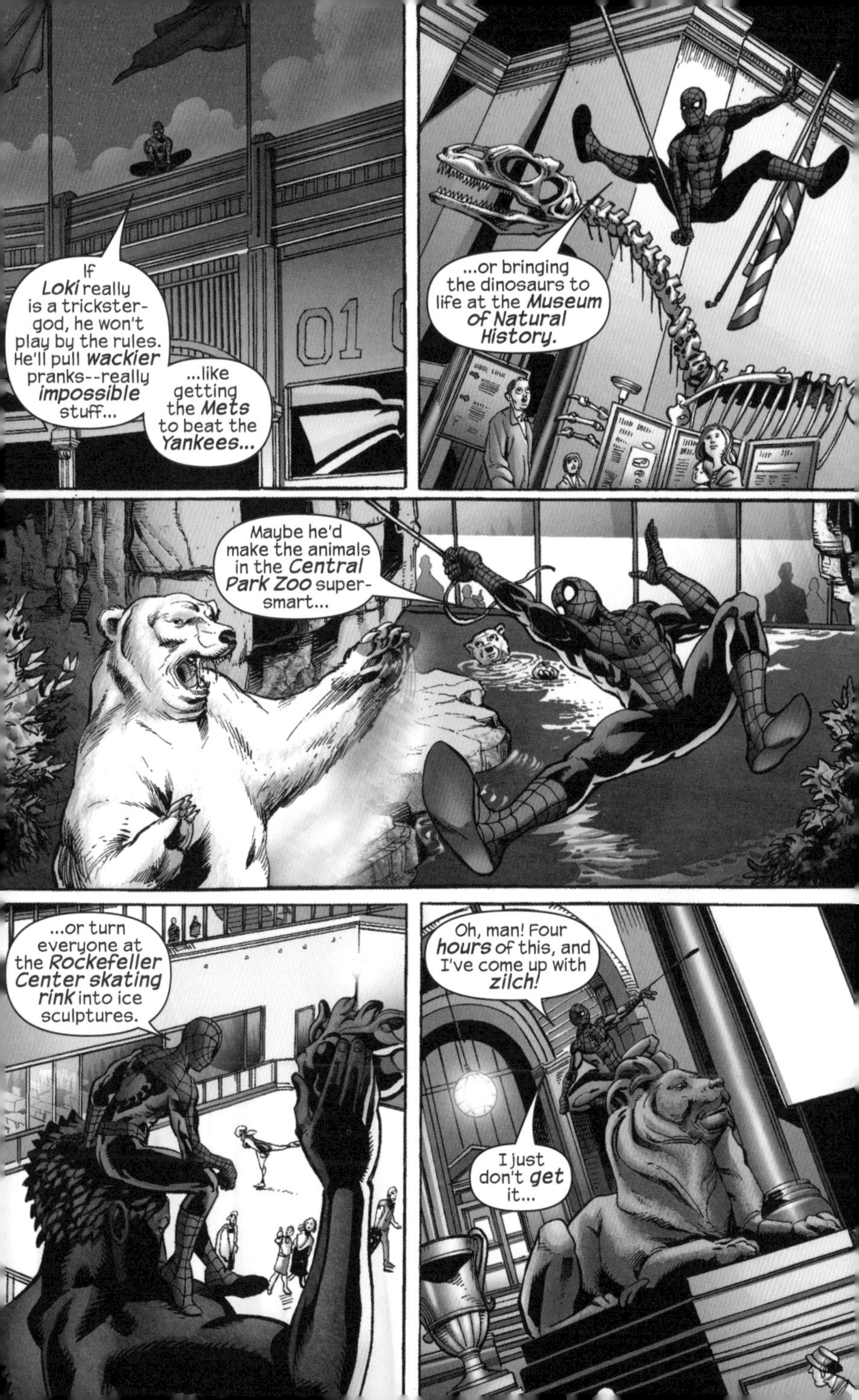
If Loki really is a trickster-god, he won't play by the rules. He'll pull wackier pranks--really impossible stuff...
...like getting the Mets to beat the Yankees...
...or bringing the dinosaurs to life at the Museum of Natural History.
Maybe he'd make the animals in the Central Park Zoo super-smart...
...or turn everyone at the Rockefeller Center skating rink into ice sculptures.
Oh, man! Four hours of this, and I've come up with zilch!
I just don't get it...

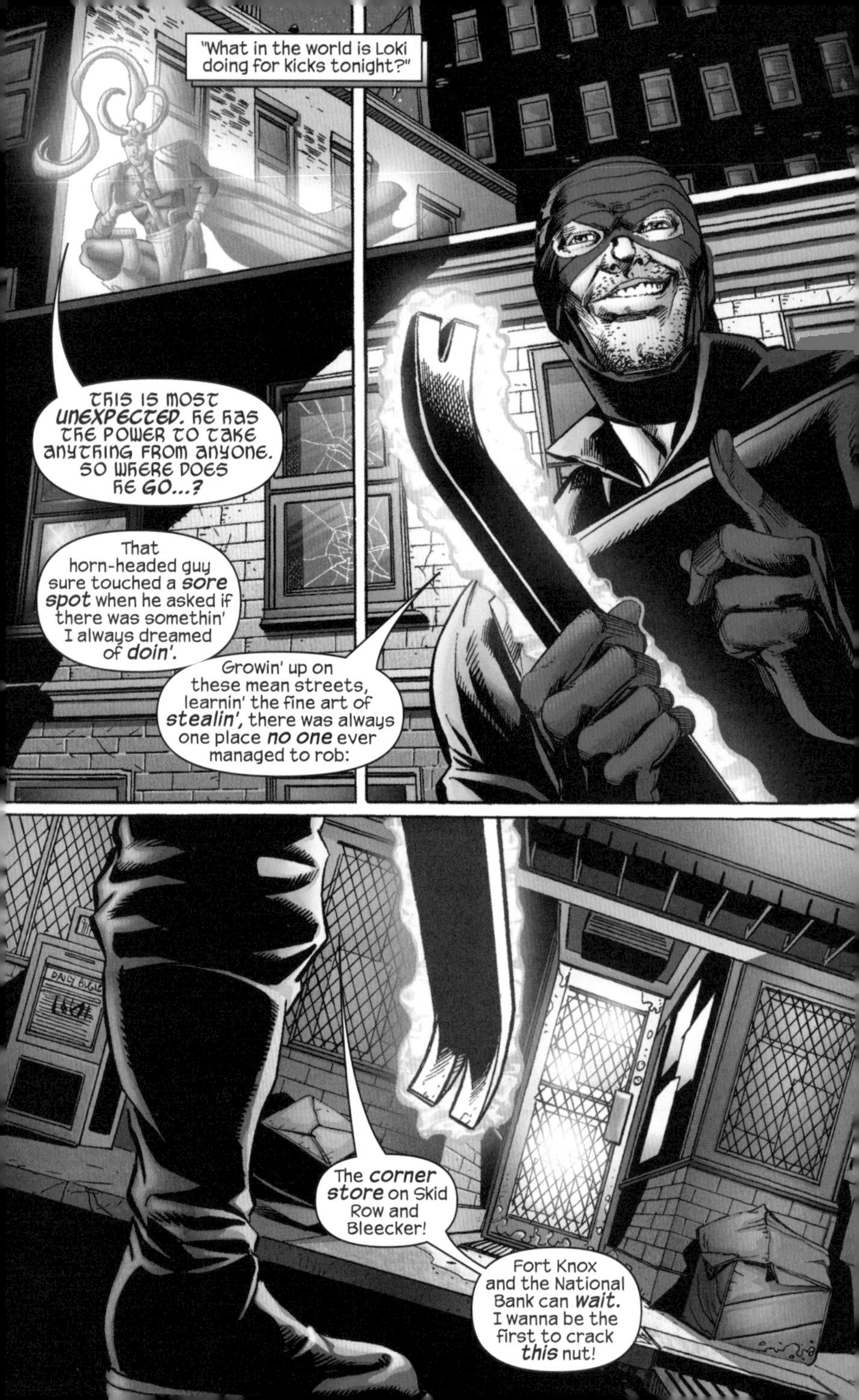
"What in the world is Loki doing for kicks tonight?"
THIS IS MOST UNEXPECTED. HE HAS THE POWER TO TAKE ANYTHING FROM ANYONE. SO WHERE DOES HE GO...?
That horn-headed guy sure touched a sore spot when he asked if there was somethin' I always dreamed of doin'.
Growin' up on these mean streets, learnin' the fine art of stealin', there was always one place no one ever managed to rob:
DAILY BUGLE
The corner store on Skid Row and Bleecker!
Fort Knox and the National Bank can wait. I wanna be the first to crack this nut!

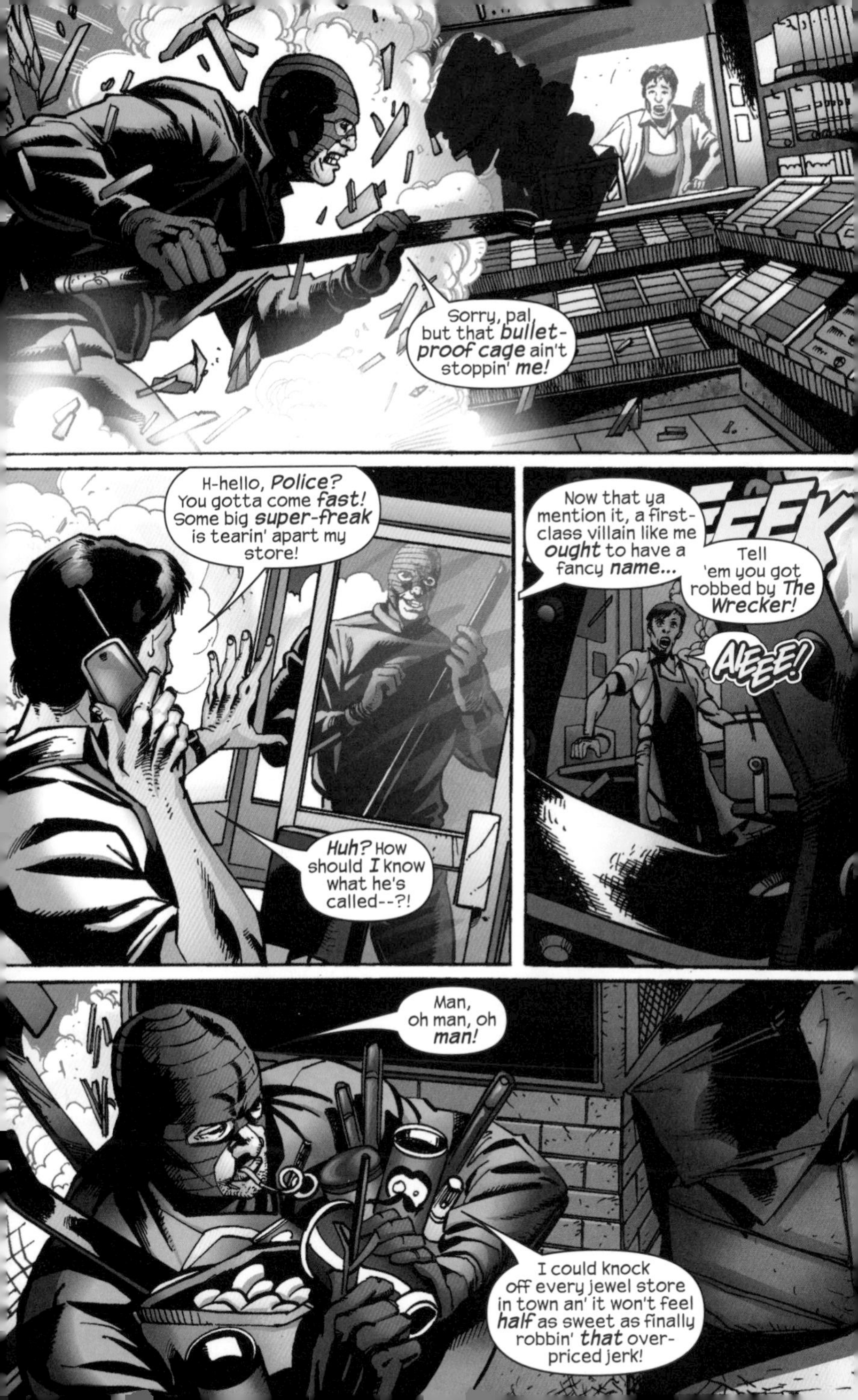
Sorry, pal, but that bullet-proof cage ain't stoppin' me!
H-hello, Police? You gotta come fast! Some big super-freak is tearin' apart my store!
Huh? How should I know what he's called--?!
Now that ya mention it, a first-class villain like me ought to have a fancy name...
Tell 'em you got robbed by The Wrecker!
EEEK
AIEEE!
Man, oh man, oh man!
I could knock off every jewel store in town an' it won't feel half as sweet as finally robbin' that over-priced jerk!

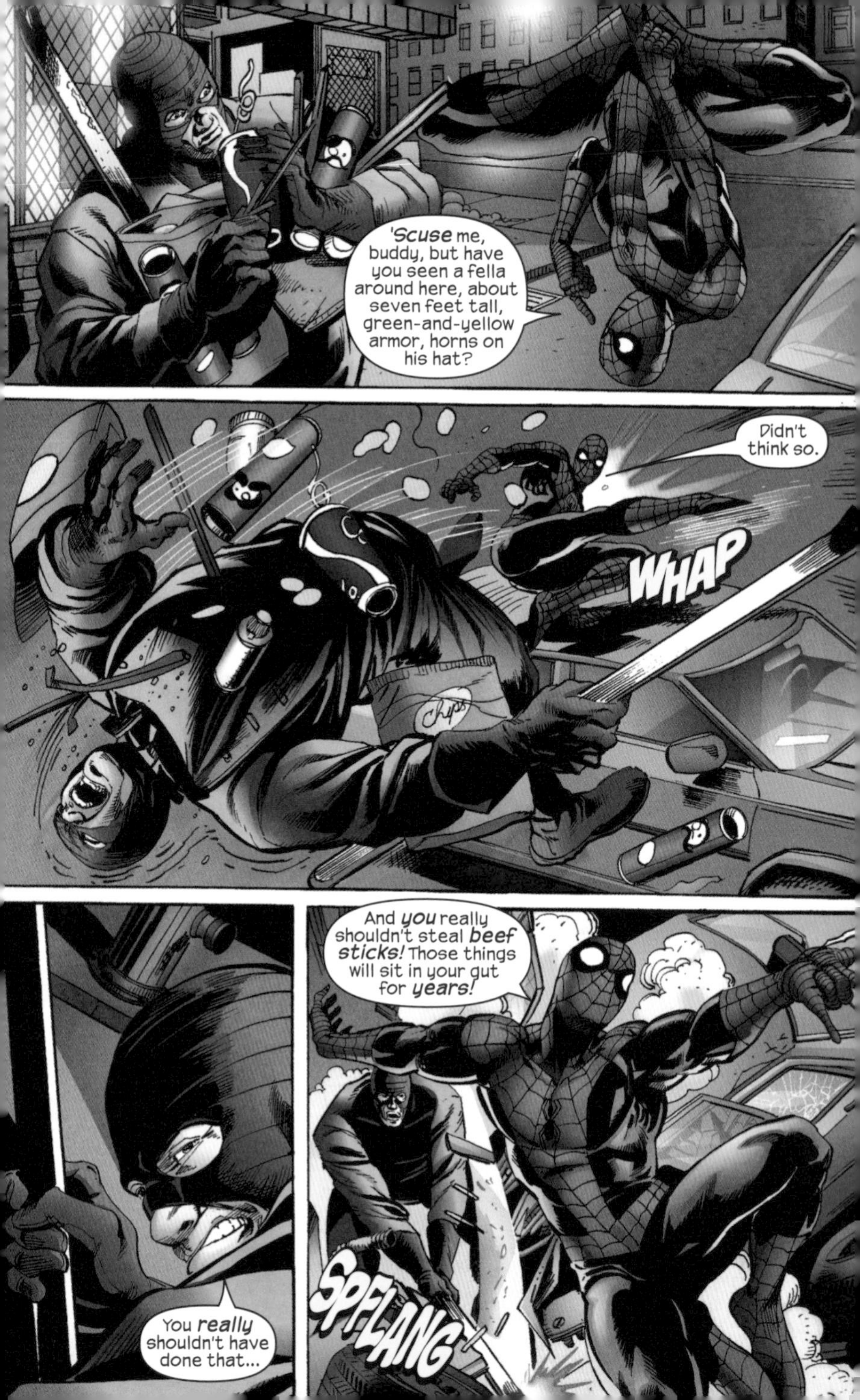
'Scuse me, buddy, but have you seen a fella around here, about seven feet tall, green-and-yellow armor, horns on his hat?
Didn't think so.
WHAP
You really shouldn't have done that...
And you really shouldn't steal beef sticks! Those things will sit in your gut for years!
SPFLANG

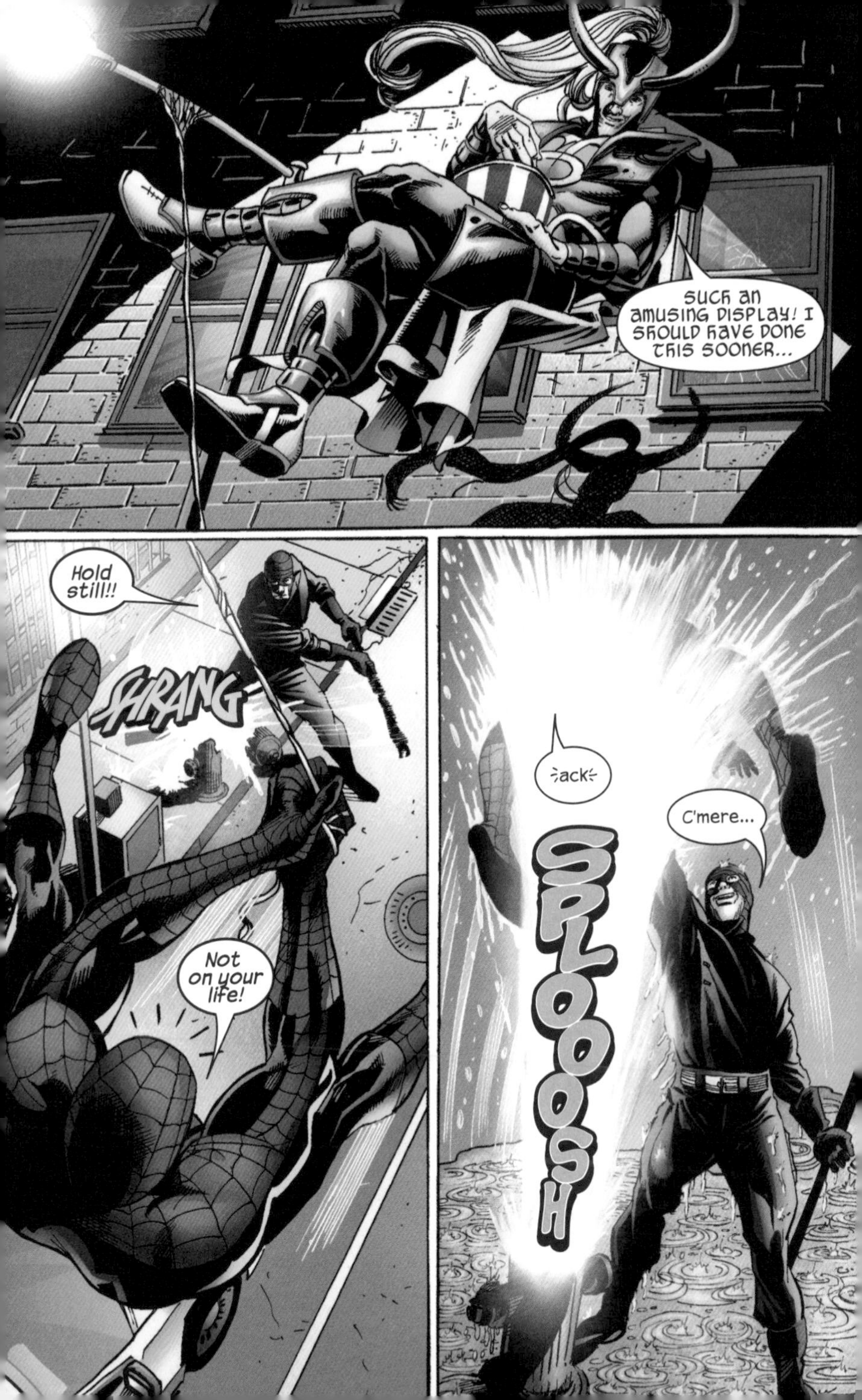
SUCH AN AMUSING DISPLAY! I SHOULD HAVE DONE THIS SOONER...
Hold still!!
SHRANG
Not on your life!
ack
C'mere...
SPLOOOOSH

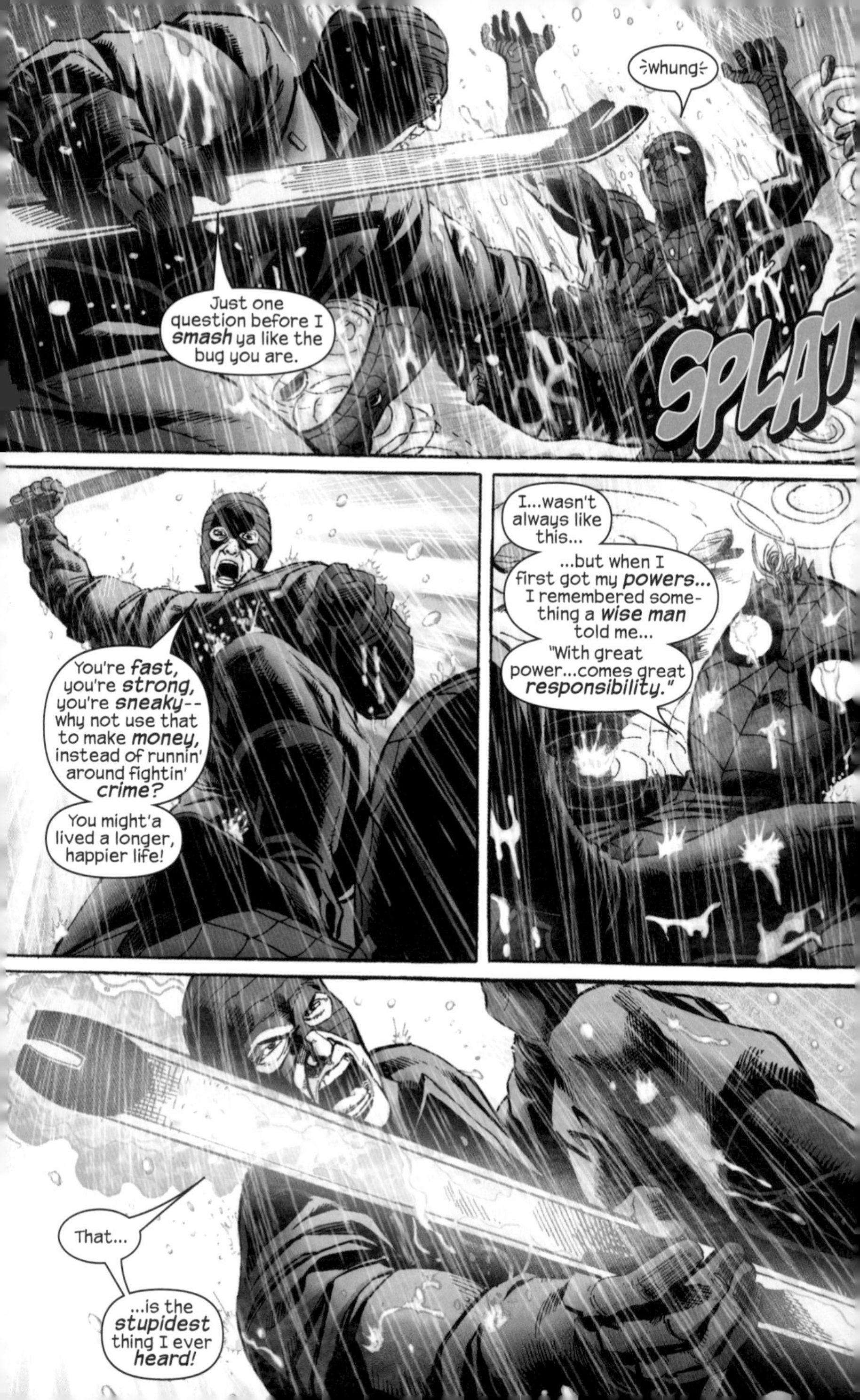
whung
Just one question before I smash ya like the bug you are.
SPLAT
You're fast, you're strong, you're sneaky-- why not use that to make money, instead of runnin' around fightin' crime?
You might'a lived a longer, happier life!
I...wasn't always like this...
...but when I first got my powers... I remembered some-thing a wise man told me...
"With great power...comes great responsibility."
That...
...is the stupidest thing I ever heard!

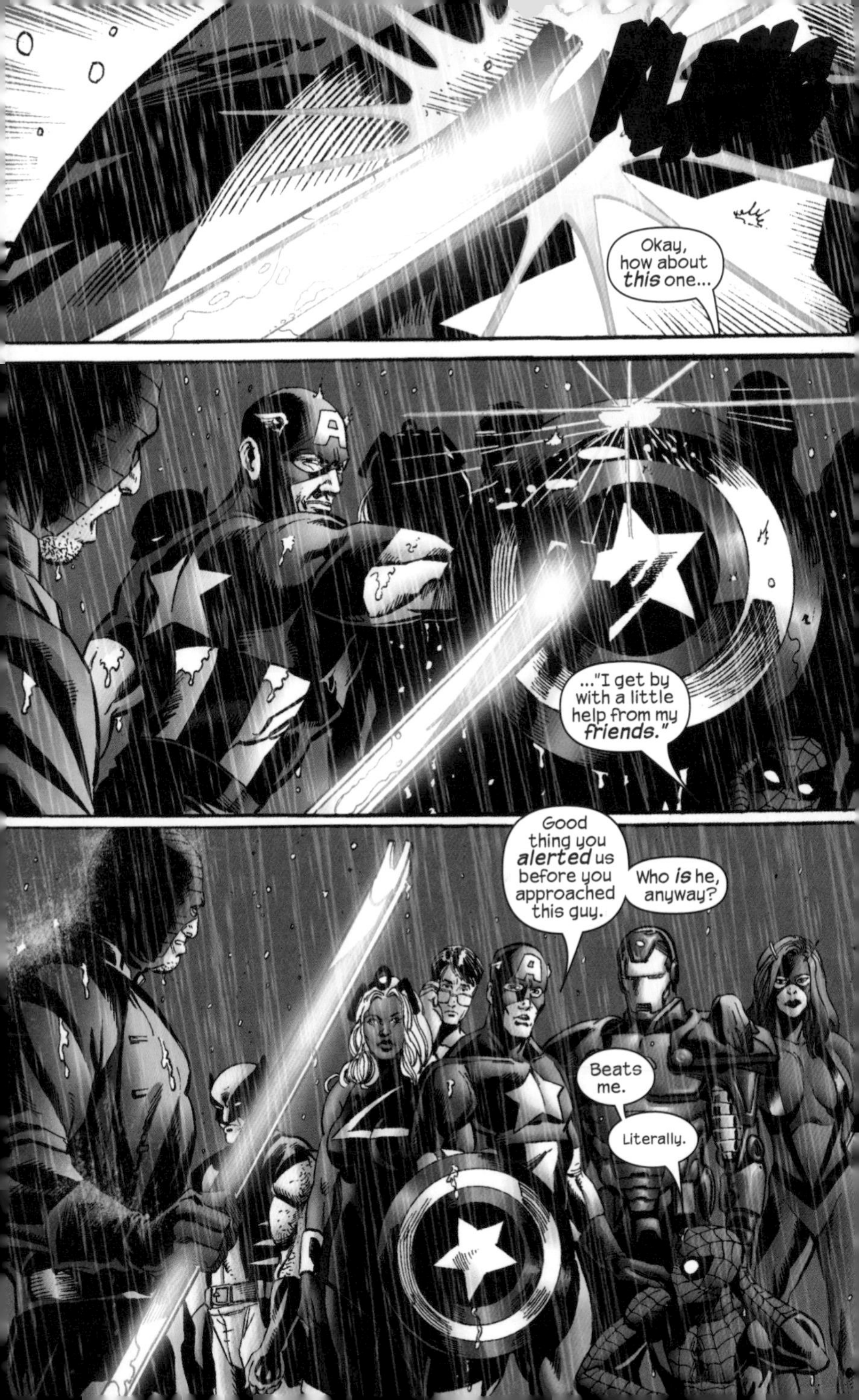
Okay, how about this one...
..."I get by with a little help from my friends."
Good thing you alerted us before you approached this guy.
Who is he, anyway?
Beats me.
Literally.

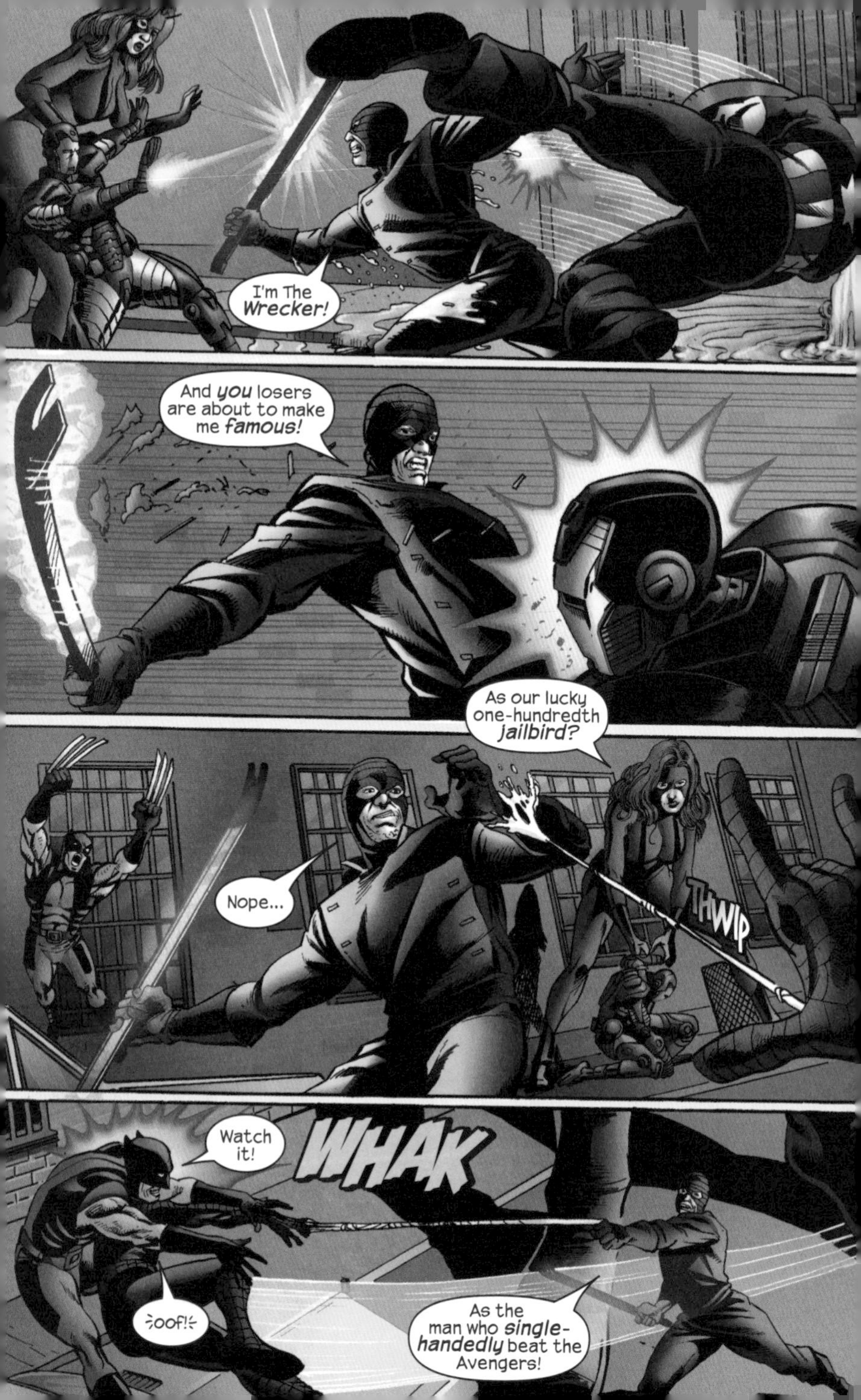
I'm The Wrecker!
And you losers are about to make me famous!
As our lucky one-hundredth jailbird?
Nope...
THWIP
Watch it!
WHAK
oof!
As the man who single-handedly beat the Avengers!

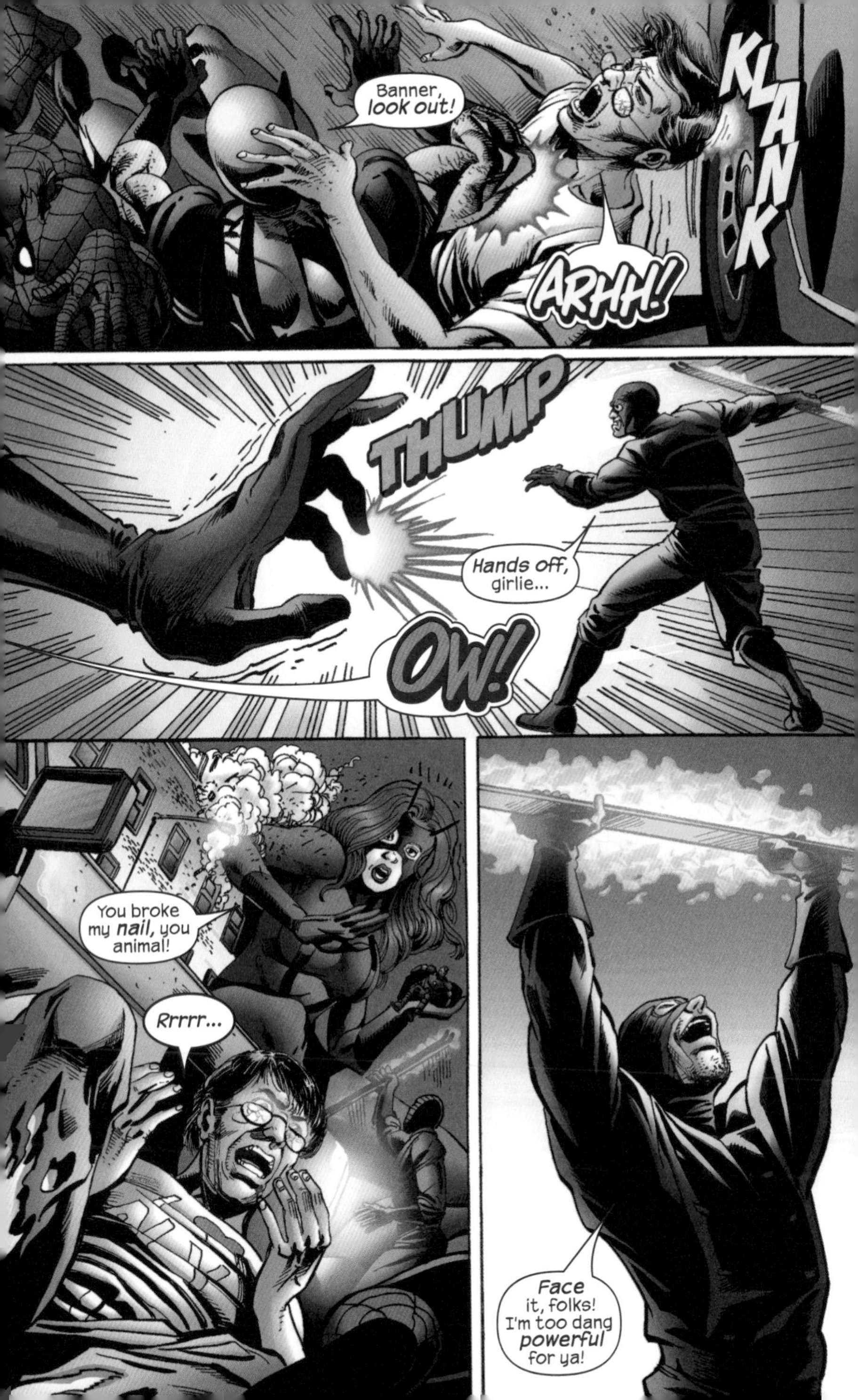

Banner, look out!
KLANK
ARHH!
THUMP
Hands off, girlie...
OW!
You broke my nail, you animal!
Rrrrr...
Face it, folks! I'm too dang powerful for ya!

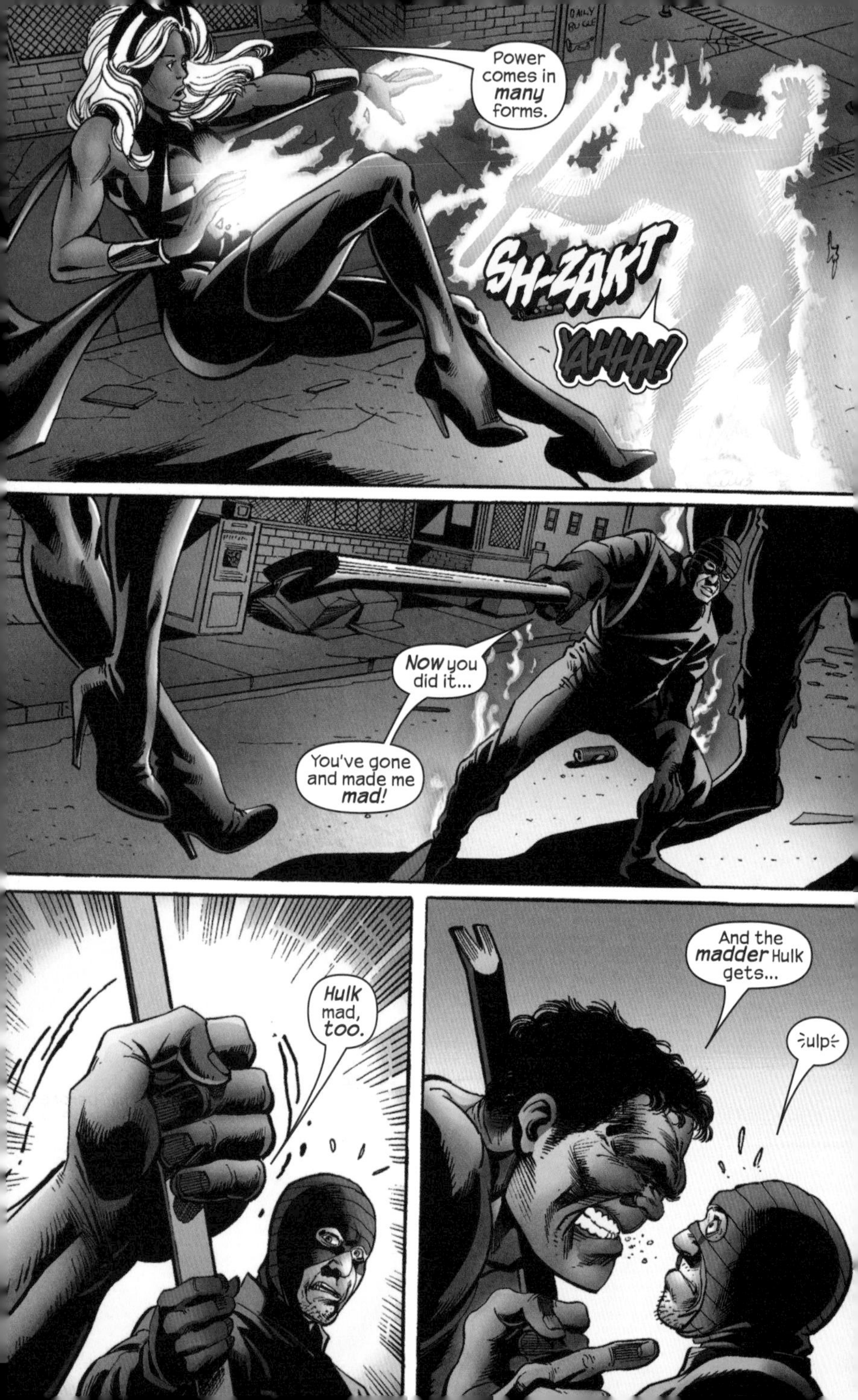
Power comes in *many* forms.
SH-ZAKT
YAHHH!
NOW you did it...
You've gone and made me *mad!*
Hulk mad, *too.*
And the *madder* Hulk gets...
ulp

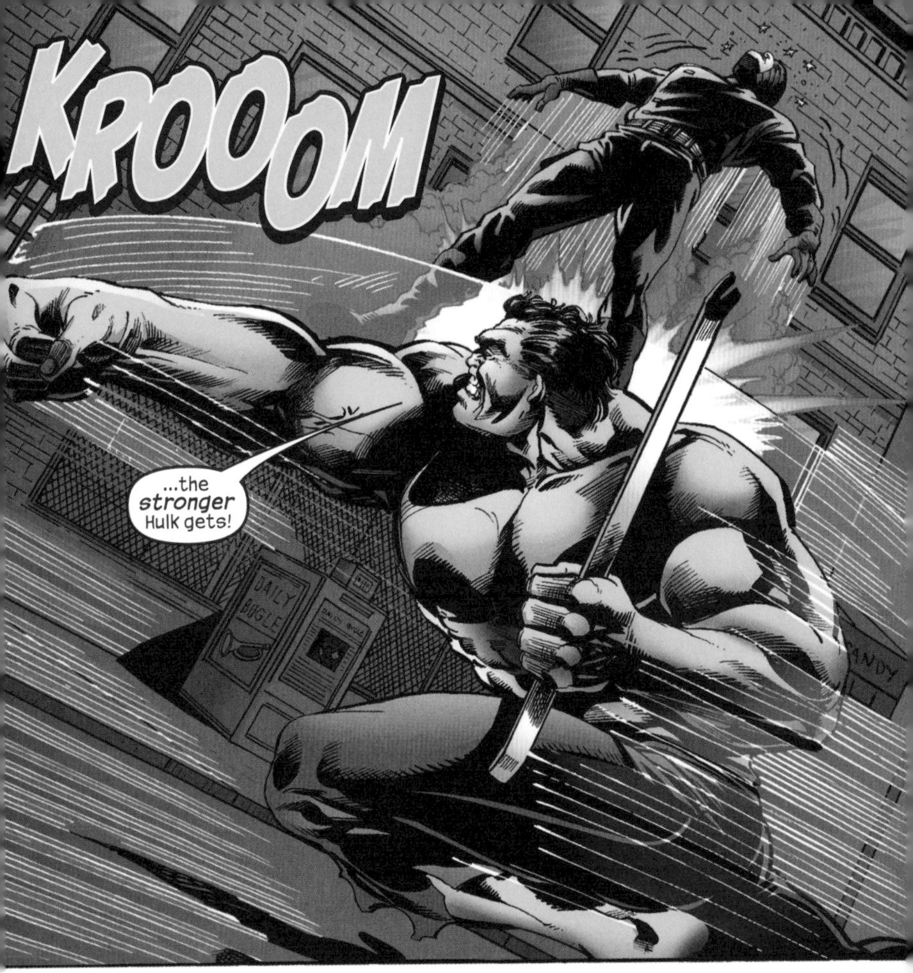
KROOOOM
...the stronger Hulk gets!
DAILY BUGLE
CANDY

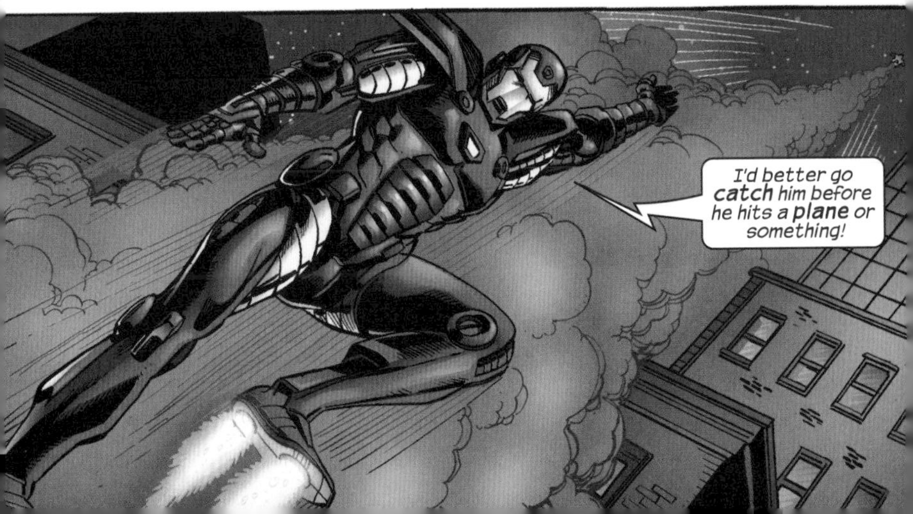
I'd better go catch him before he hits a plane or something!

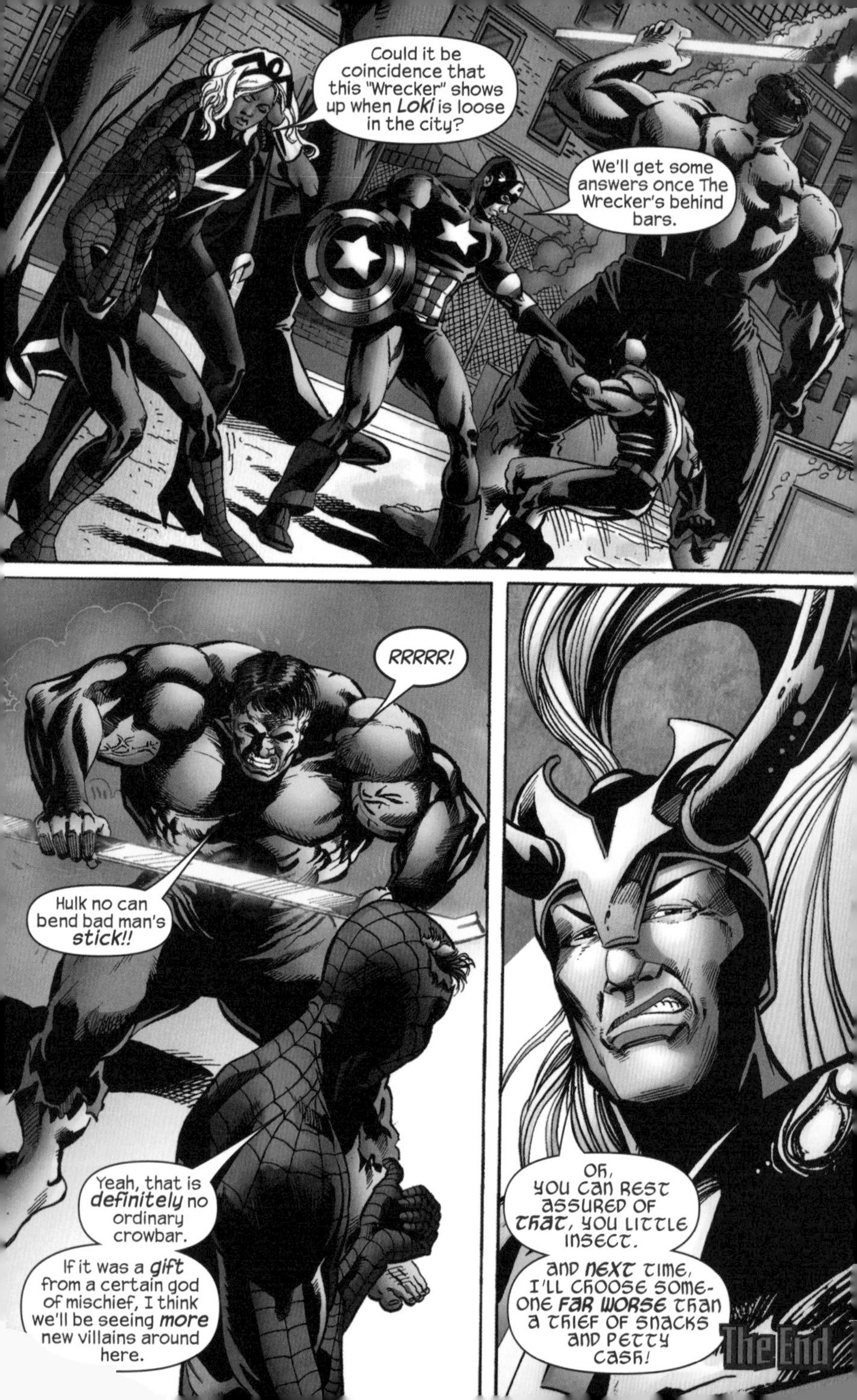
Could it be coincidence that this "Wrecker" shows up when *Loki* is loose in the city?
We'll get some answers once The Wrecker's behind bars.
RRRRR!
Hulk no can bend bad man's *stick!!*
Yeah, that is *definitely* no ordinary crowbar.
If it was a *gift* from a certain god of mischief, I think we'll be seeing *more* new villains around here.
Oh, you can rest assured of *that*, you little insect.
And *next* time, I'll choose some-one *far worse* than a thief of snacks and petty cash!
The End

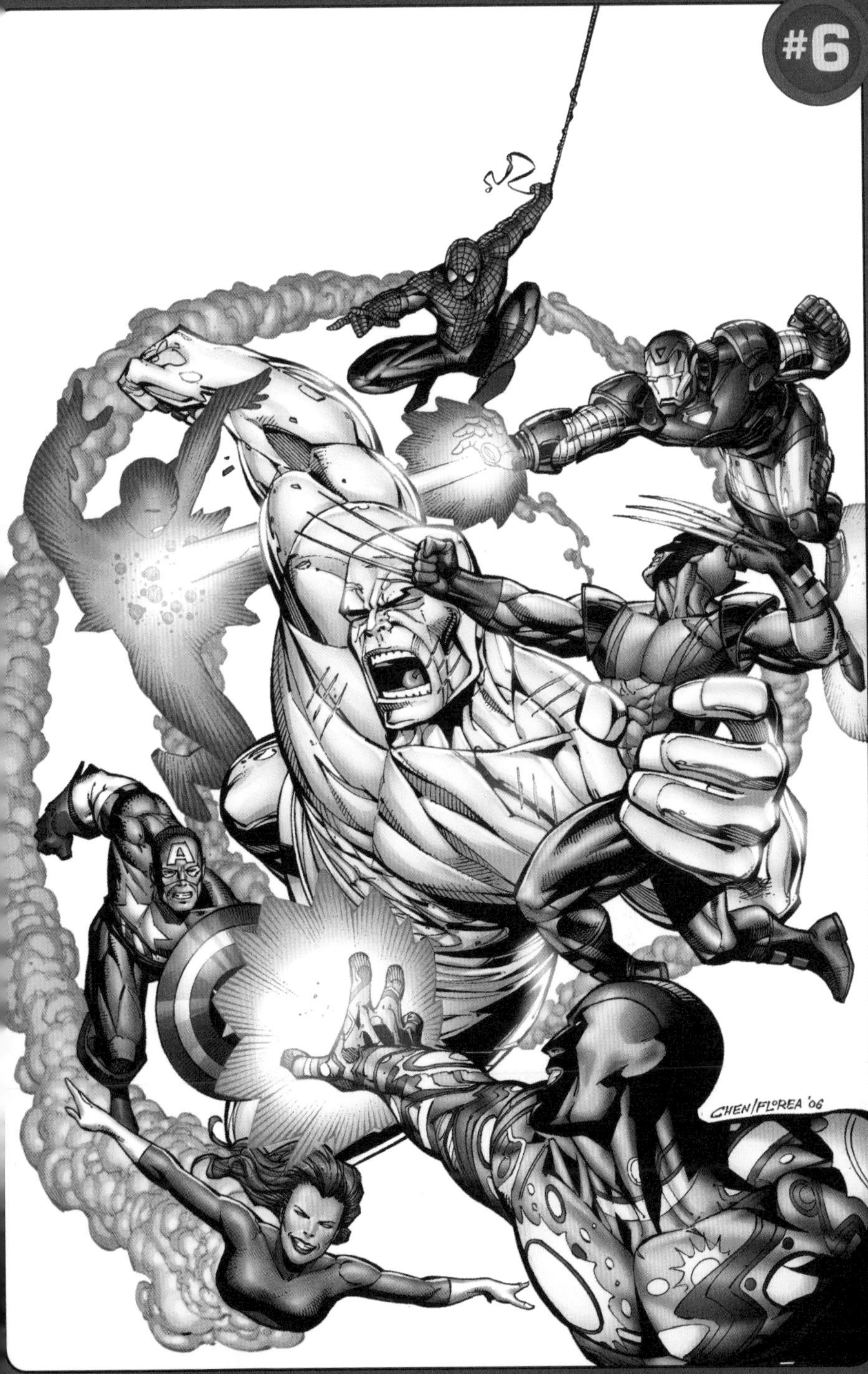

#6
CHEN/FLOREA '06

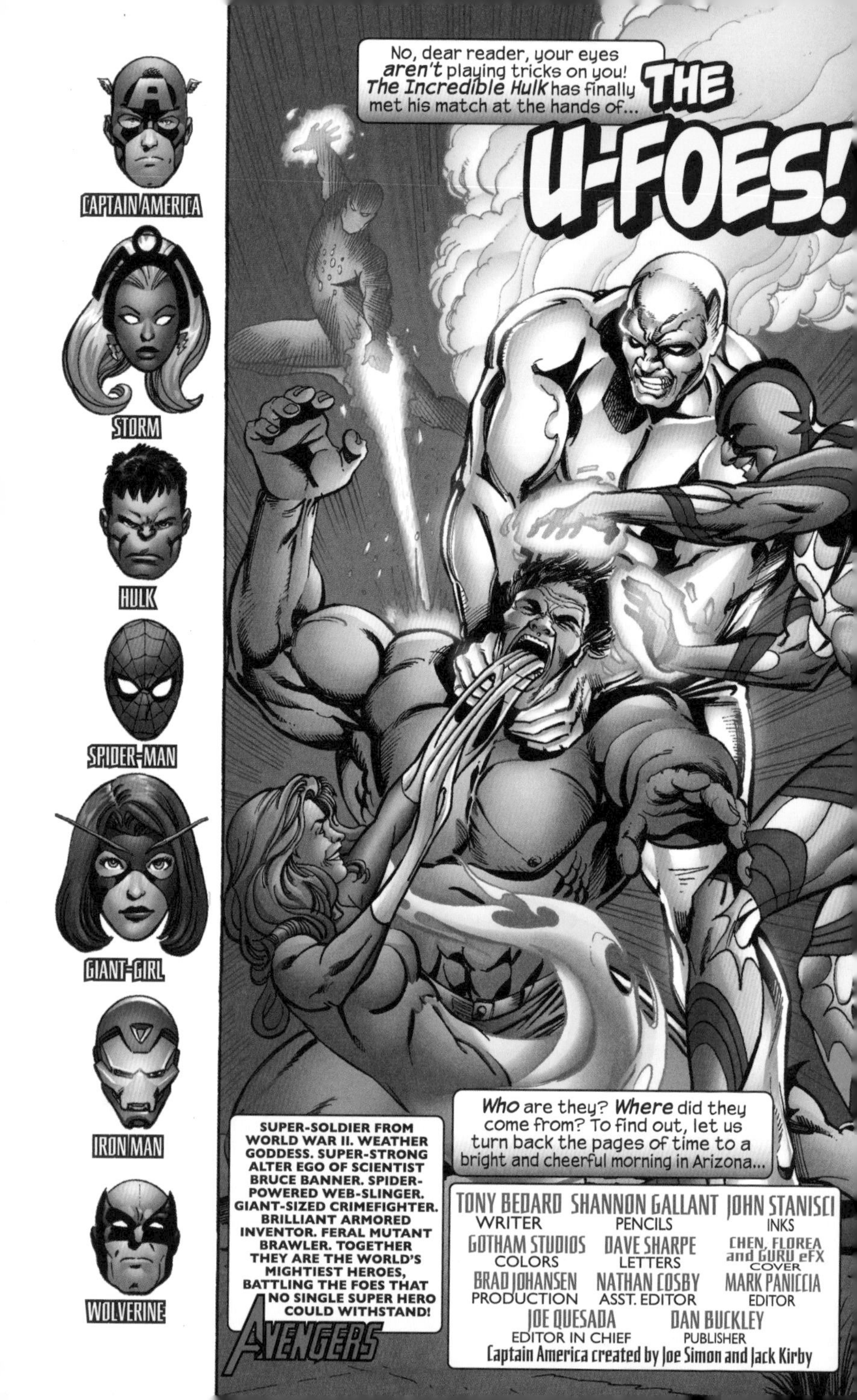
CAPTAIN AMERICA
STORM
HULK
SPIDER-MAN
GIANT-GIRL
IRON MAN
WOLVERINE
No, dear reader, your eyes aren't playing tricks on you! The Incredible Hulk has finally met his match at the hands of...
THE U-FOES!
Who are they? Where did they come from? To find out, let us turn back the pages of time to a bright and cheerful morning in Arizona...
SUPER-SOLDIER FROM WORLD WAR II. WEATHER GODDESS. SUPER-STRONG ALTER EGO OF SCIENTIST BRUCE BANNER. SPIDER-POWERED WEB-SLINGER. GIANT-SIZED CRIMEFIGHTER. BRILLIANT ARMORED INVENTOR. FERAL MUTANT BRAWLER. TOGETHER THEY ARE THE WORLD'S MIGHTIEST HEROES, BATTLING THE FOES THAT NO SINGLE SUPER HERO COULD WITHSTAND!
AVENGERS
TONY BEDARD WRITER
SHANNON GALLANT PENCILS
JOHN STANISCI INKS
GOTHAM STUDIOS COLORS
DAVE SHARPE LETTERS
CHEN, FLOREA and GURU eFX COVER
BRAD JOHANSEN PRODUCTION
NATHAN COSBY ASST. EDITOR
MARK PANICCIA EDITOR
JOE QUESADA EDITOR IN CHIEF
DAN BUCKLEY PUBLISHER
Captain America created by Joe Simon and Jack Kirby

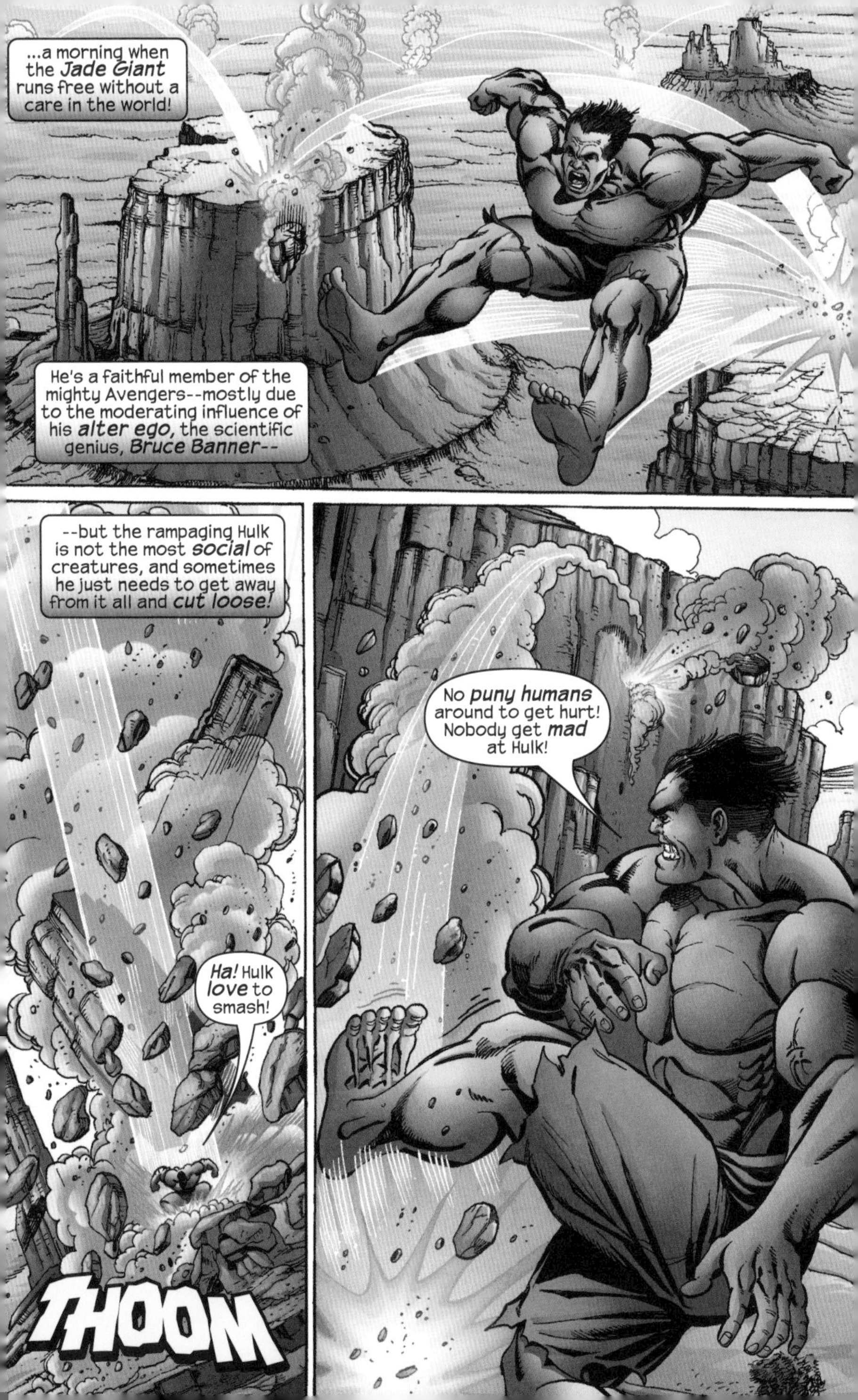
...a morning when the *Jade Giant* runs free without a care in the world!
He's a faithful member of the mighty Avengers--mostly due to the moderating influence of his *alter ego,* the scientific genius, *Bruce Banner*--
--but the rampaging Hulk is not the most *social* of creatures, and sometimes he just needs to get away from it all and *cut loose!*
Ha! Hulk *love* to smash!
THOOM
No *puny humans* around to get hurt! Nobody get *mad* at Hulk!

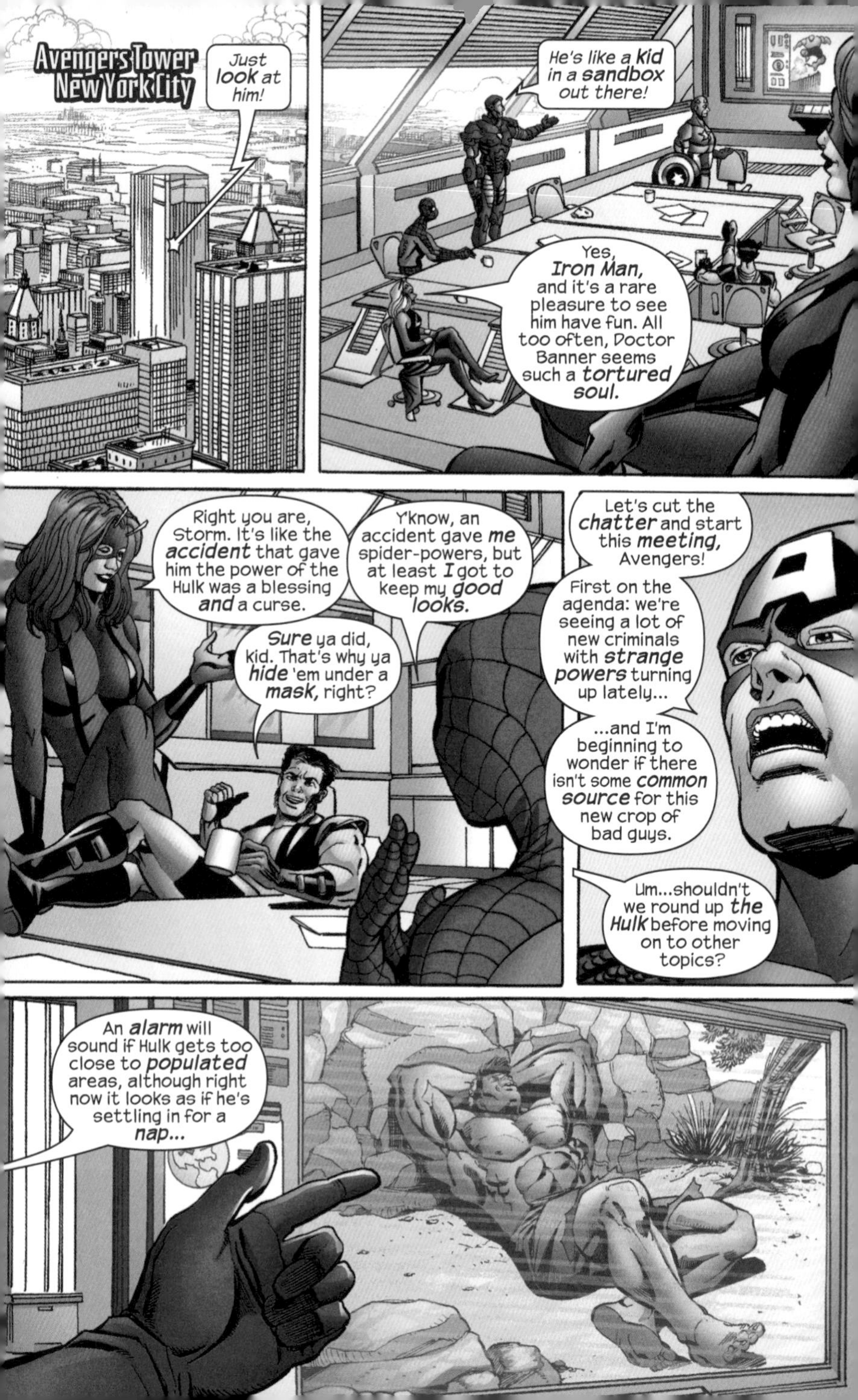
Avengers Tower New York City
Just look at him!
He's like a kid in a sandbox out there!
Yes, Iron Man, and it's a rare pleasure to see him have fun. All too often, Doctor Banner seems such a tortured soul.
Right you are, Storm. It's like the accident that gave him the power of the Hulk was a blessing and a curse.
Y'know, an accident gave me spider-powers, but at least I got to keep my good looks.
Sure ya did, kid. That's why ya hide 'em under a mask, right?
Let's cut the chatter and start this meeting, Avengers!
First on the agenda: we're seeing a lot of new criminals with strange powers turning up lately...
...and I'm beginning to wonder if there isn't some common source for this new crop of bad guys.
Um...shouldn't we round up the Hulk before moving on to other topics?
An alarm will sound if Hulk gets too close to populated areas, although right now it looks as if he's settling in for a nap...

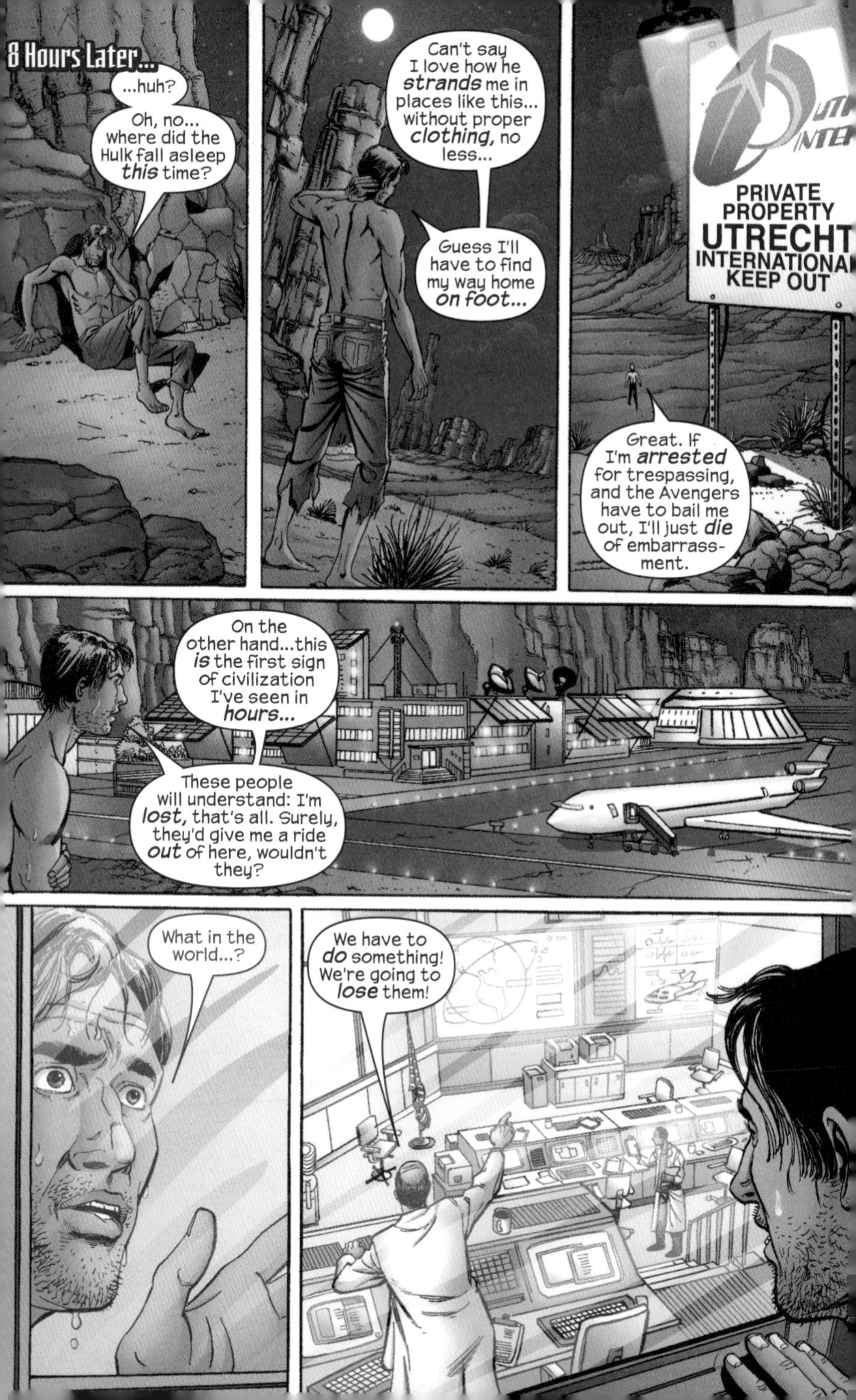
8 Hours Later...
...huh?
Oh, no... where did the Hulk fall asleep this time?
Can't say I love how he strands me in places like this... without proper clothing, no less...
Guess I'll have to find my way home on foot...
PRIVATE PROPERTY UTRECHT INTERNATIONAL KEEP OUT
Great. If I'm arrested for trespassing, and the Avengers have to bail me out, I'll just die of embarrass- ment.
On the other hand...this is the first sign of civilization I've seen in hours...
These people will understand: I'm lost, that's all. Surely, they'd give me a ride out of here, wouldn't they?
What in the world...?
We have to do something! We're going to lose them!

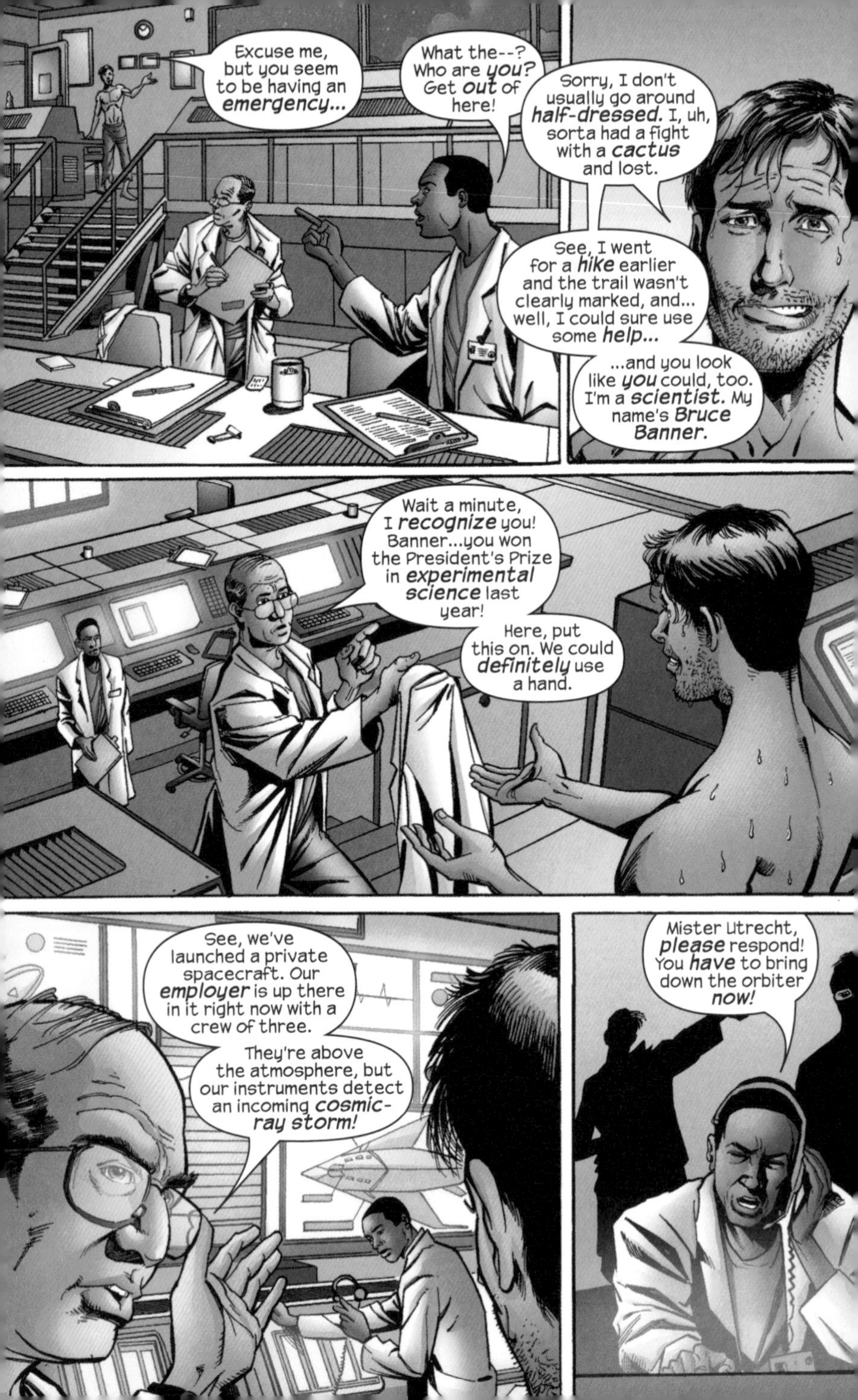
Excuse me, but you seem to be having an *emergency*...
What the--? Who are *you*? Get *out* of here!
Sorry, I don't usually go around *half-dressed*. I, uh, sorta had a fight with a *cactus* and lost.
See, I went for a *hike* earlier and the trail wasn't clearly marked, and... well, I could sure use some *help*...
...and you look like *you* could, too. I'm a *scientist*. My name's *Bruce Banner*.
Wait a minute, I *recognize* you! Banner...you won the President's Prize in *experimental science* last year!
Here, put this on. We could *definitely* use a hand.
See, we've launched a private spacecraft. Our *employer* is up there in it right now with a crew of three.
They're above the atmosphere, but our instruments detect an incoming *cosmic-ray storm*!
Mister Utrecht, *please* respond! You *have* to bring down the orbiter *now*!

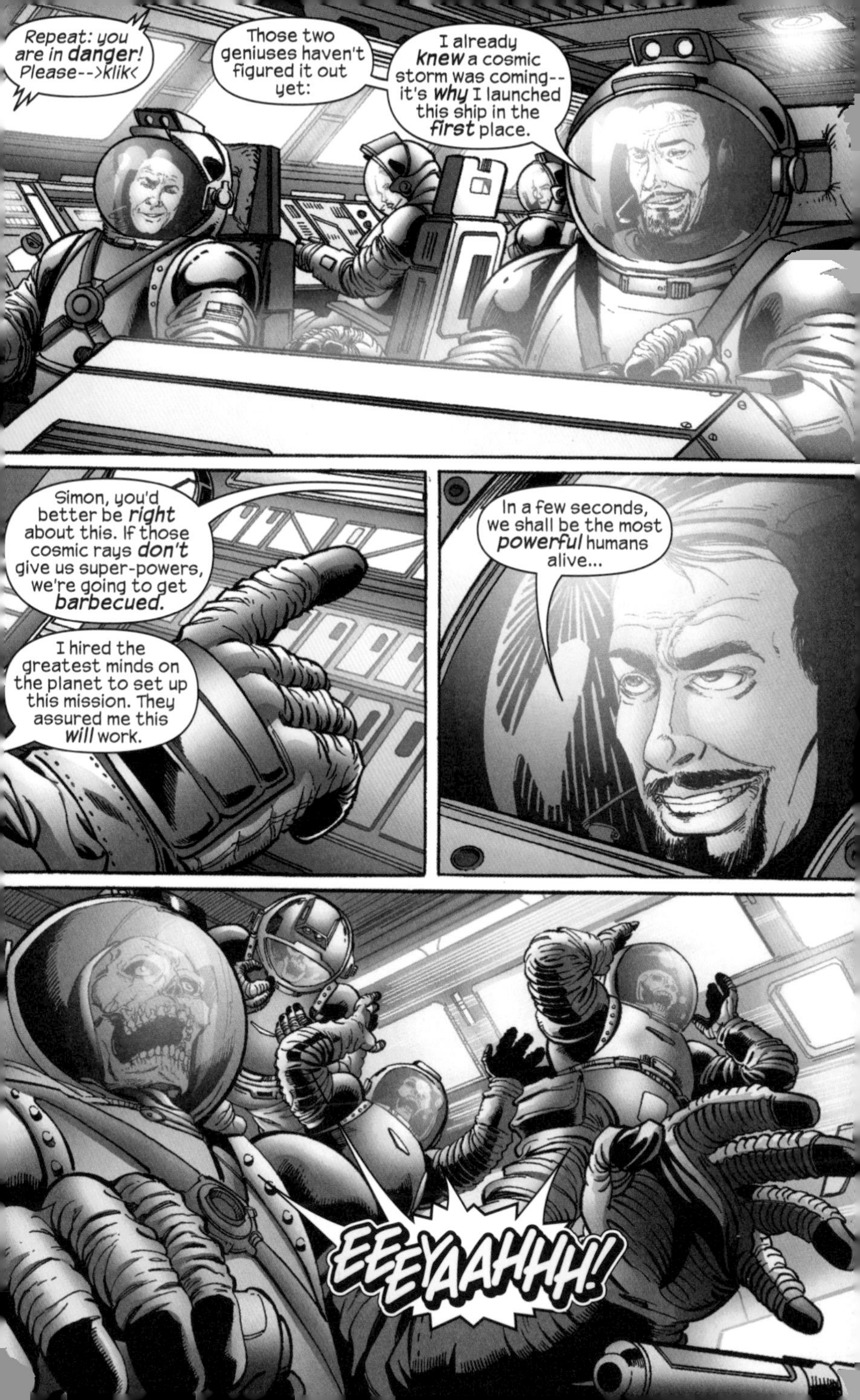
Repeat: you are in danger! Please-->klik<
Those two geniuses haven't figured it out yet:
I already knew a cosmic storm was coming-- it's why I launched this ship in the first place.
Simon, you'd better be right about this. If those cosmic rays don't give us super-powers, we're going to get barbecued.
I hired the greatest minds on the planet to set up this mission. They assured me this will work.
In a few seconds, we shall be the most powerful humans alive...
EEEYAAHHH!

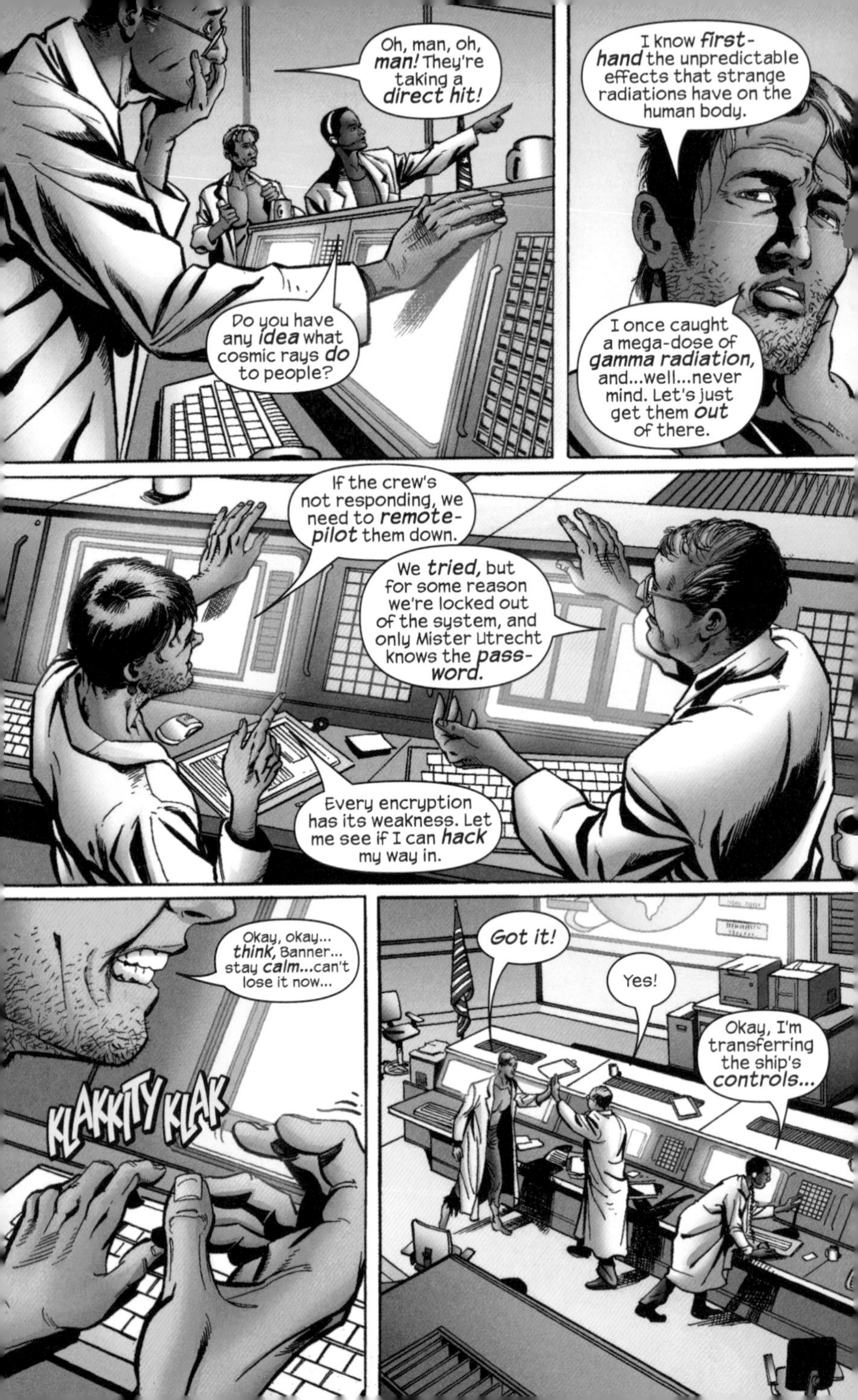
Oh, man, oh, man! They're taking a direct hit!
Do you have any idea what cosmic rays do to people?
I know first-hand the unpredictable effects that strange radiations have on the human body.
I once caught a mega-dose of gamma radiation, and...well...never mind. Let's just get them out of there.
If the crew's not responding, we need to remote-pilot them down.
We tried, but for some reason we're locked out of the system, and only Mister Utrecht knows the pass-word.
Every encryption has its weakness. Let me see if I can hack my way in.
Okay, okay... think, Banner... stay calm...can't lose it now...
KLAKKITY KLAK
Got it!
Yes!
Okay, I'm transferring the ship's controls...

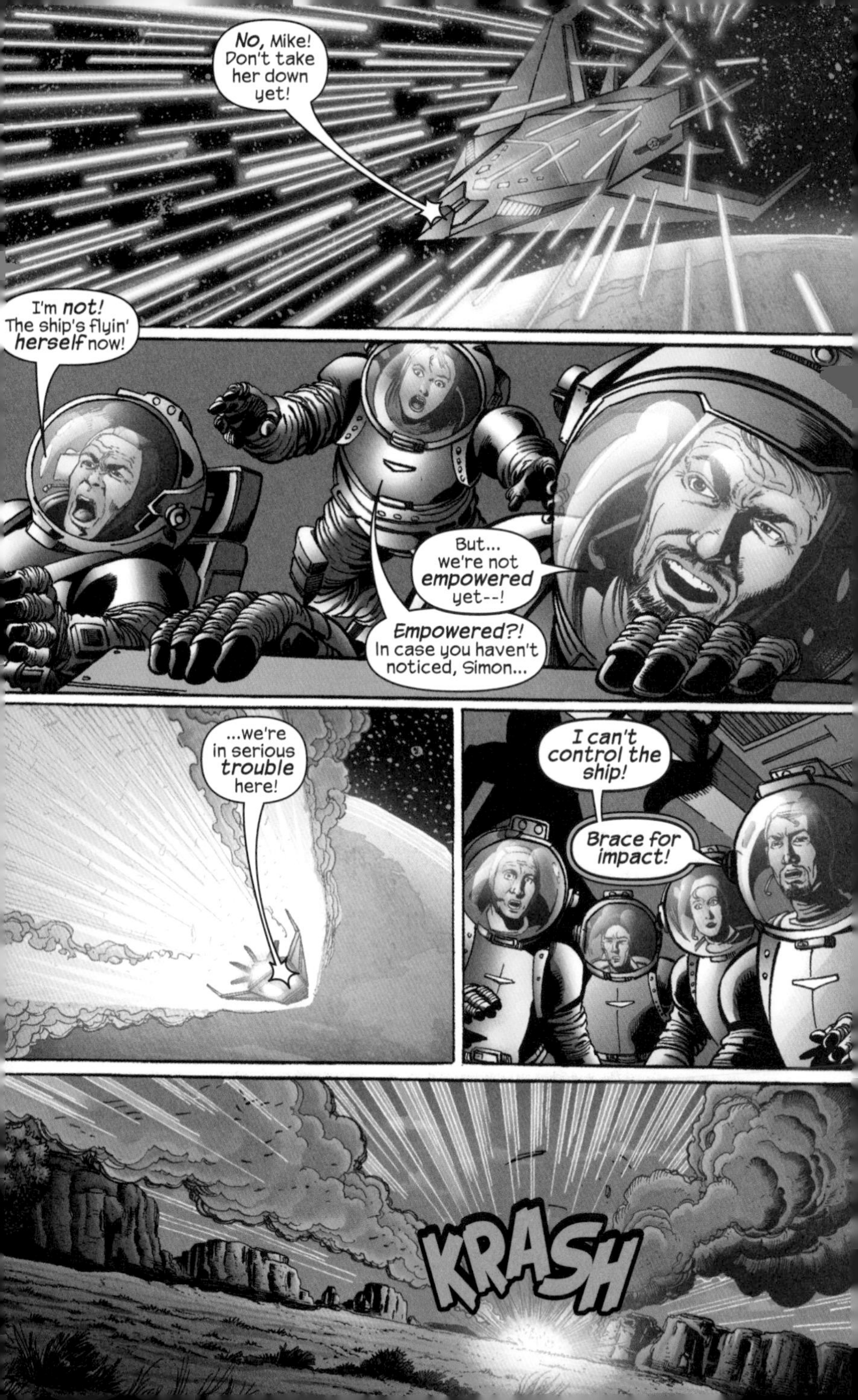
No, Mike! Don't take her down yet!
I'm not! The ship's flyin' herself now!
But... we're not empowered yet--!
Empowered?! In case you haven't noticed, Simon...
...we're in serious trouble here!
I can't control the ship!
Brace for impact!
KRASH

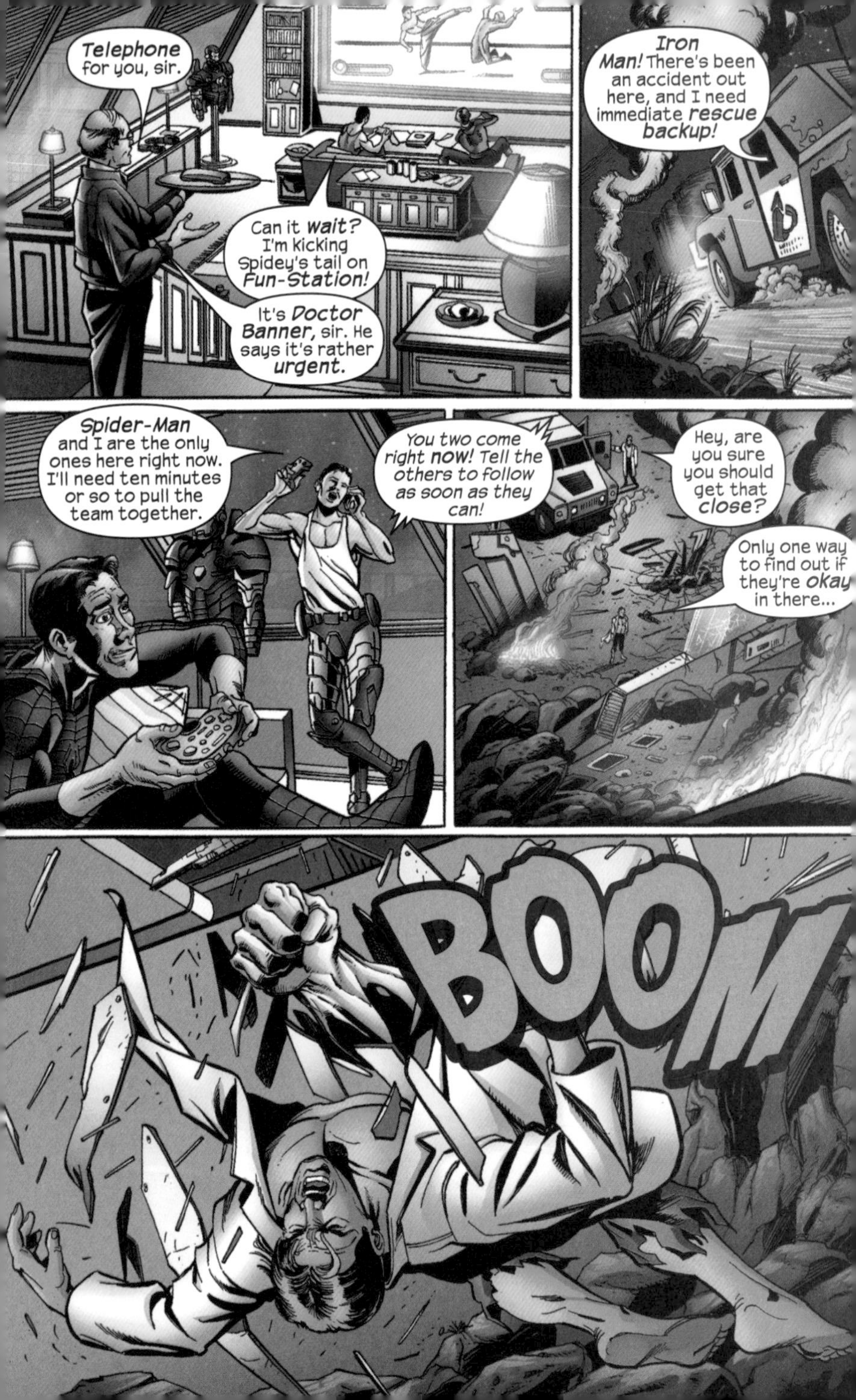
Telephone for you, sir.
Can it wait? I'm kicking Spidey's tail on Fun-Station!
It's Doctor Banner, sir. He says it's rather urgent.
Iron Man! There's been an accident out here, and I need immediate rescue backup!
Spider-Man and I are the only ones here right now. I'll need ten minutes or so to pull the team together.
You two come right now! Tell the others to follow as soon as they can!
Hey, are you sure you should get that close?
Only one way to find out if they're okay in there...
BOOM

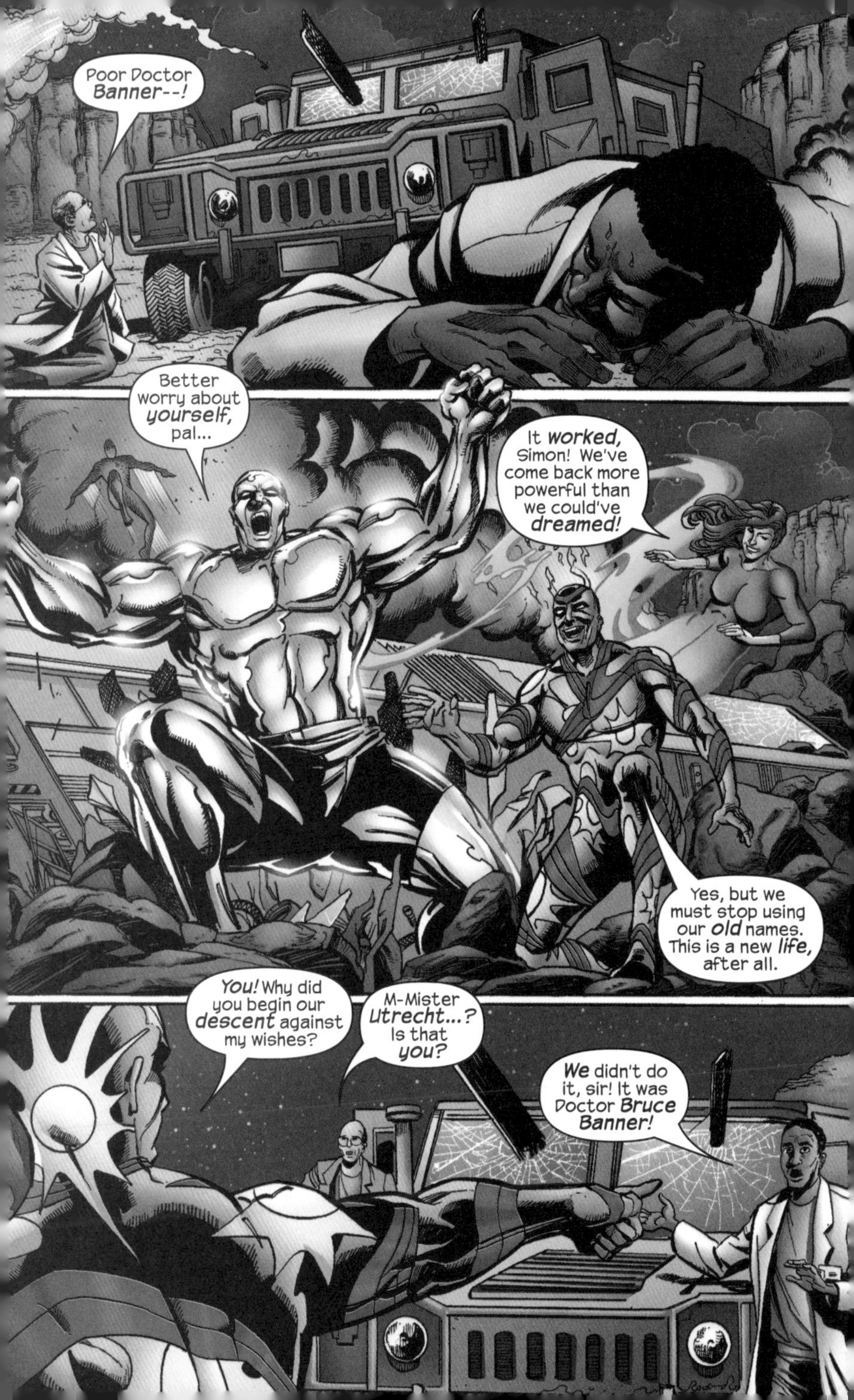
Poor Doctor Banner--!
Better worry about yourself, pal...
It worked, Simon! We've come back more powerful than we could've dreamed!
Yes, but we must stop using our old names. This is a new life, after all.
You! Why did you begin our descent against my wishes?
M-Mister Utrecht...? Is that you?
We didn't do it, sir! It was Doctor Bruce Banner!

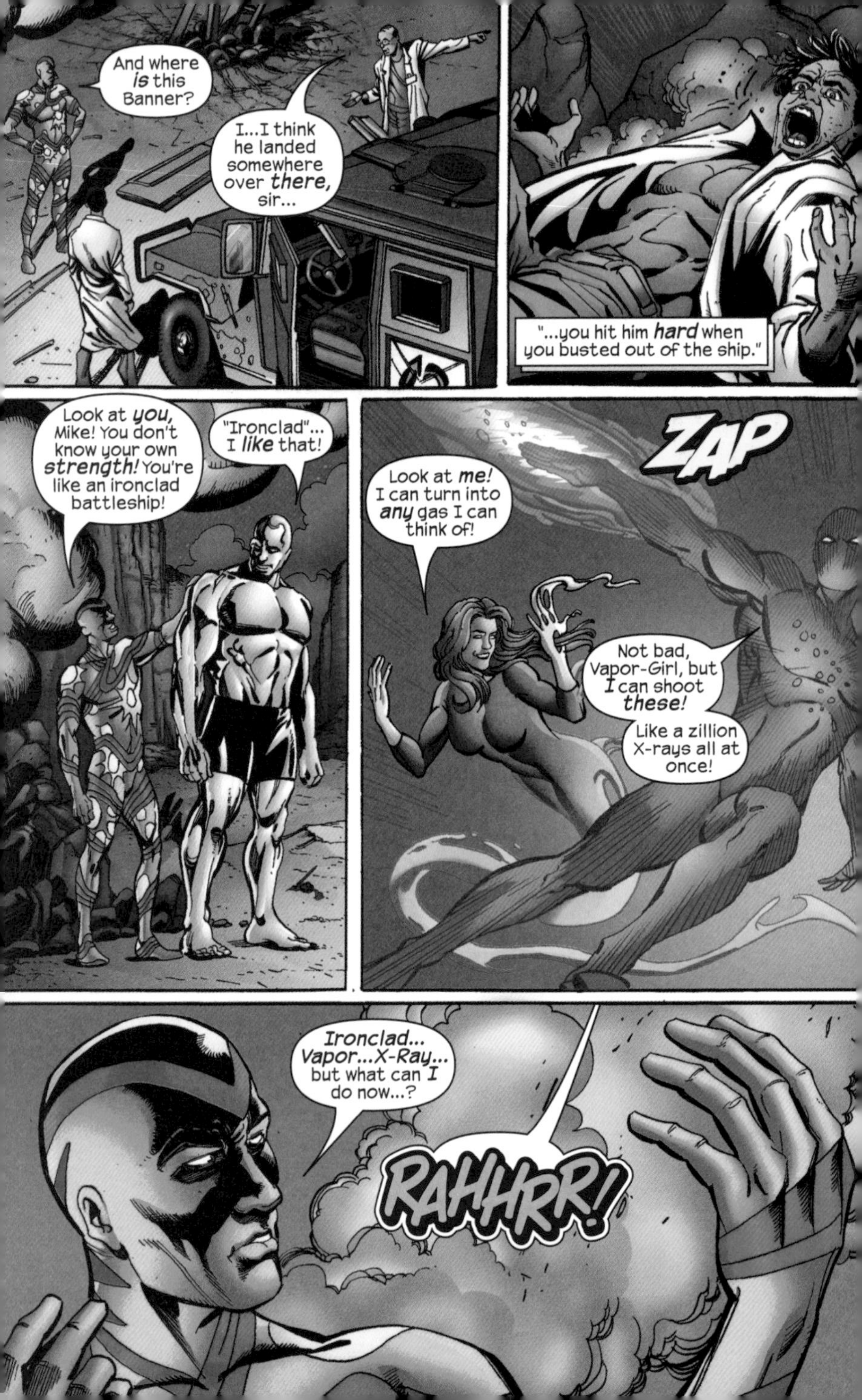
And where is this Banner?
I...I think he landed somewhere over there, sir...
"...you hit him hard when you busted out of the ship."
Look at you, Mike! You don't know your own strength! You're like an ironclad battleship!
"Ironclad"... I like that!
ZAP
Look at me! I can turn into any gas I can think of!
Not bad, Vapor-Girl, but I can shoot these!
Like a zillion X-rays all at once!
Ironclad... Vapor...X-Ray... but what can I do now...?
RAHHRR!

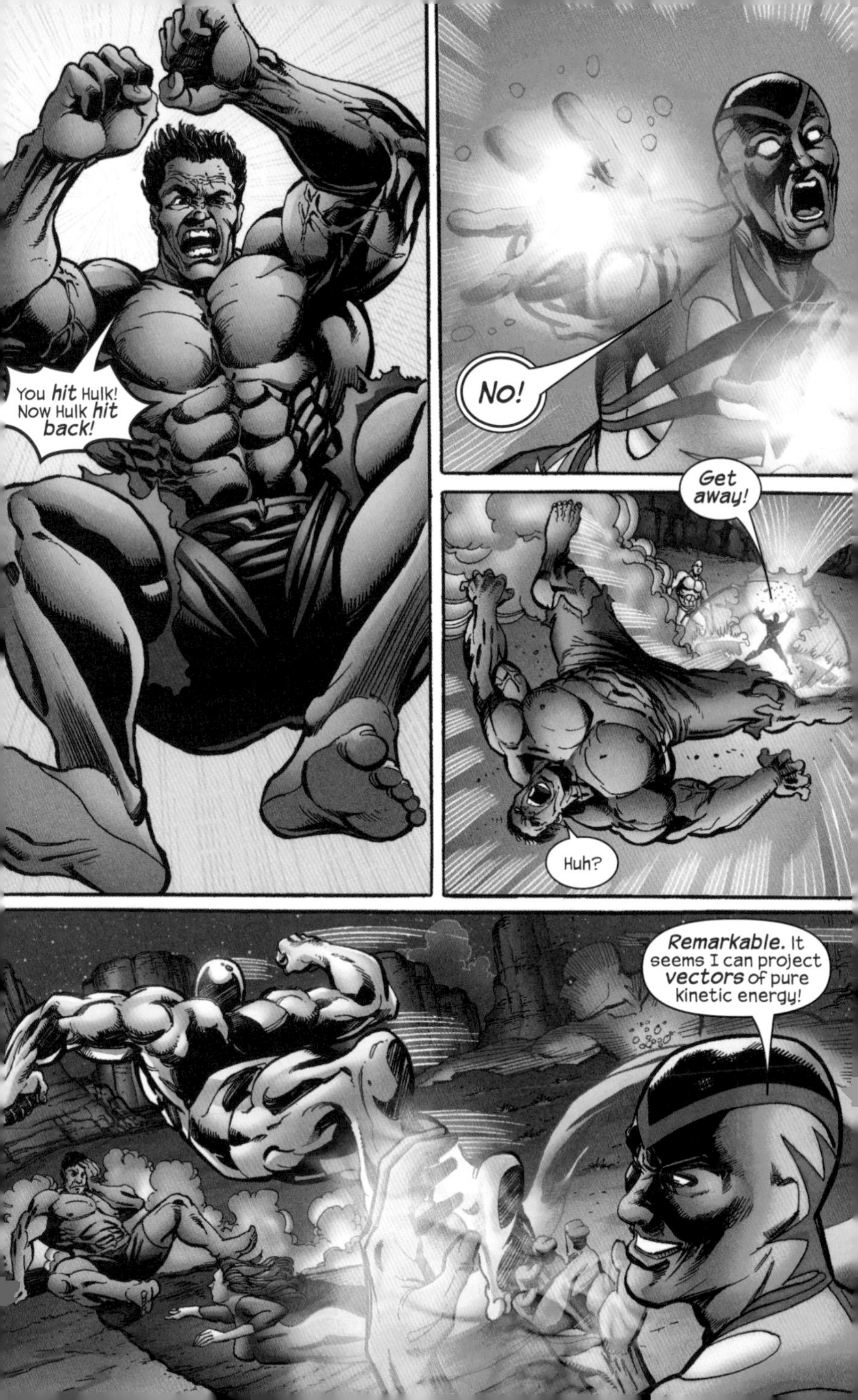
You hit Hulk! Now Hulk hit back!
No!
Get away!
Huh?
Remarkable. It seems I can project vectors of pure kinetic energy!

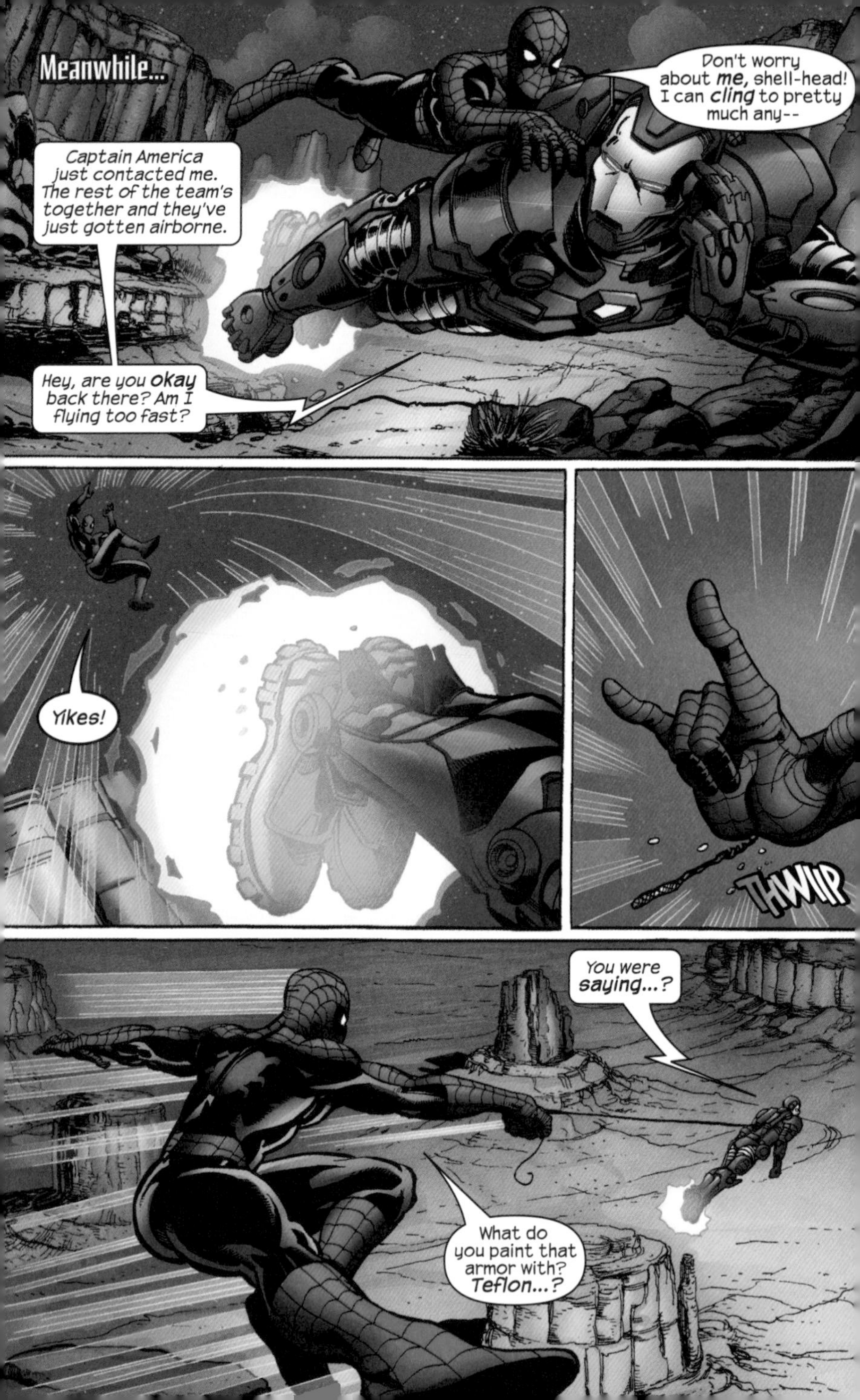
Meanwhile...
Captain America just contacted me. The rest of the team's together and they've just gotten airborne.
Hey, are you okay back there? Am I flying too fast?
Don't worry about me, shell-head! I can cling to pretty much any--
Yikes!
THWIP
You were saying...?
What do you paint that armor with? Teflon...?

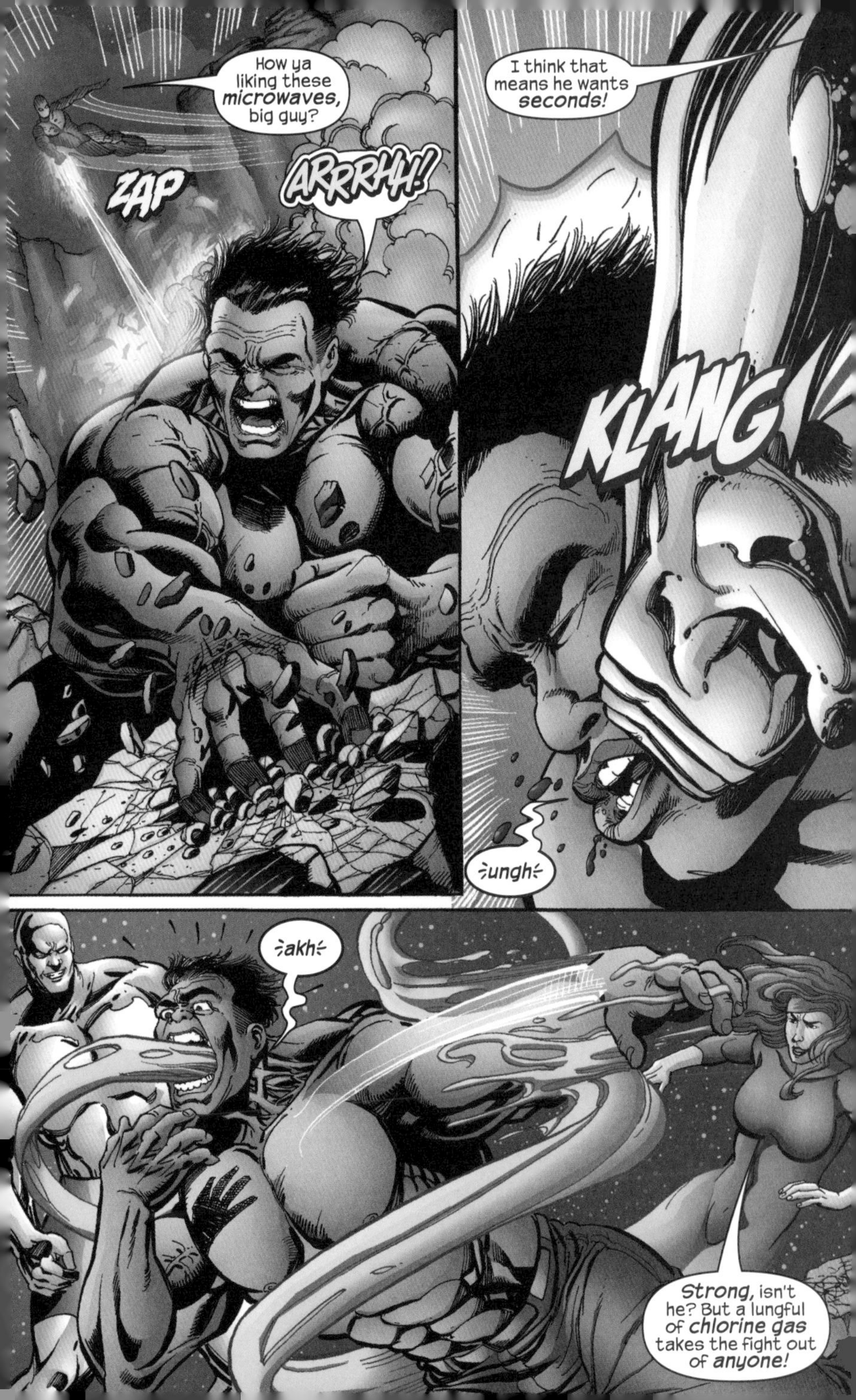
How ya liking these microwaves, big guy?
ZAP
ARRRHH!
I think that means he wants seconds!
KLANG
ungh
akh
Strong, isn't he? But a lungful of chlorine gas takes the fight out of anyone!

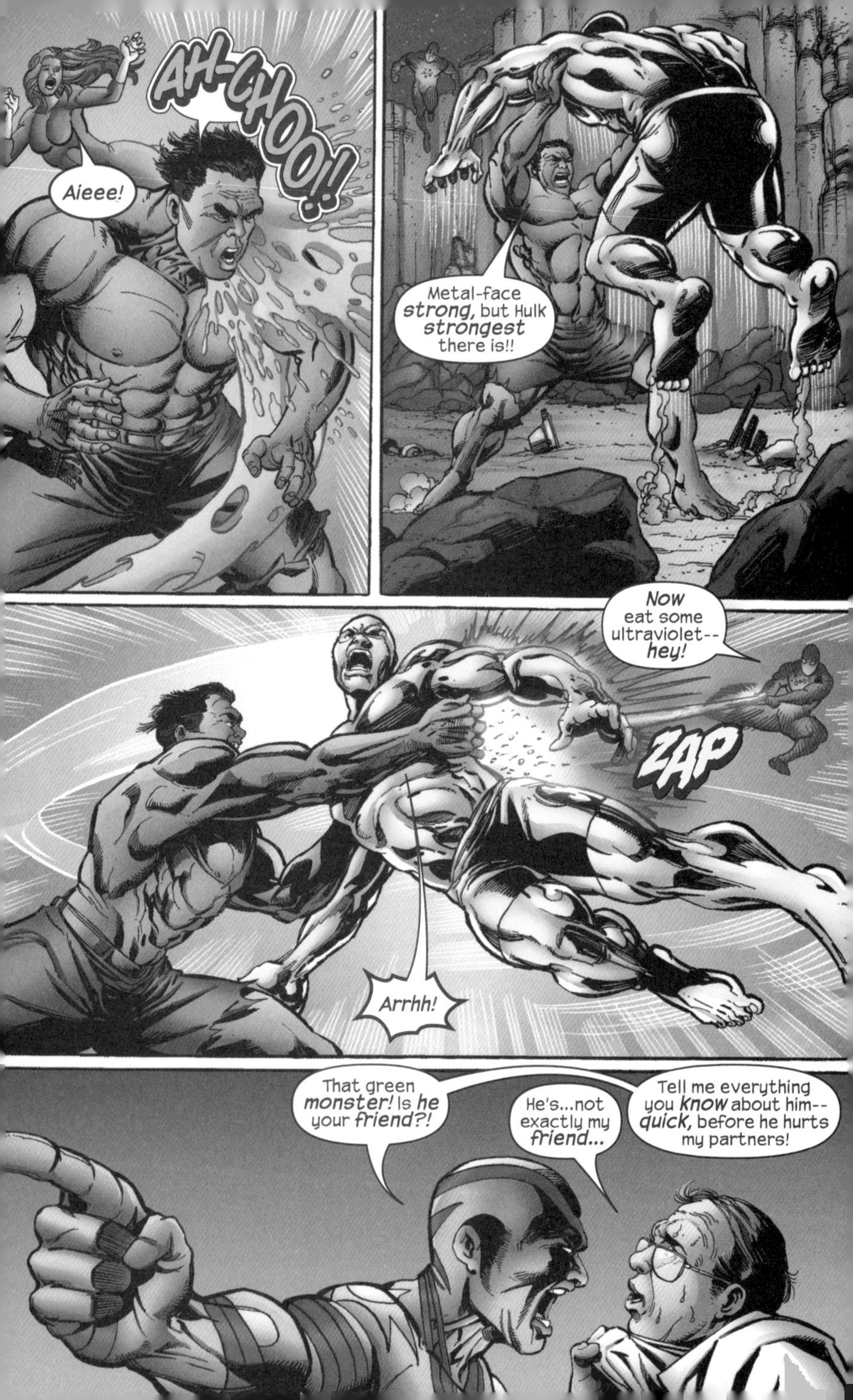
AH-CHOO!!
Aieee!
Metal-face strong, but Hulk strongest there is!!
Now eat some ultraviolet--hey!
ZAP
Arrhh!
That green monster! Is he your friend?!
He's...not exactly my friend...
Tell me everything you know about him--quick, before he hurts my partners!

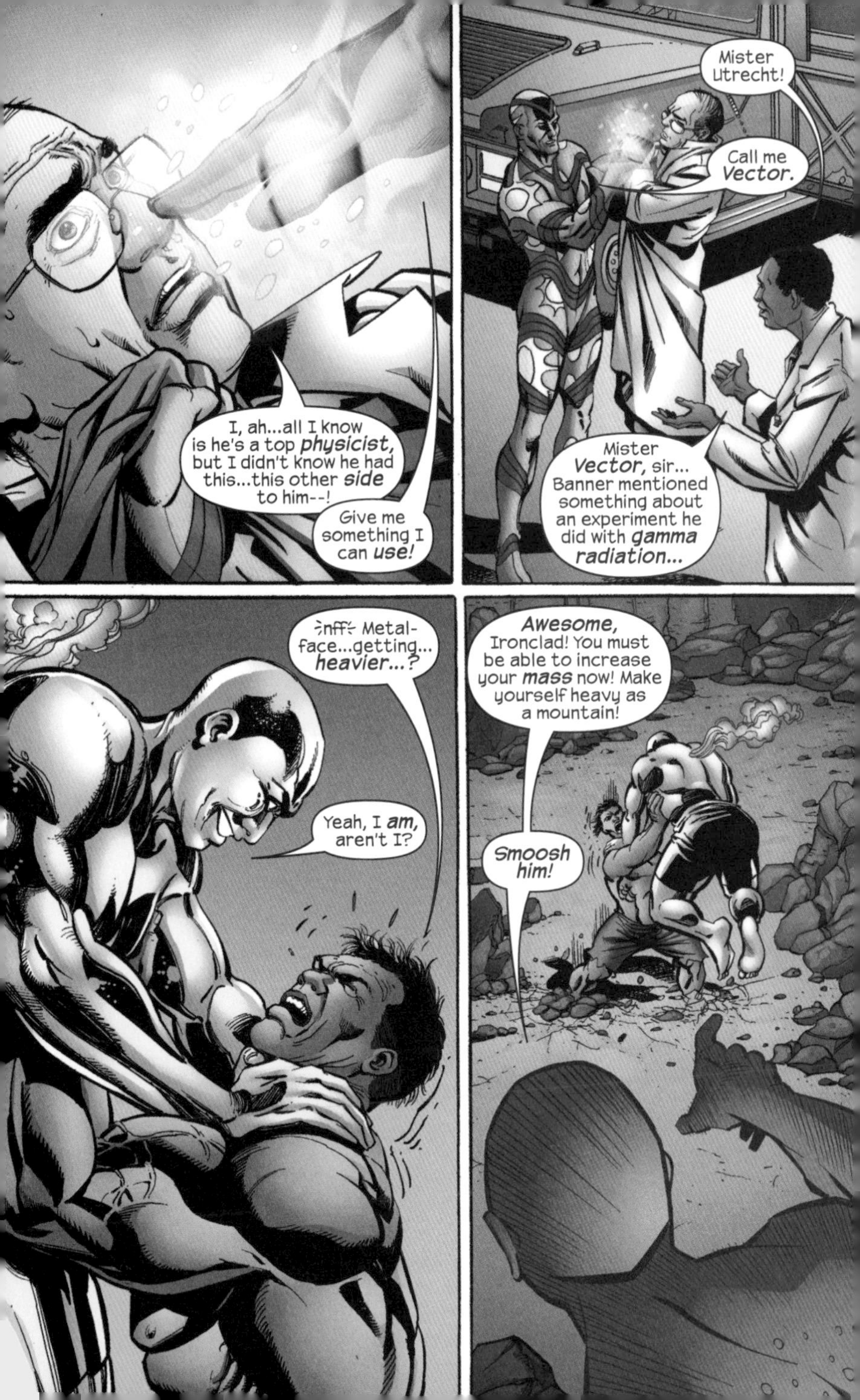
I, ah...all I know is he's a top *physicist*, but I didn't know he had this...this other *side* to him--!
Give me something I can *use!*
Mister Utrecht!
Call me *Vector.*
Mister *Vector,* sir... Banner mentioned something about an experiment he did with *gamma radiation...*
nff Metal-face...getting... *heavier...?*
Yeah, I *am,* aren't I?
Awesome, Ironclad! You must be able to increase your *mass* now! Make yourself heavy as a mountain!
Smoosh him!

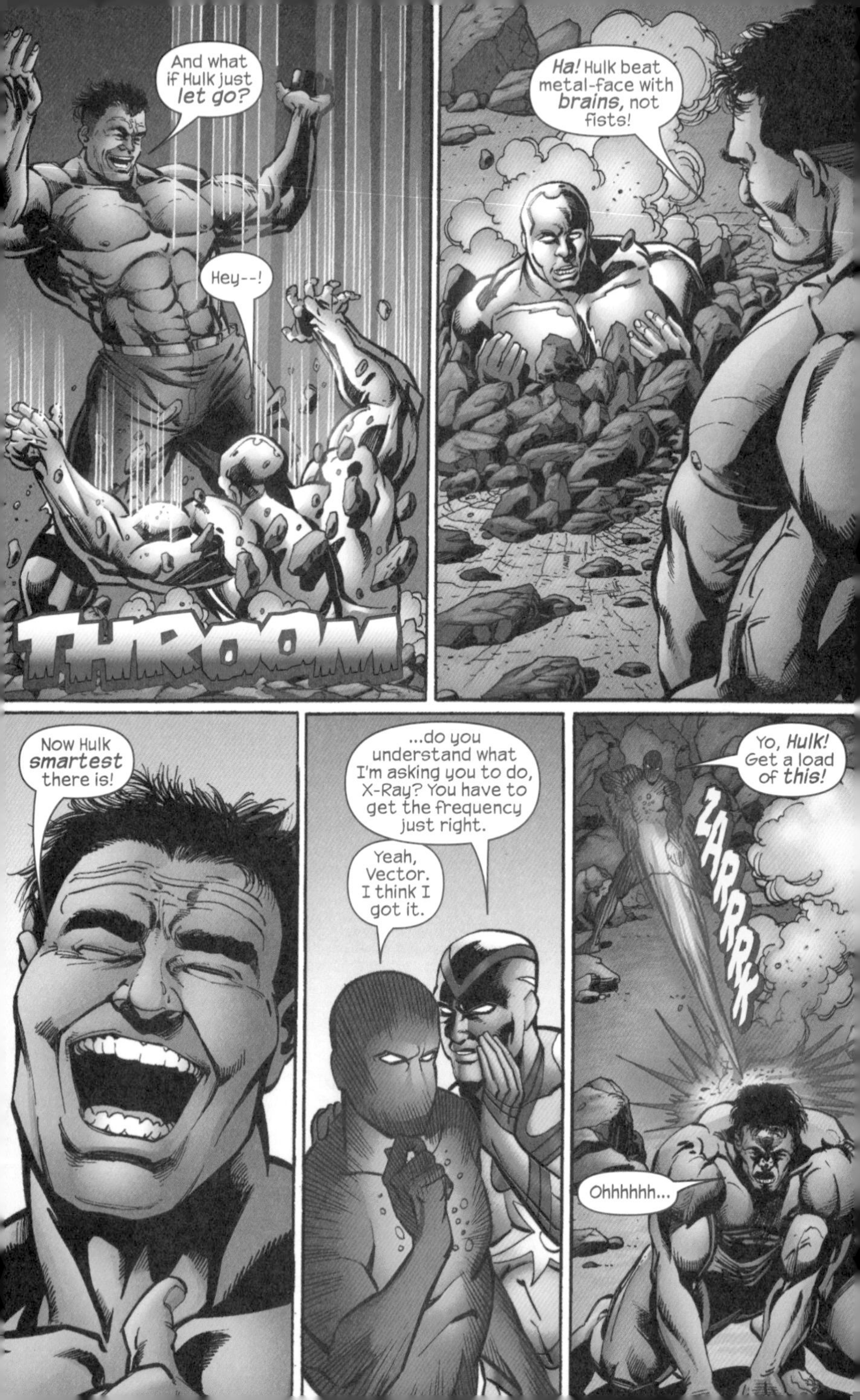
And what if Hulk just *let go?*
Hey--!
THROOM
Ha! Hulk beat metal-face with **brains,** not fists!
Now Hulk **smartest** there is!
...do you understand what I'm asking you to do, X-Ray? You have to get the frequency just right.
Yeah, Vector. I think I got it.
Yo, **Hulk!** Get a load of **this!**
ZARRRK
Ohhhhhh...

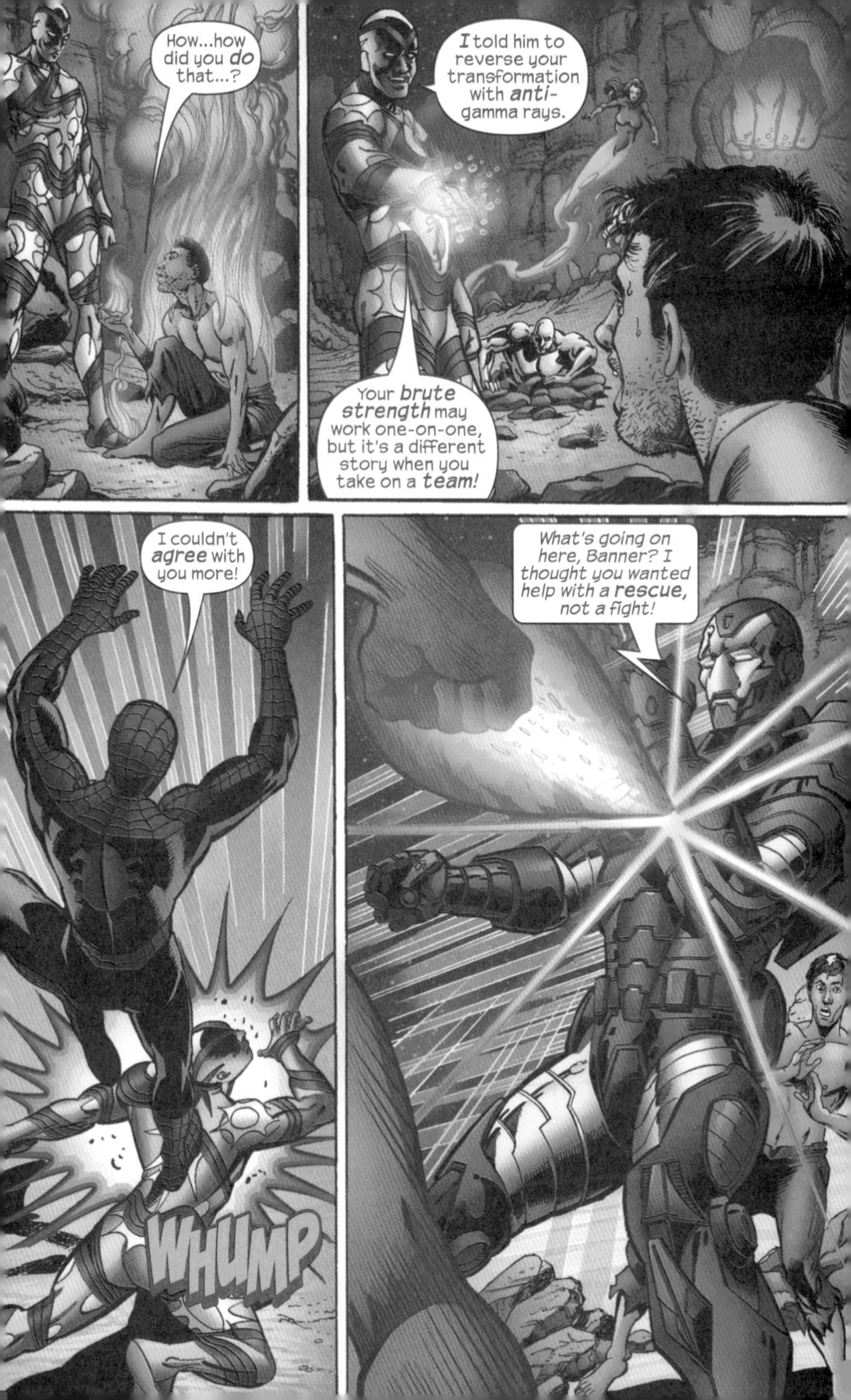
How...how did you do that...?
I told him to reverse your transformation with anti-gamma rays.
Your brute strength may work one-on-one, but it's a different story when you take on a team!
I couldn't agree with you more!
WHUMP
What's going on here, Banner? I thought you wanted help with a rescue, not a fight!

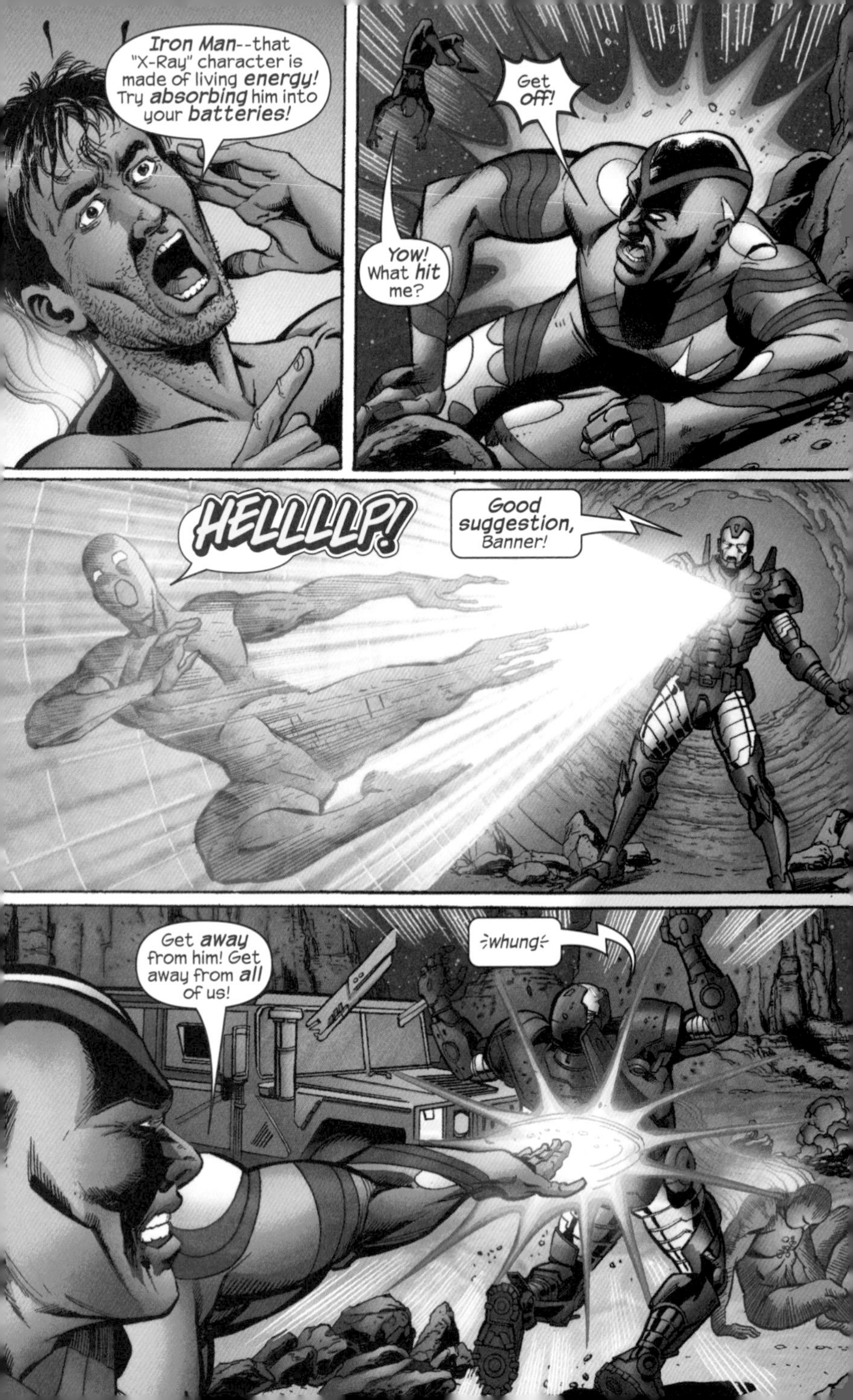

Iron Man--that "X-Ray" character is made of living energy! Try absorbing him into your batteries!
Get off!
Yow! What hit me?
HELLLLP!
Good suggestion, Banner!
Get away from him! Get away from all of us!
whung

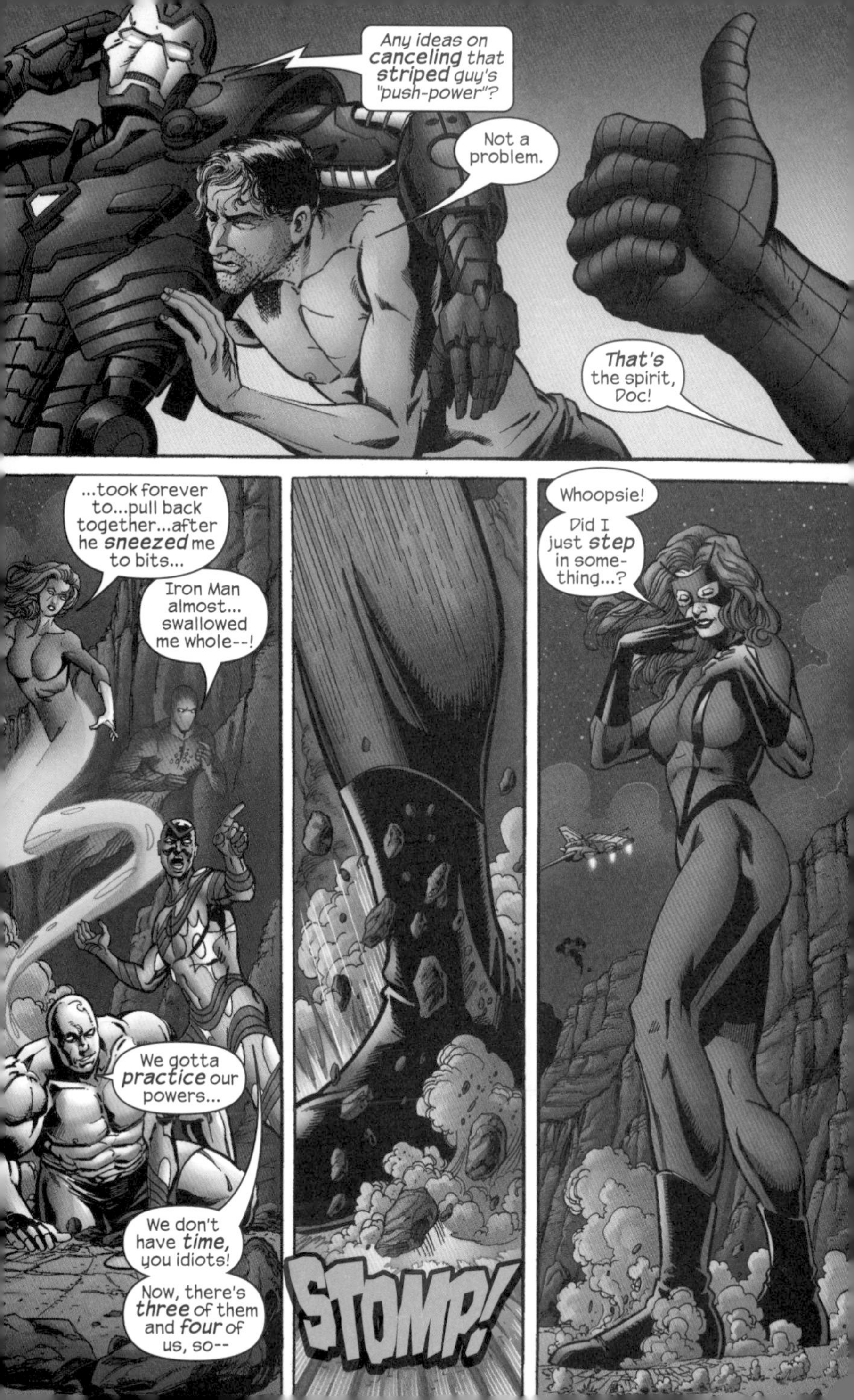
Any ideas on canceling that striped guy's "push-power"?
Not a problem.
That's the spirit, Doc!
...took forever to...pull back together...after he sneezed me to bits...
Iron Man almost... swallowed me whole--!
We gotta practice our powers...
We don't have time, you idiots!
Now, there's three of them and four of us, so--
STOMP!
Whoopsie!
Did I just step in some-thing...?

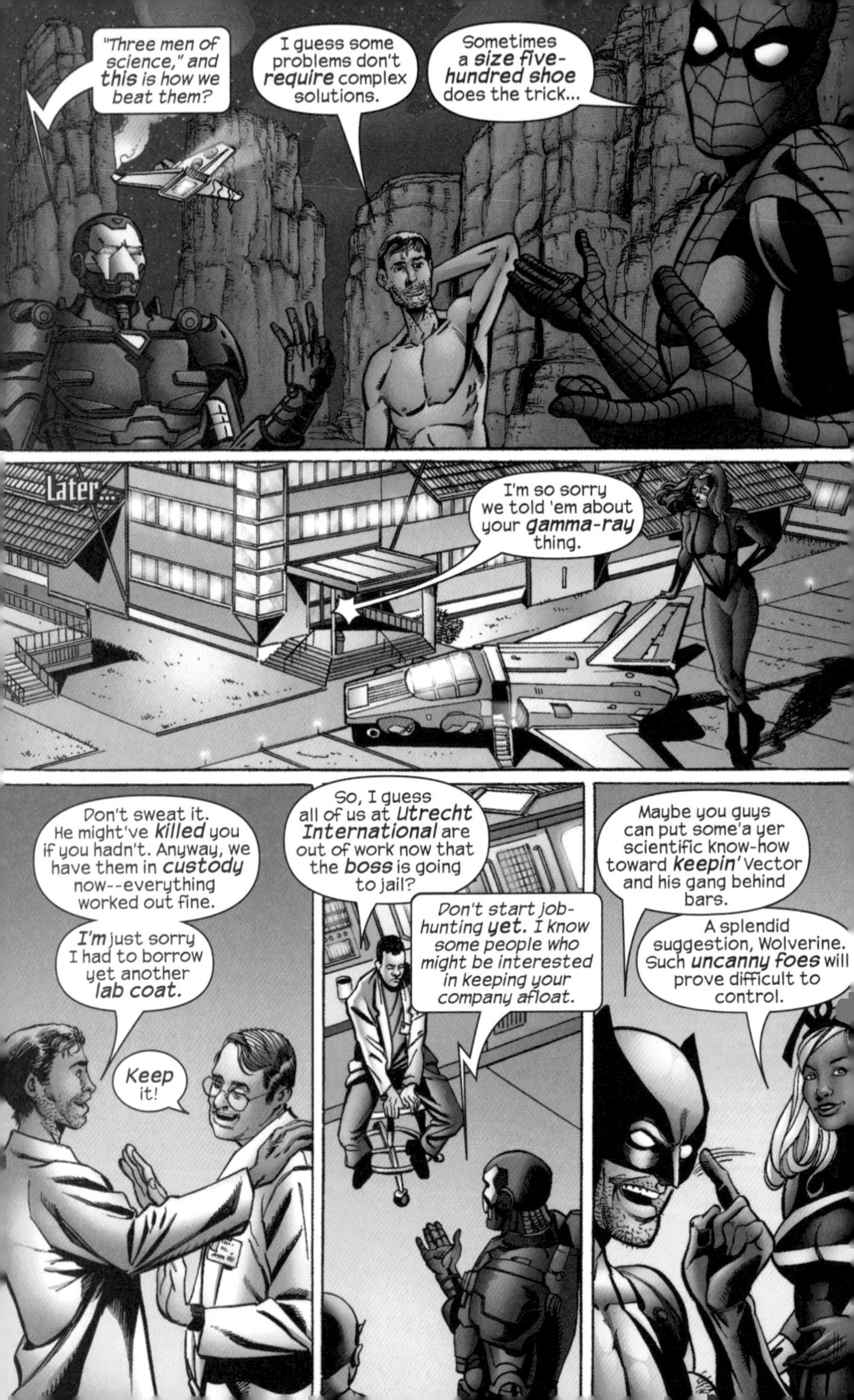
"Three men of science," and this is how we beat them?
I guess some problems don't require complex solutions.
Sometimes a size five-hundred shoe does the trick...
Later...
I'm so sorry we told 'em about your gamma-ray thing.
Don't sweat it. He might've killed you if you hadn't. Anyway, we have them in custody now--everything worked out fine.
I'm just sorry I had to borrow yet another lab coat.
Keep it!
So, I guess all of us at Utrecht International are out of work now that the boss is going to jail?
Don't start job-hunting yet. I know some people who might be interested in keeping your company afloat.
Maybe you guys can put some'a yer scientific know-how toward keepin' Vector and his gang behind bars.
A splendid suggestion, Wolverine. Such uncanny foes will prove difficult to control.

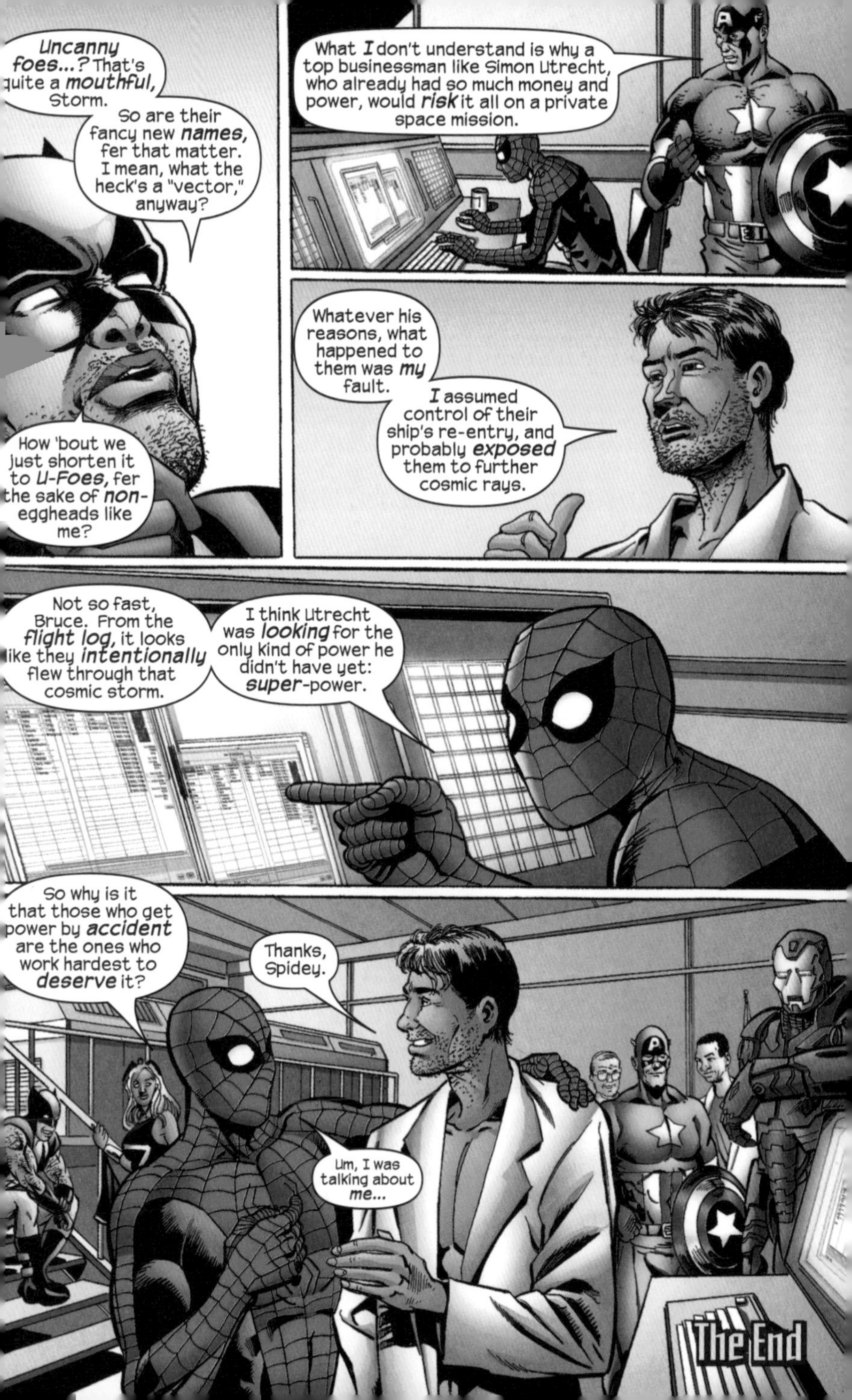
Uncanny foes...? That's quite a mouthful, Storm.
So are their fancy new names, fer that matter. I mean, what the heck's a "vector," anyway?
How 'bout we just shorten it to U-Foes, fer the sake of non-eggheads like me?
What I don't understand is why a top businessman like Simon Utrecht, who already had so much money and power, would risk it all on a private space mission.
Whatever his reasons, what happened to them was my fault.
I assumed control of their ship's re-entry, and probably exposed them to further cosmic rays.
Not so fast, Bruce. From the flight log, it looks like they intentionally flew through that cosmic storm.
I think Utrecht was looking for the only kind of power he didn't have yet: super-power.
So why is it that those who get power by accident are the ones who work hardest to deserve it?
Thanks, Spidey.
Um, I was talking about me...
The End

#7

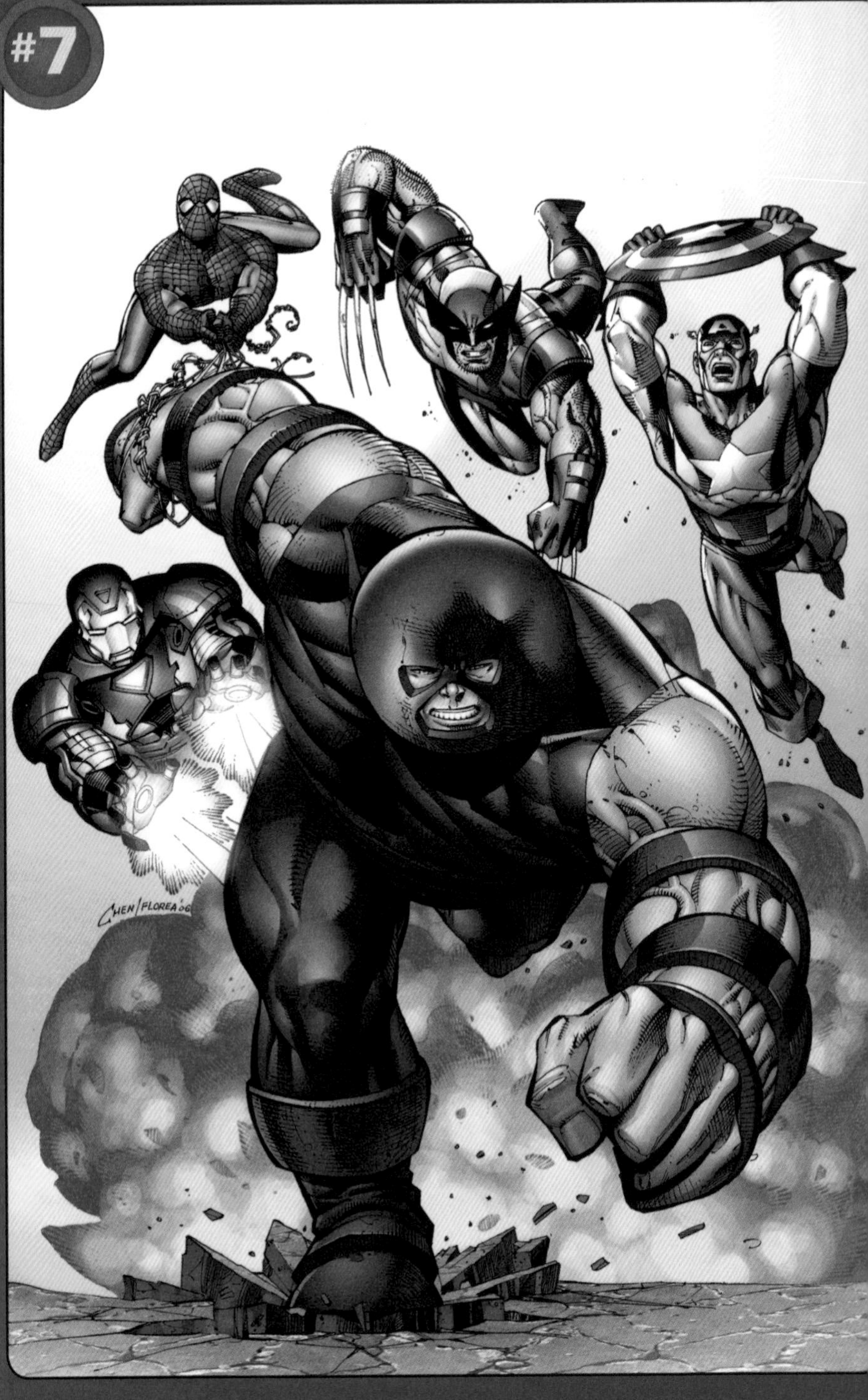
CHEN/FLOREA '06

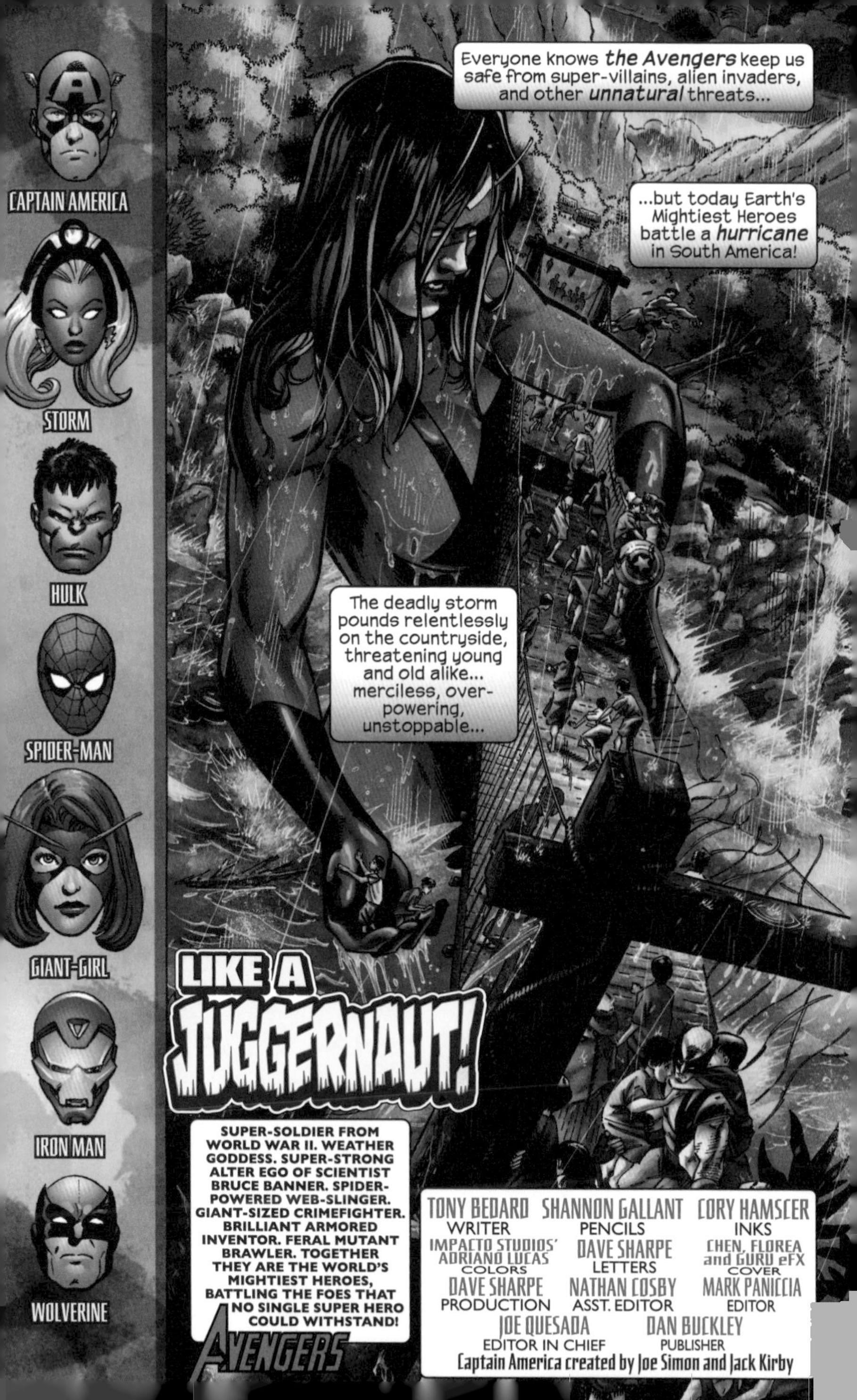

CAPTAIN AMERICA
STORM
HULK
SPIDER-MAN
GIANT-GIRL
IRON MAN
WOLVERINE
Everyone knows the Avengers keep us safe from super-villains, alien invaders, and other unnatural threats...
...but today Earth's Mightiest Heroes battle a hurricane in South America!
The deadly storm pounds relentlessly on the countryside, threatening young and old alike... merciless, over-powering, unstoppable...
LIKE A JUGGERNAUT!
SUPER-SOLDIER FROM WORLD WAR II. WEATHER GODDESS. SUPER-STRONG ALTER EGO OF SCIENTIST BRUCE BANNER. SPIDER-POWERED WEB-SLINGER. GIANT-SIZED CRIMEFIGHTER. BRILLIANT ARMORED INVENTOR. FERAL MUTANT BRAWLER. TOGETHER THEY ARE THE WORLD'S MIGHTIEST HEROES, BATTLING THE FOES THAT NO SINGLE SUPER HERO COULD WITHSTAND!
AVENGERS
TONY BEDARD WRITER
SHANNON GALLANT PENCILS
CORY HAMSCER INKS
IMPACTO STUDIOS' ADRIANO LUCAS COLORS
DAVE SHARPE LETTERS
CHEN, FLOREA and GURU eFX COVER
DAVE SHARPE PRODUCTION
NATHAN COSBY ASST. EDITOR
MARK PANICCIA EDITOR
JOE QUESADA EDITOR IN CHIEF
DAN BUCKLEY PUBLISHER
Captain America created by Joe Simon and Jack Kirby

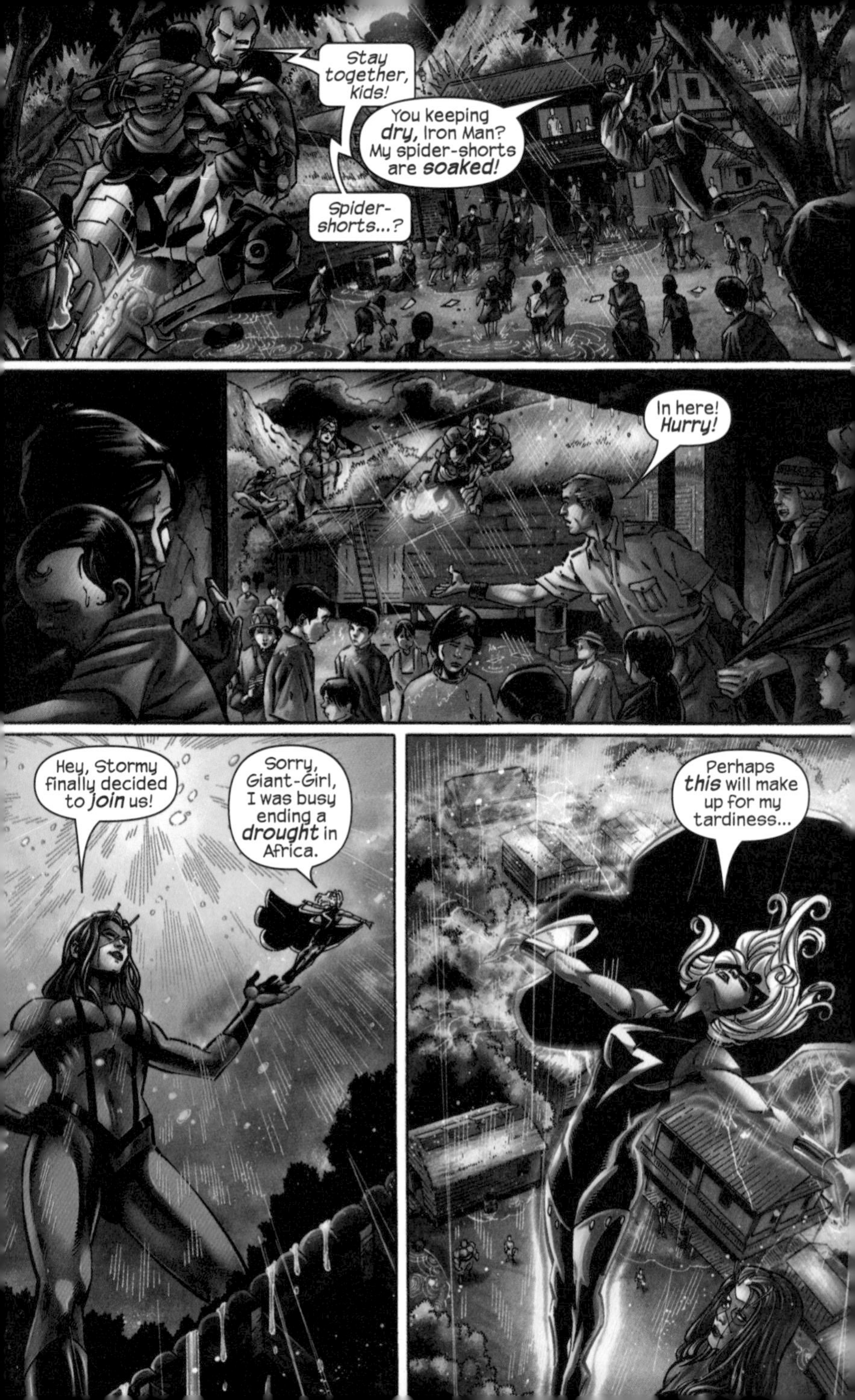
Stay together, kids!
You keeping dry, Iron Man? My spider-shorts are soaked!
Spider-shorts...?
In here! Hurry!
Hey, Stormy finally decided to join us!
Sorry, Giant-Girl, I was busy ending a drought in Africa.
Perhaps this will make up for my tardiness...

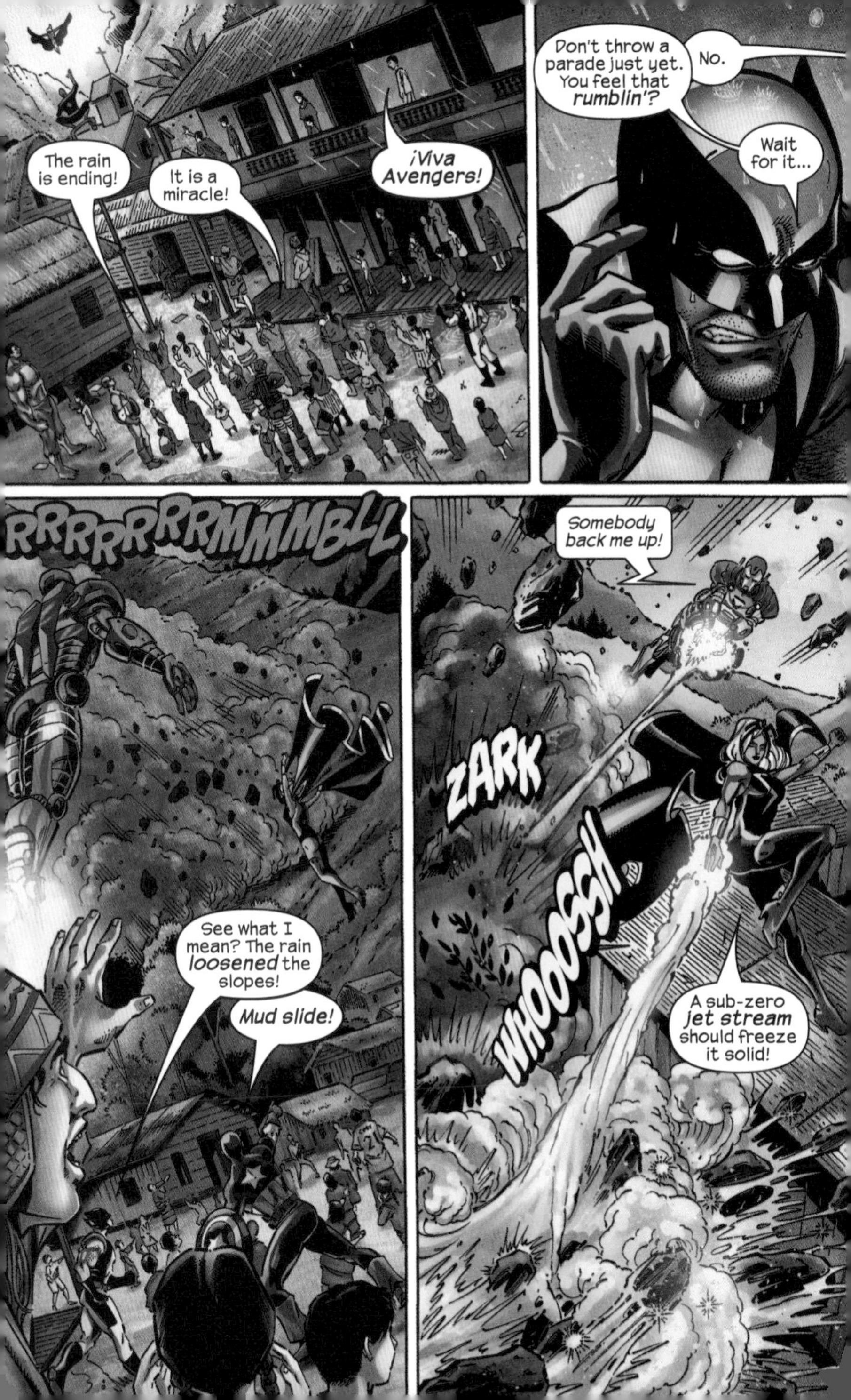
The rain is ending!
It is a miracle!
¡Viva Avengers!
Don't throw a parade just yet. You feel that rumblin'?
No.
Wait for it...
RRRRRRRMMMBLL
See what I mean? The rain loosened the slopes!
Mud slide!
Somebody back me up!
ZARK
WHOOOSSH
A sub-zero jet stream should freeze it solid!

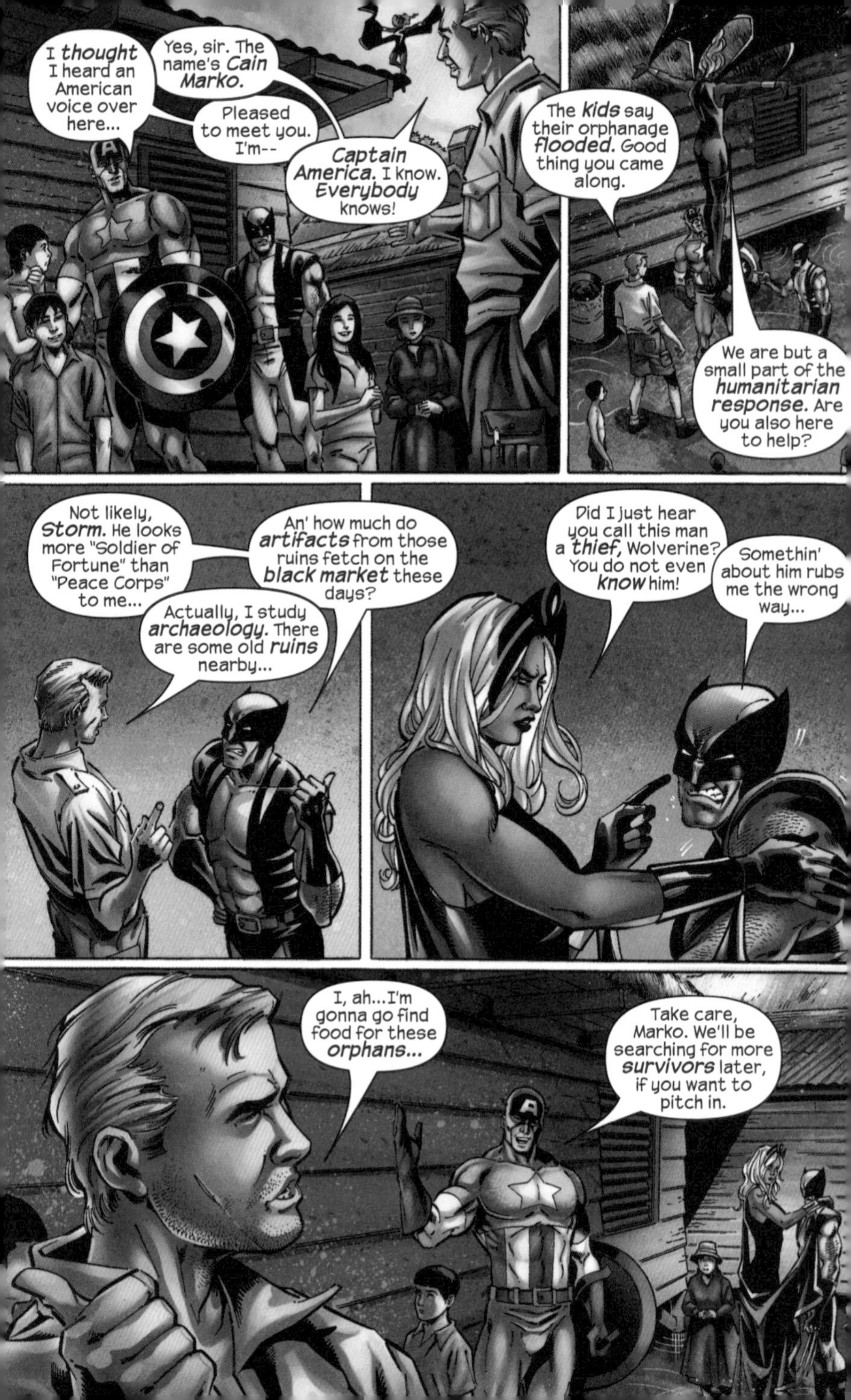

I thought I heard an American voice over here...
Yes, sir. The name's Cain Marko.
Pleased to meet you. I'm--
Captain America. I know. Everybody knows!
The kids say their orphanage flooded. Good thing you came along.
We are but a small part of the humanitarian response. Are you also here to help?
Not likely, Storm. He looks more "Soldier of Fortune" than "Peace Corps" to me...
An' how much do artifacts from those ruins fetch on the black market these days?
Actually, I study archaeology. There are some old ruins nearby...
Did I just hear you call this man a thief, Wolverine? You do not even know him!
Somethin' about him rubs me the wrong way...
I, ah...I'm gonna go find food for these orphans...
Take care, Marko. We'll be searching for more survivors later, if you want to pitch in.

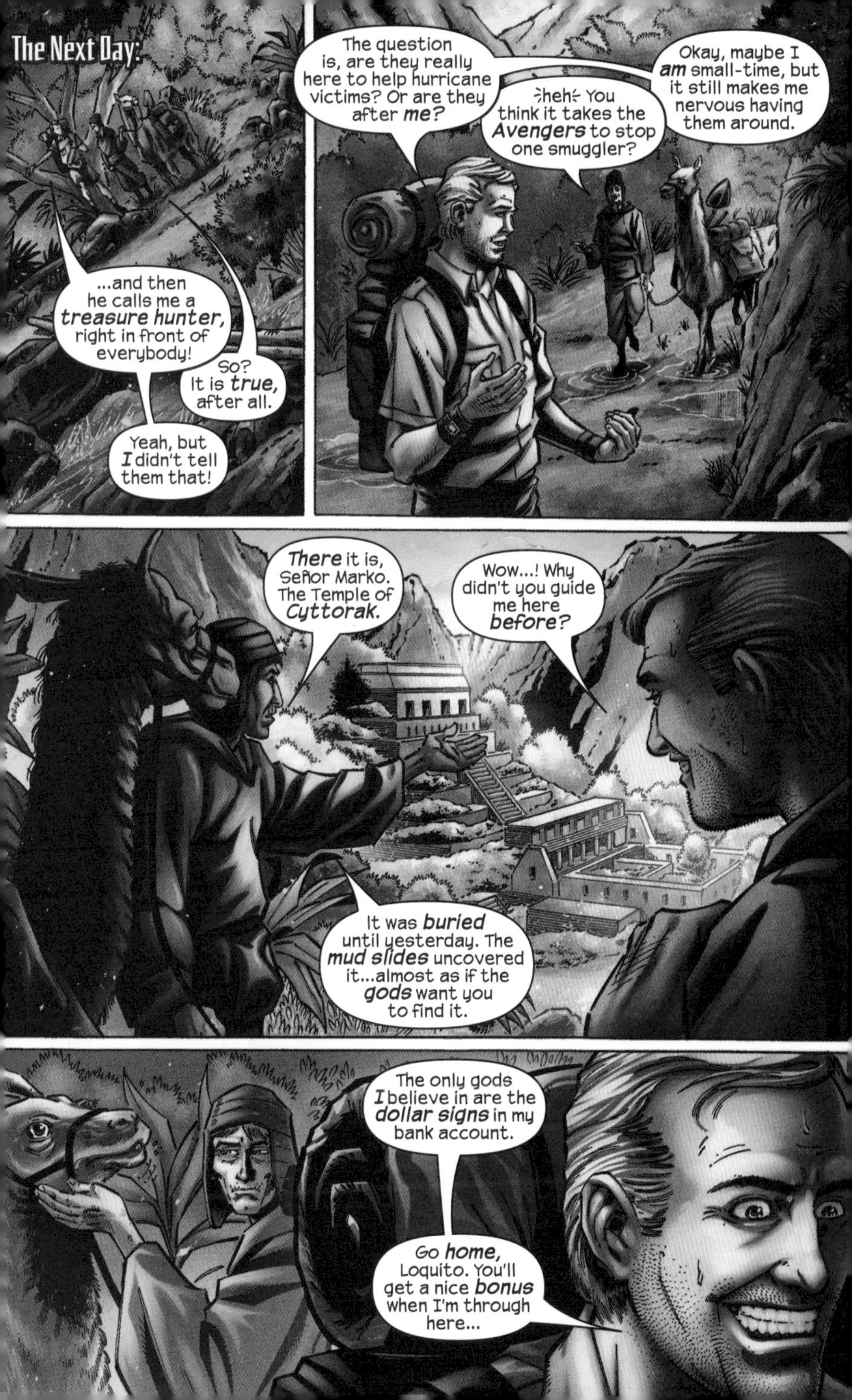
The Next Day:
...and then he calls me a treasure hunter, right in front of everybody!
So? It is true, after all.
Yeah, but I didn't tell them that!
The question is, are they really here to help hurricane victims? Or are they after me?
=heh= You think it takes the Avengers to stop one smuggler?
Okay, maybe I am small-time, but it still makes me nervous having them around.
There it is, Señor Marko. The Temple of Cyttorak.
Wow...! Why didn't you guide me here before?
It was buried until yesterday. The mud slides uncovered it...almost as if the gods want you to find it.
The only gods I believe in are the dollar signs in my bank account.
Go home, Loquito. You'll get a nice bonus when I'm through here...

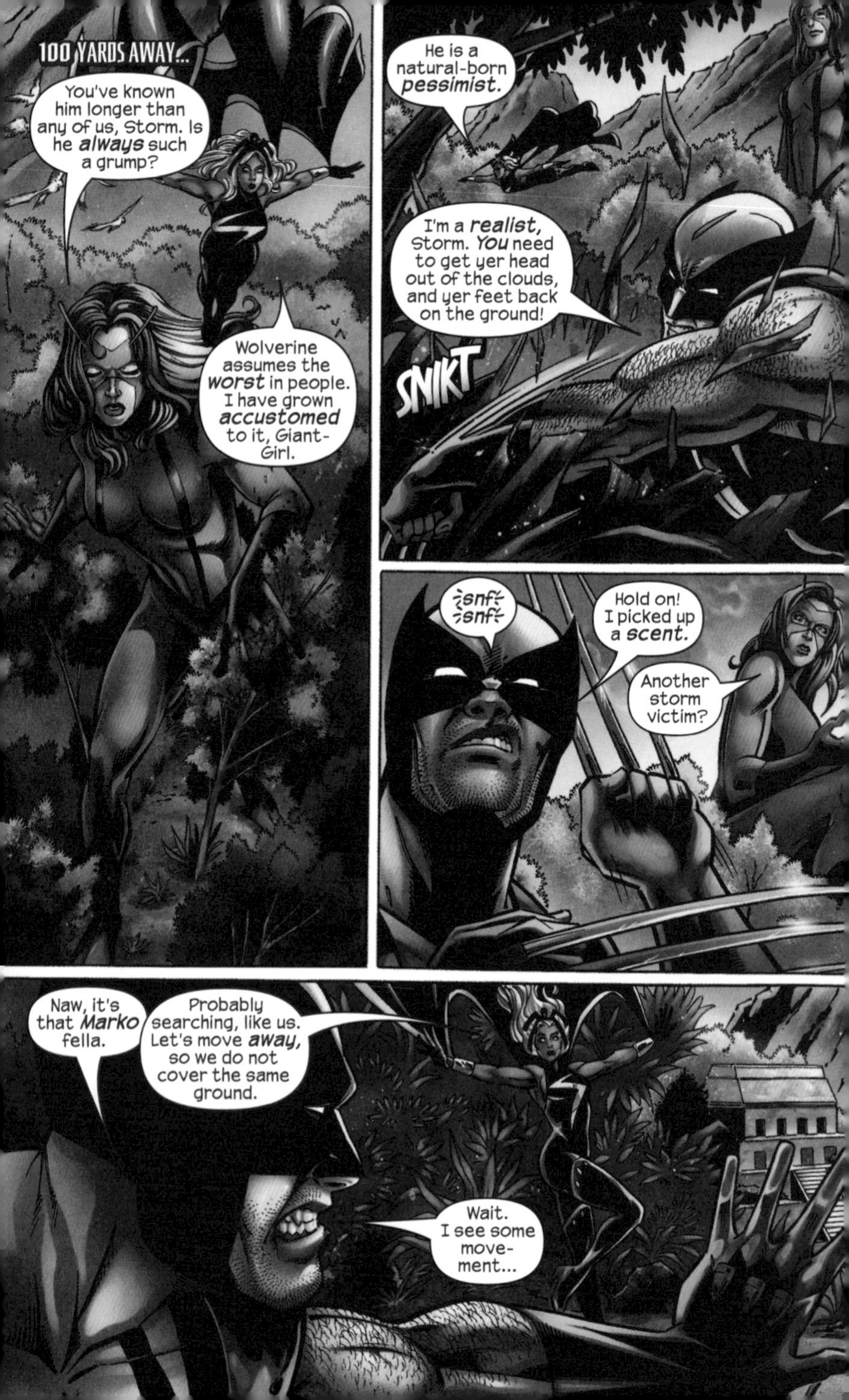
100 YARDS AWAY...
You've known him longer than any of us, Storm. Is he *always* such a grump?
Wolverine assumes the *worst* in people. I have grown *accustomed* to it, Giant-Girl.
He is a natural-born *pessimist.*
I'm a *realist,* Storm. *You* need to get yer head out of the clouds, and yer feet back on the ground!
SNIKT
snf *snf*
Hold on! I picked up a *scent.*
Another storm victim?
Naw, it's that *Marko* fella.
Probably searching, like us. Let's move *away,* so we do not cover the same ground.
Wait. I see some move-ment...

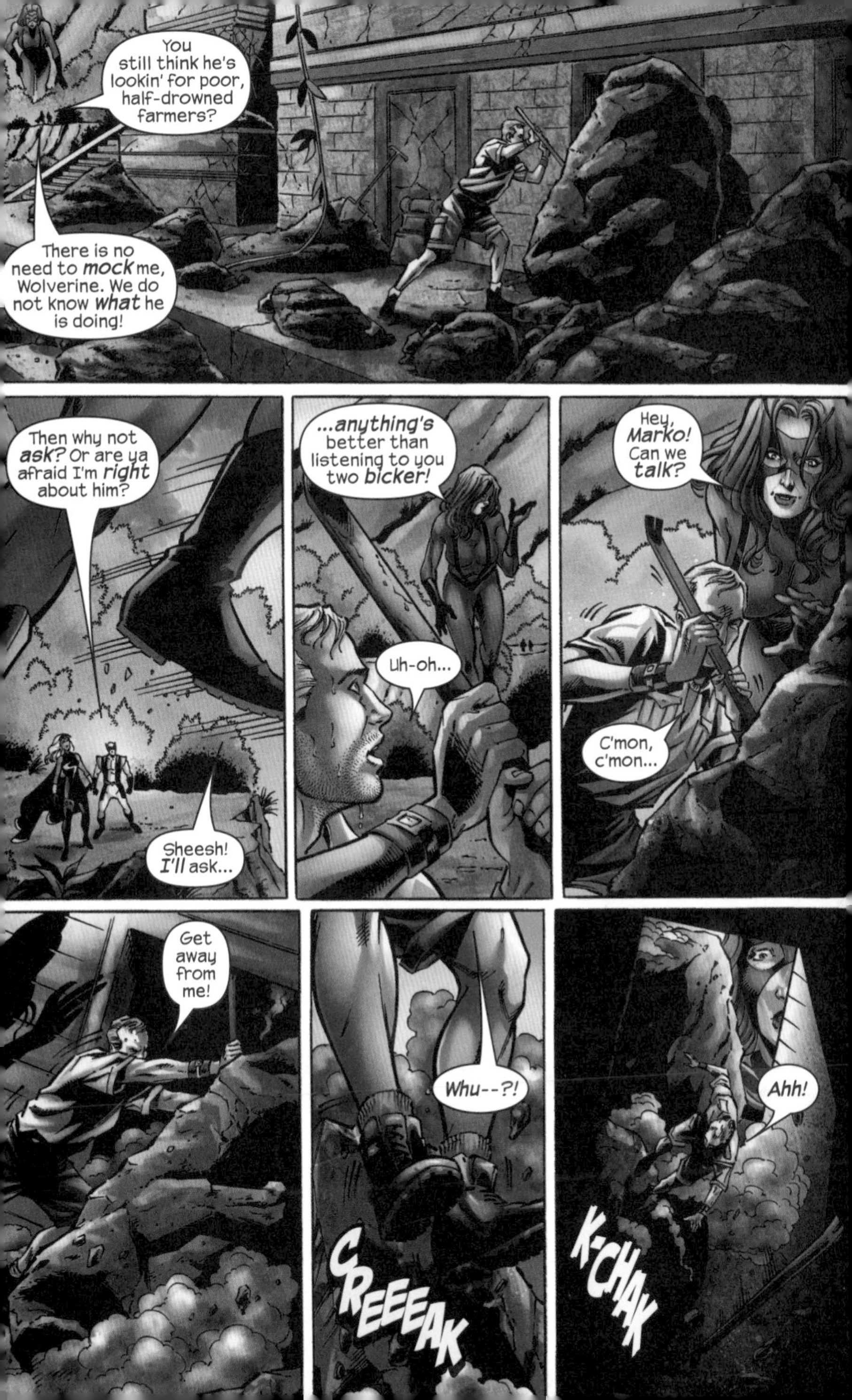
You still think he's lookin' for poor, half-drowned farmers?
There is no need to *mock* me, Wolverine. We do not know *what* he is doing!
Then why not *ask?* Or are ya afraid I'm *right* about him?
Sheesh! *I'll* ask...
...*anything's* better than listening to you two *bicker!*
Uh-oh...
Hey, *Marko!* Can we *talk?*
C'mon, c'mon...
Get away from me!
Whu--?!
CREEEAK
Ahh!
K-CHAK

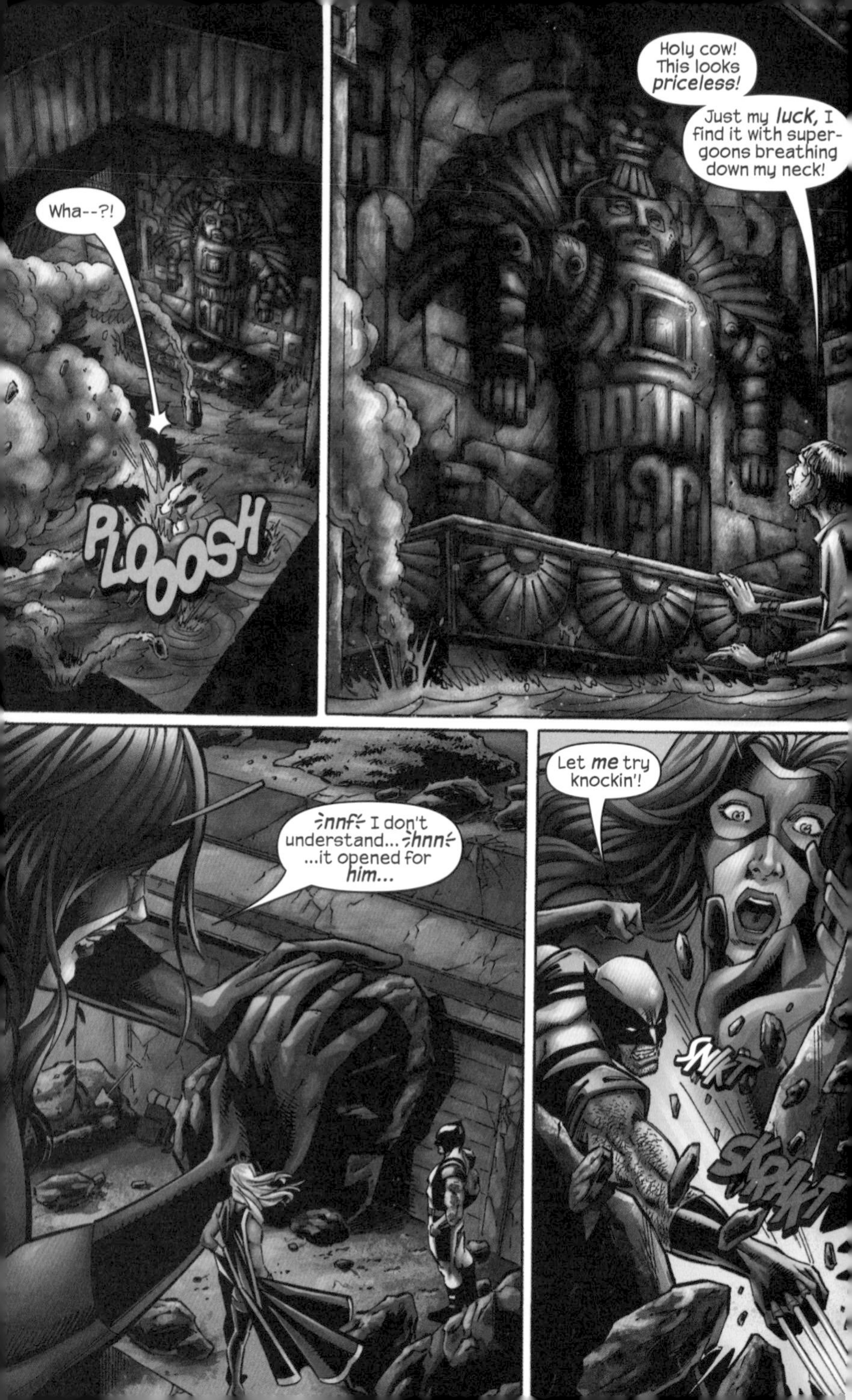
Wha--?!
PLOOOSH
Holy cow! This looks priceless!
Just my luck, I find it with super-goons breathing down my neck!
≈nnf≈ I don't understand... ≈hnn≈ ...it opened for him...
Let me try knockin'!
SNIKT
SKRAKT

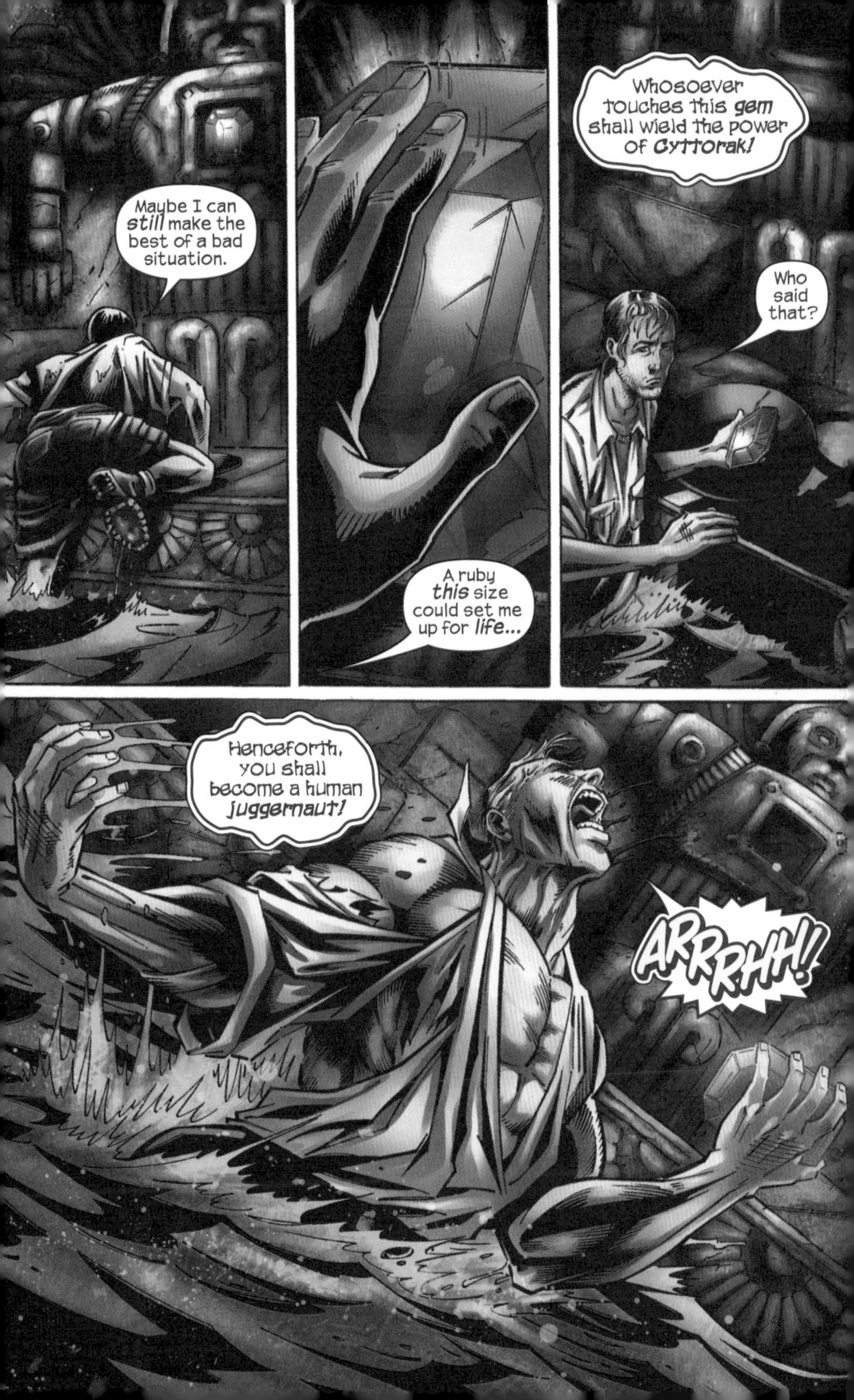
Maybe I can still make the best of a bad situation.
A ruby this size could set me up for life...
Whosoever touches this gem shall wield the power of Cyttorak!
Who said that?
Henceforth, you shall become a human juggernaut!
ARRRHH!!

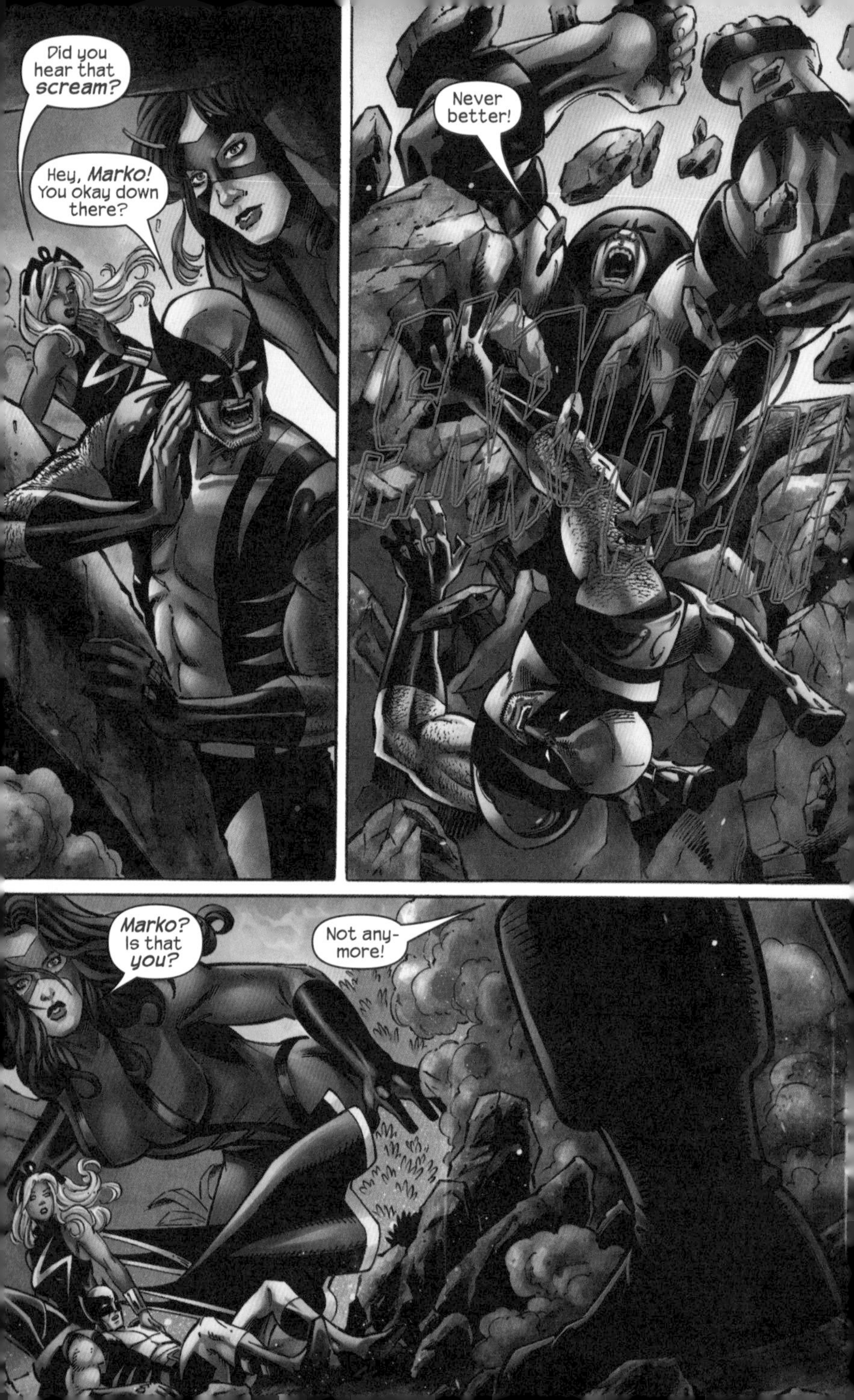
Did you hear that scream?
Hey, Marko! You okay down there?
Never better!
Marko? Is that you?
Not any-more!

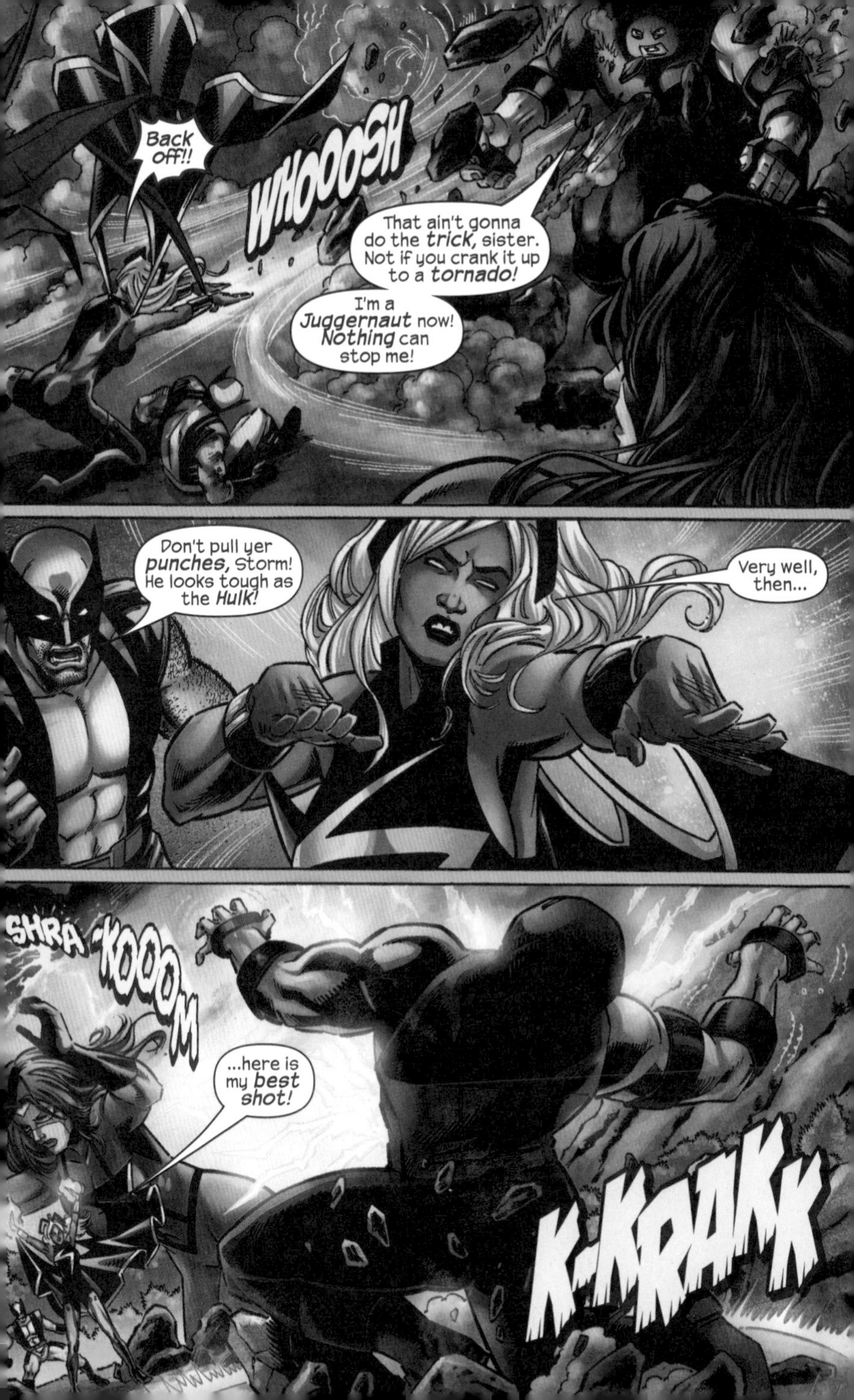

Back off!!
WHOOOSH
That ain't gonna do the trick, sister. Not if you crank it up to a tornado!
I'm a Juggernaut now! Nothing can stop me!
Don't pull yer punches, Storm! He looks tough as the Hulk!
Very well, then...
SHRA-KOOOM
...here is my best shot!
K-KRAKK

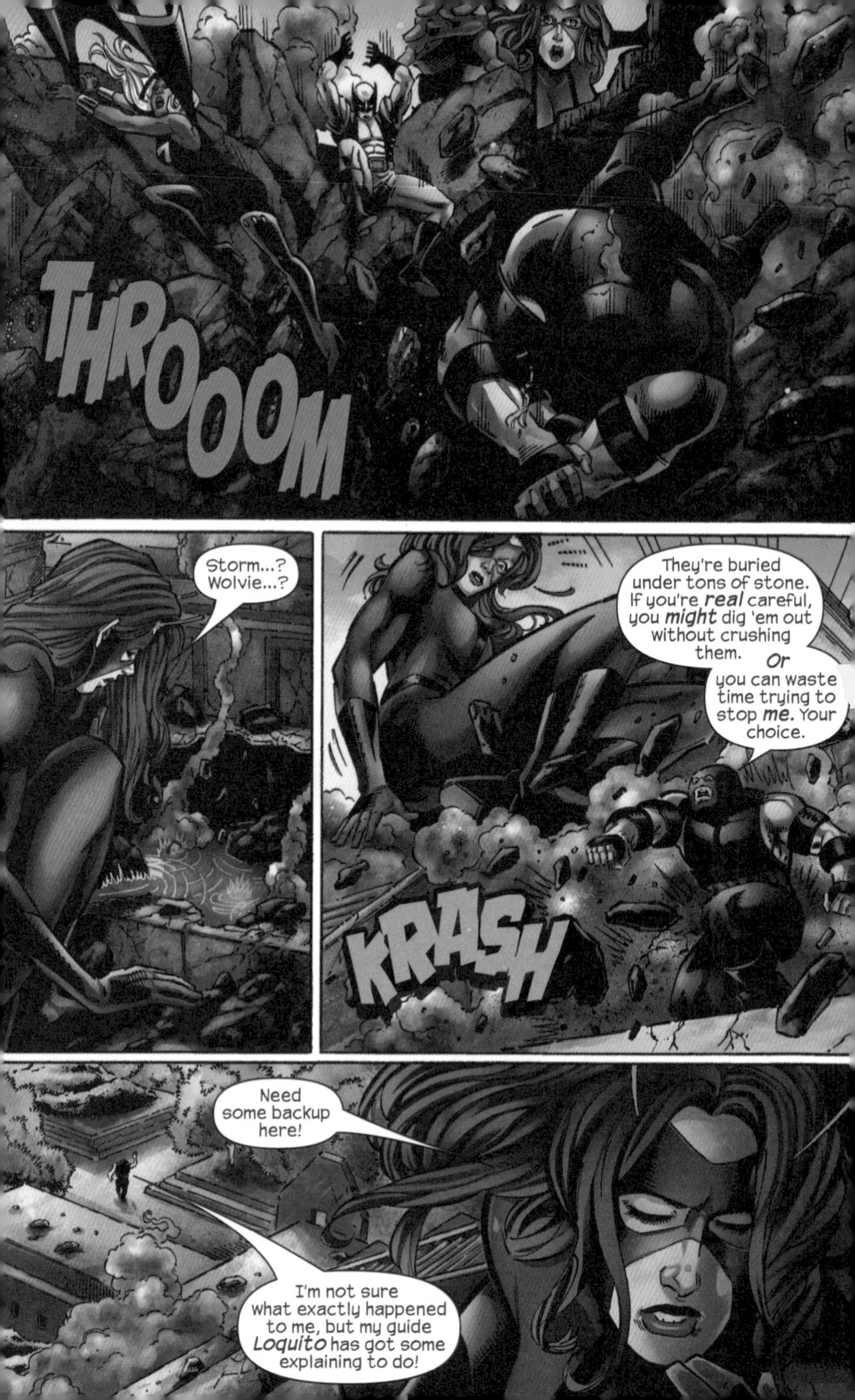

THROOOM
Storm...? Wolvie...?
They're buried under tons of stone. If you're real careful, you might dig 'em out without crushing them.
Or you can waste time trying to stop me. Your choice.
KRASH
Need some backup here!
I'm not sure what exactly happened to me, but my guide Loquito has got some explaining to do!

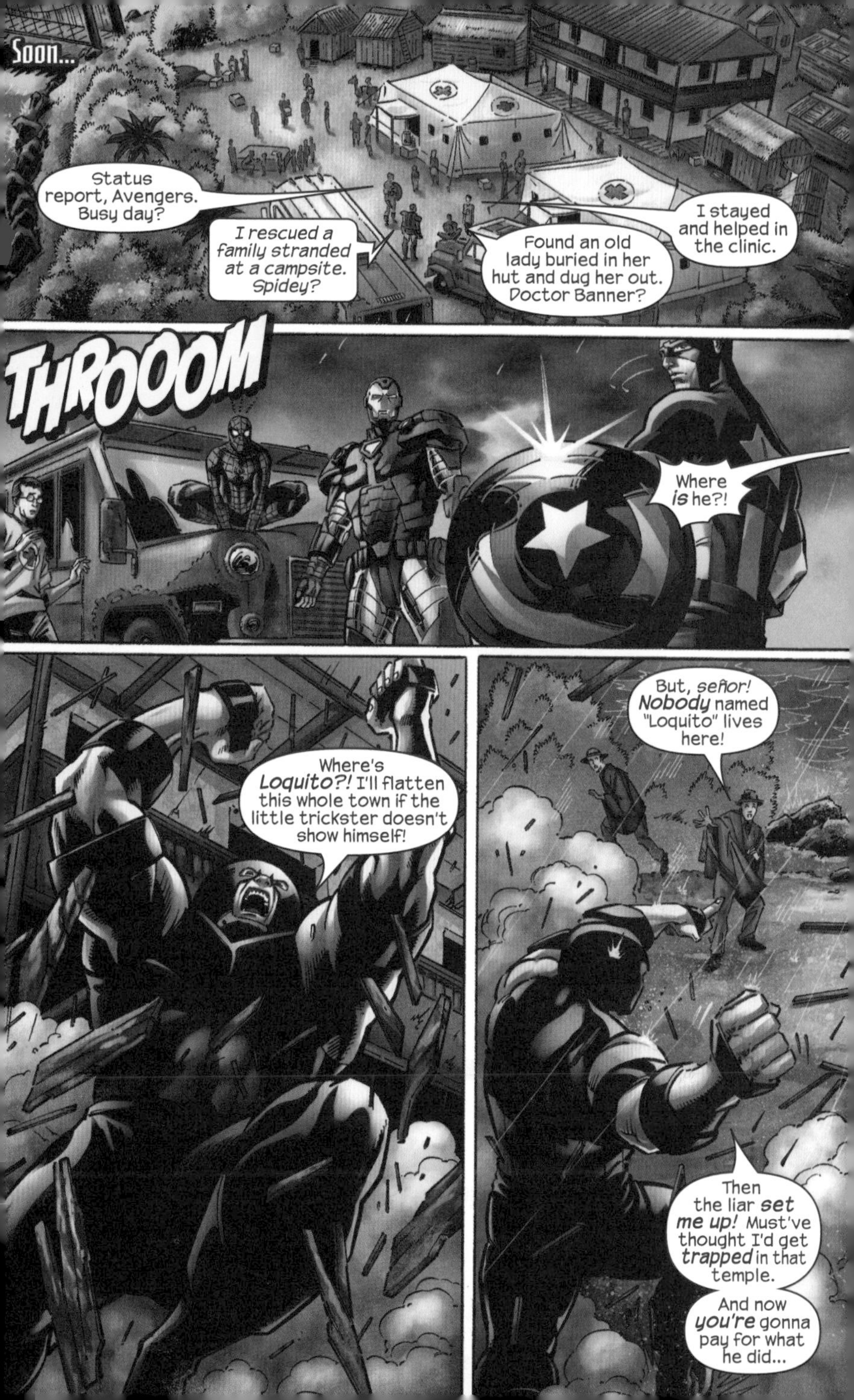
Soon...
Status report, Avengers. Busy day?
I rescued a family stranded at a campsite. Spidey?
Found an old lady buried in her hut and dug her out. Doctor Banner?
I stayed and helped in the clinic.
THROOOM
Where *is* he?!
Where's *Loquito?!* I'll flatten this whole town if the little trickster doesn't show himself!
But, *señor!* ***Nobody*** named "Loquito" lives here!
Then the liar ***set me up!*** Must've thought I'd get ***trapped*** in that temple.
And now ***you're*** gonna pay for what he did...

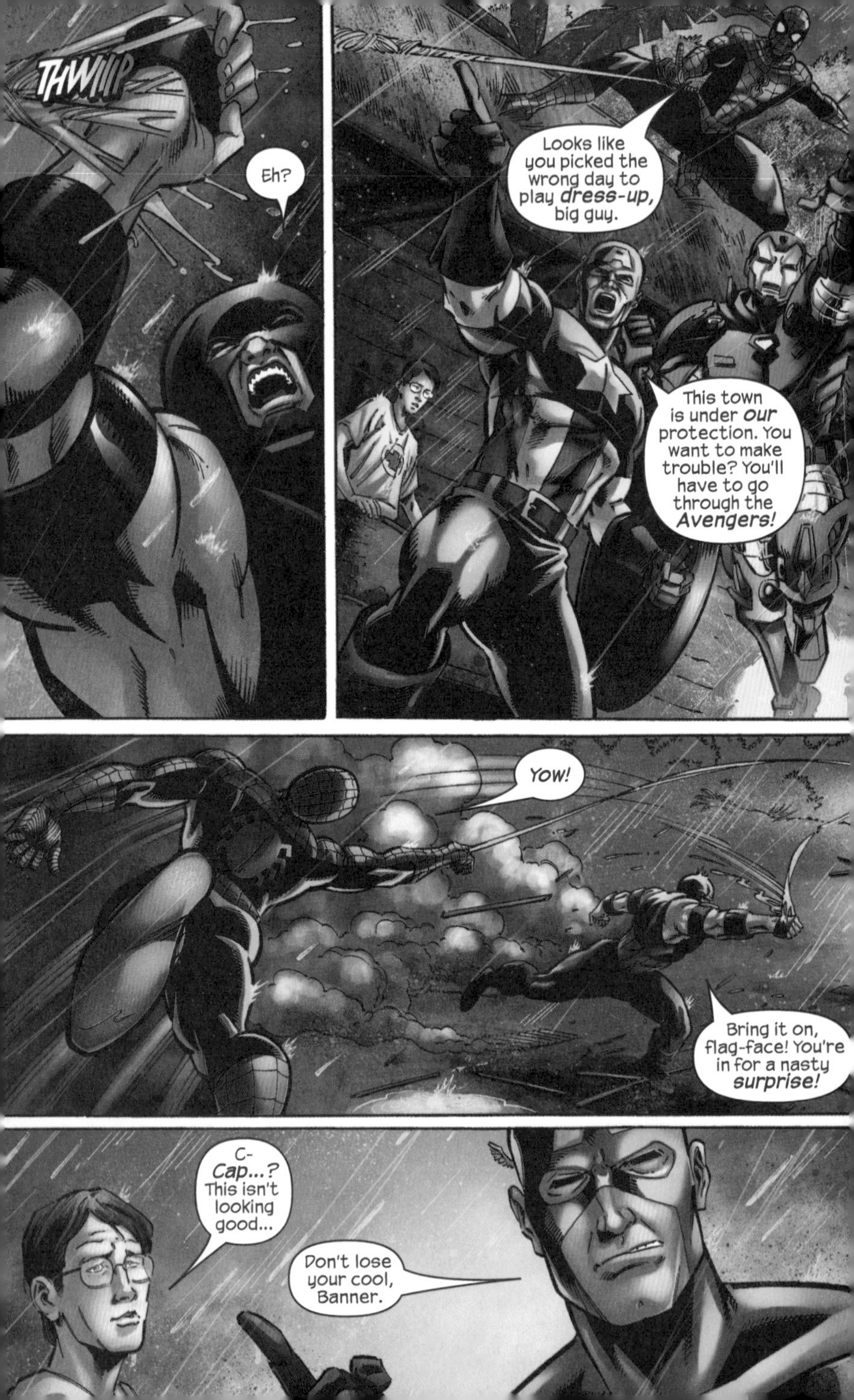

THWIIIP
Eh?
Looks like you picked the wrong day to play *dress-up,* big guy.
This town is under *our* protection. You want to make trouble? You'll have to go through the *Avengers!*
YOW!
Bring it on, flag-face! You're in for a nasty *surprise!*
C- *Cap...?* This isn't looking good...
Don't lose your cool, Banner.

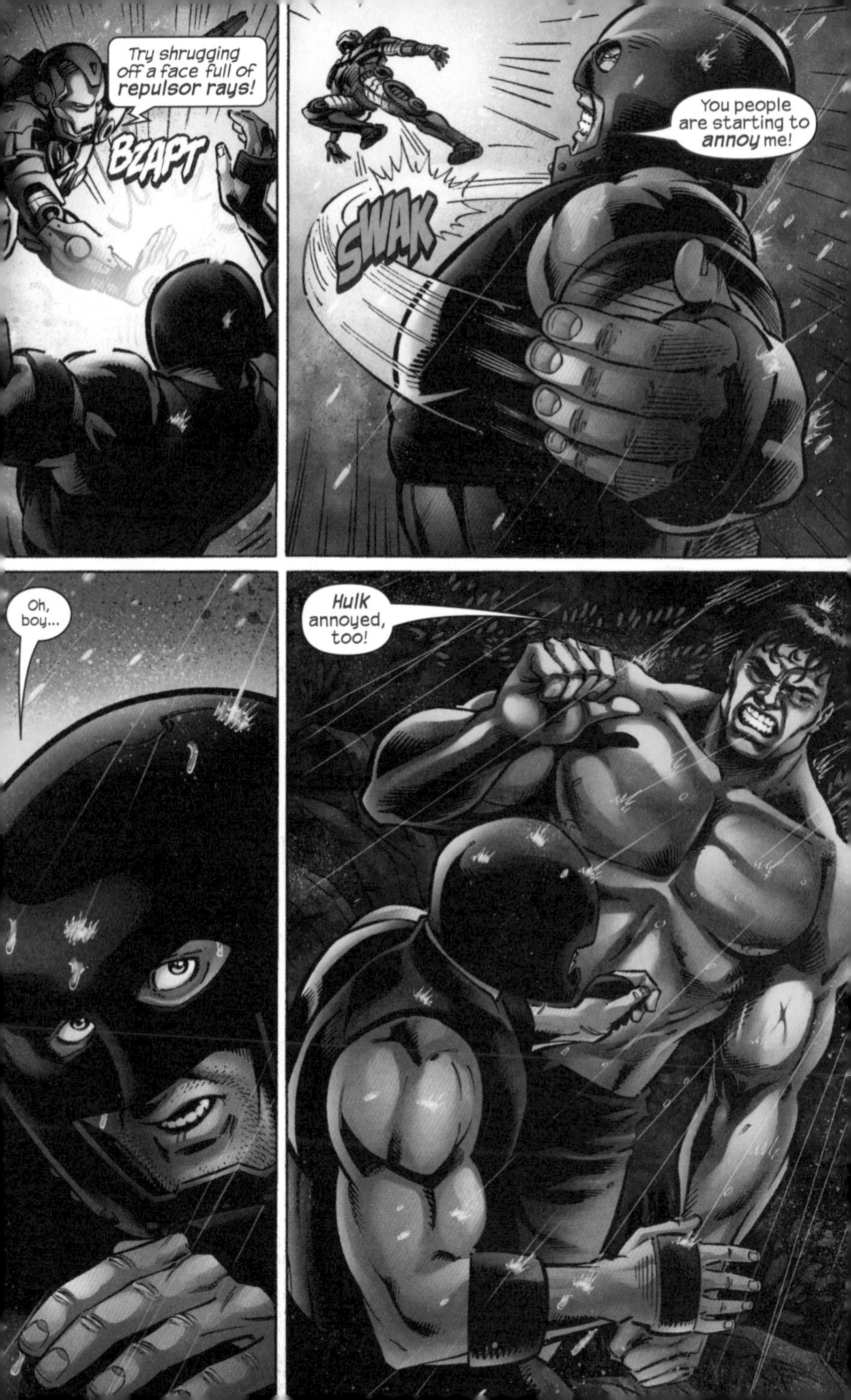
Try shrugging off a face full of repulsor rays!
BZAPT
You people are starting to annoy me!
SWAK
Oh, boy...
Hulk annoyed, too!

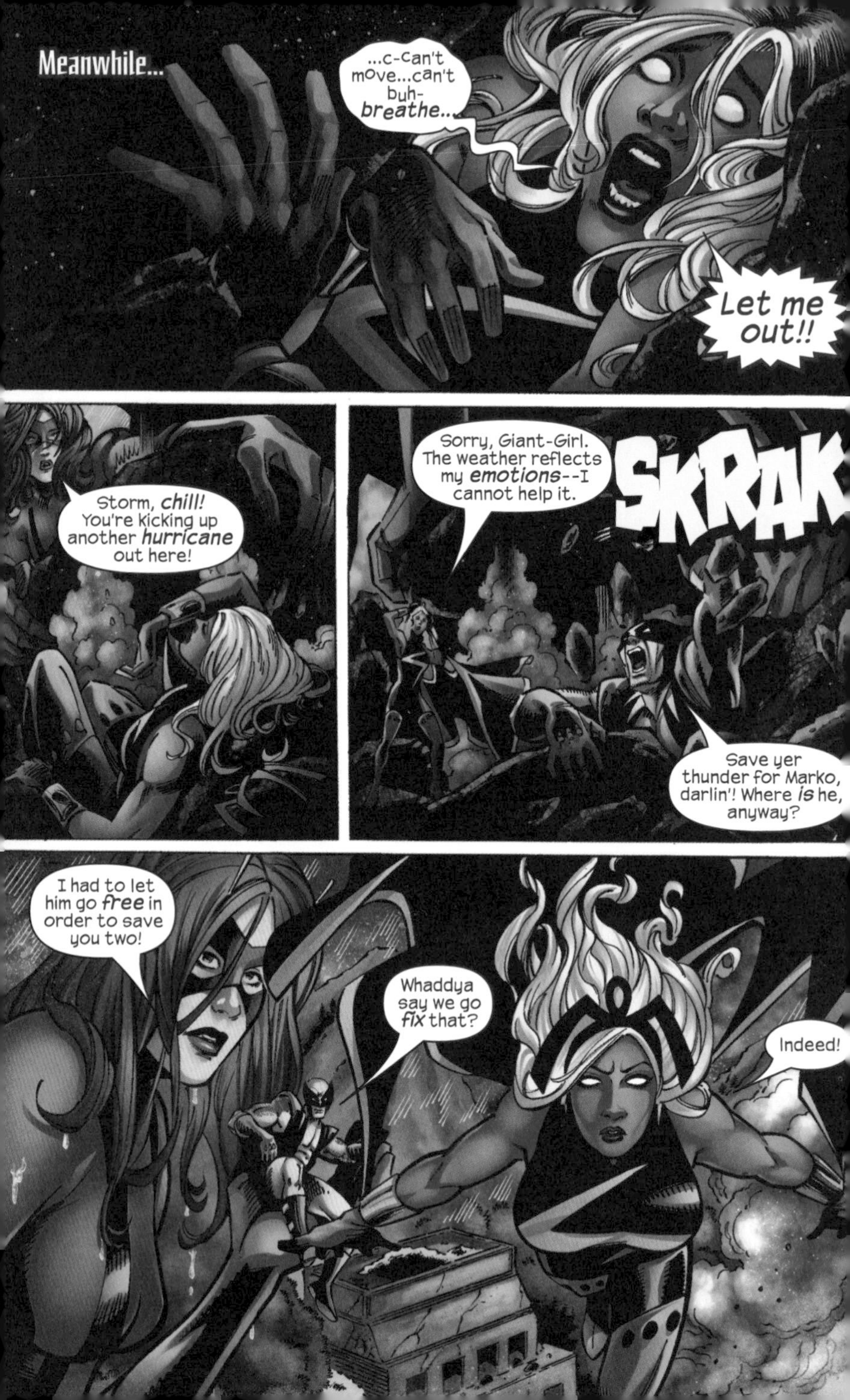
Meanwhile...
...c-can't move...can't buh-breathe...
Let me out!!
Storm, chill! You're kicking up another hurricane out here!
Sorry, Giant-Girl. The weather reflects my emotions--I cannot help it.
SKRAK
Save yer thunder for Marko, darlin'! Where is he, anyway?
I had to let him go free in order to save you two!
Whaddya say we go fix that?
Indeed!

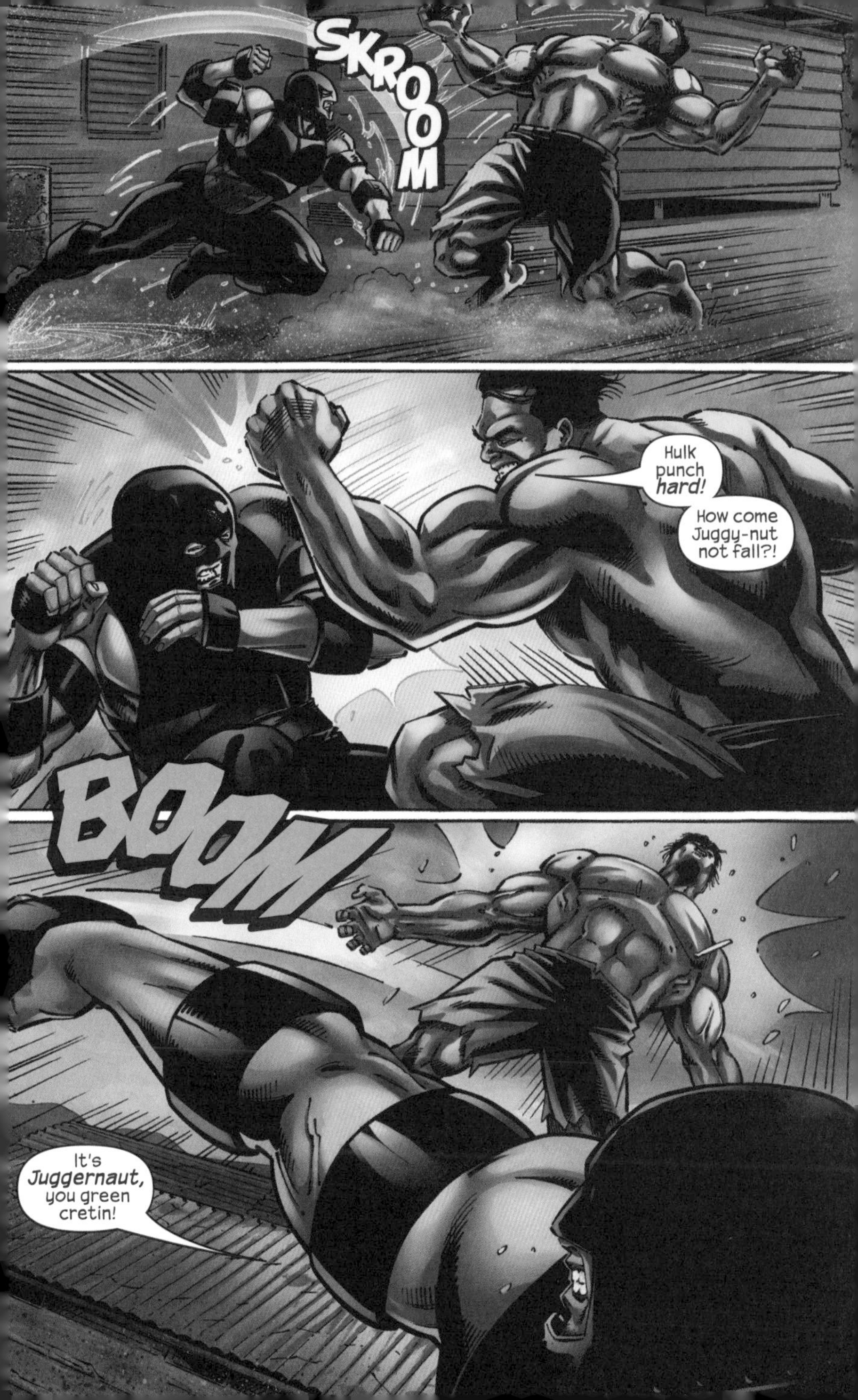
SKROOOM
Hulk punch hard!
How come Juggy-nut not fall?!
BOOM
It's Juggernaut, you green cretin!

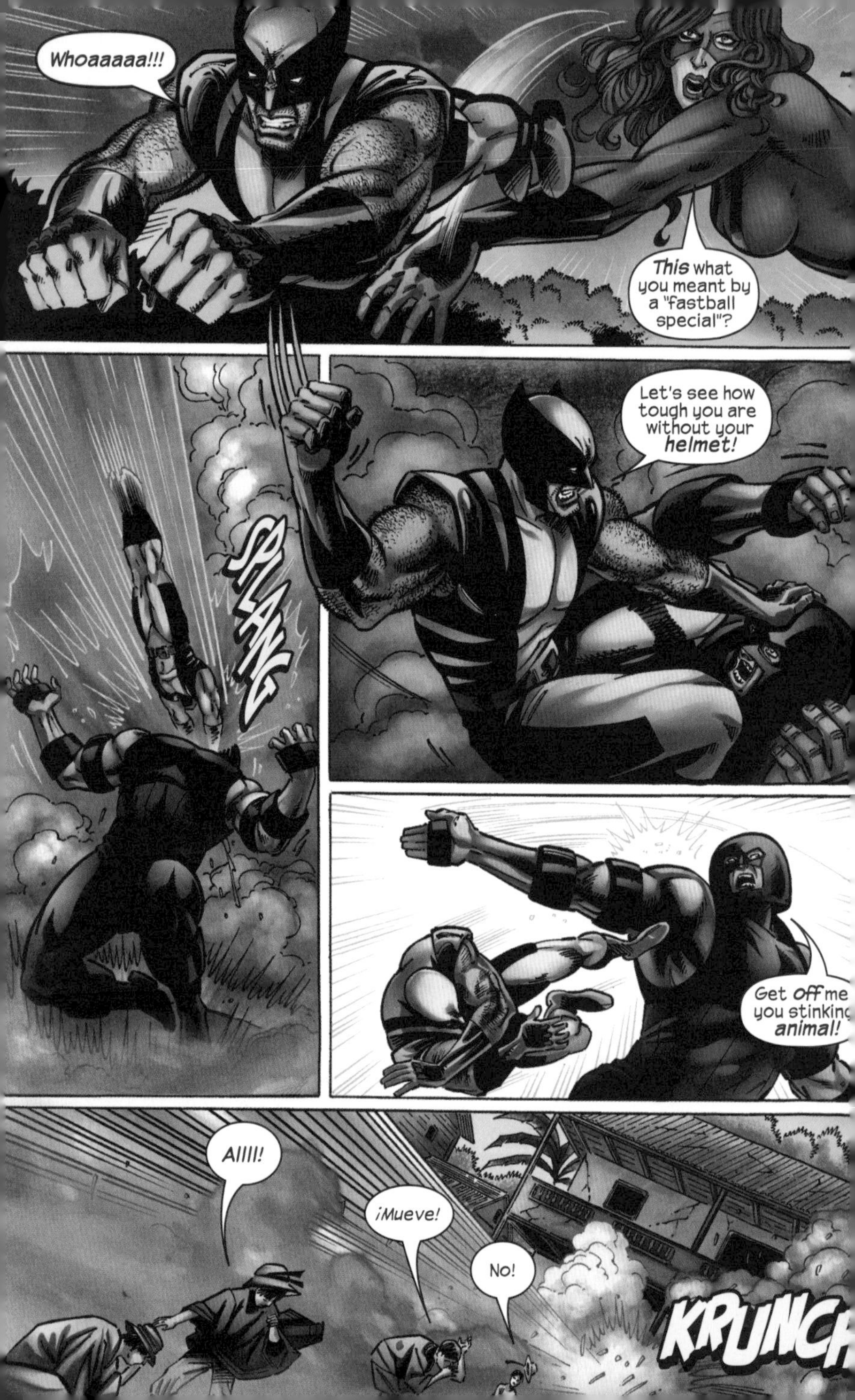
Whoaaaaa!!!
This what you meant by a "fastball special"?
SPLANG
Let's see how tough you are without your helmet!
Get off me you stinking animal!
Allll!
¡Mueve!
No!
KRUNCH

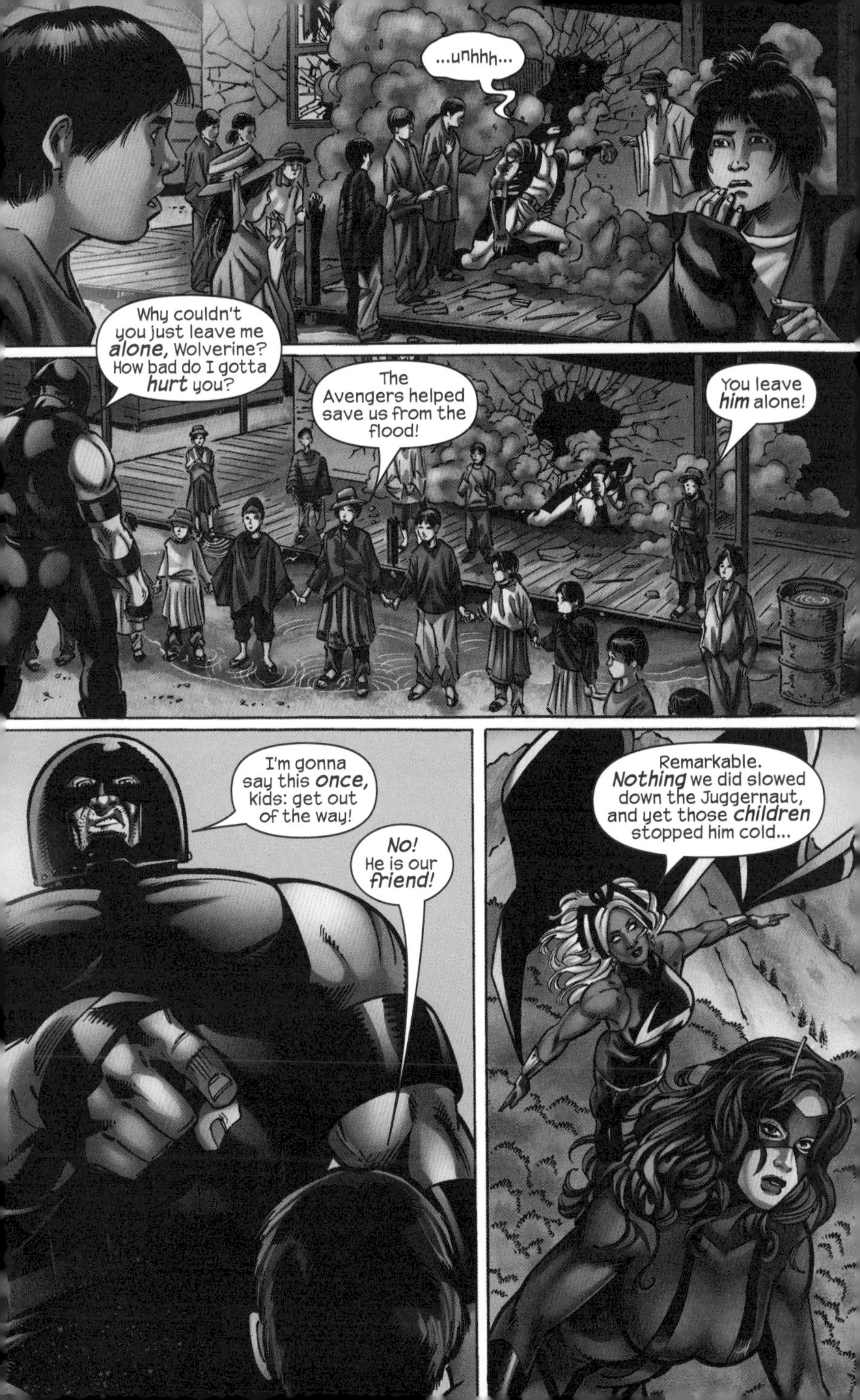
...unhhh...
Why couldn't you just leave me alone, Wolverine? How bad do I gotta hurt you?
The Avengers helped save us from the flood!
You leave him alone!
I'm gonna say this once, kids: get out of the way!
No! He is our friend!
Remarkable. Nothing we did slowed down the Juggernaut, and yet those children stopped him cold...

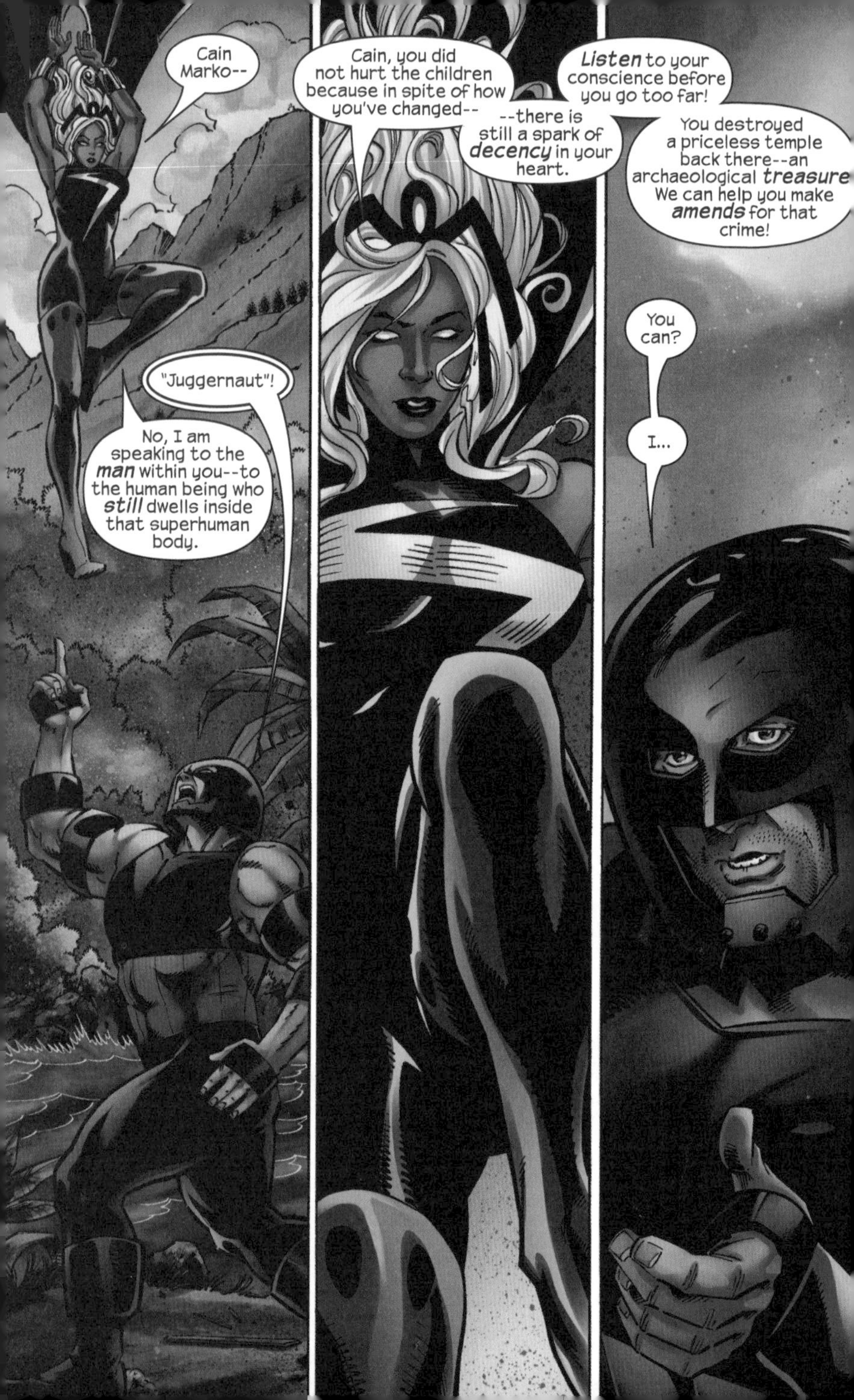
Cain Marko--
"Juggernaut"!
No, I am speaking to the man within you--to the human being who still dwells inside that superhuman body.
Cain, you did not hurt the children because in spite of how you've changed--
--there is still a spark of decency in your heart.
Listen to your conscience before you go too far!
You destroyed a priceless temple back there--an archaeological treasure. We can help you make amends for that crime!
You can?
I...

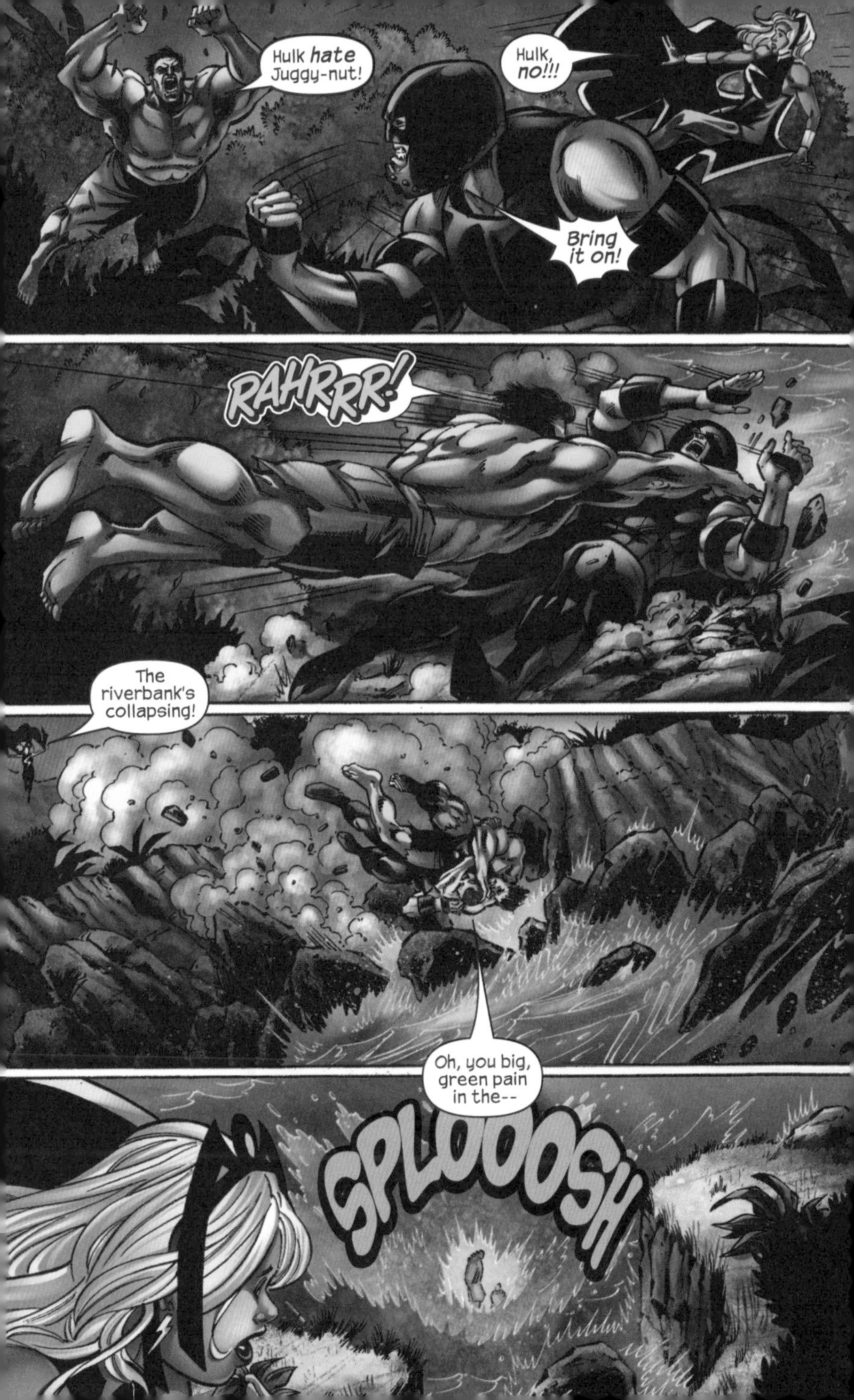
Hulk hate Juggy-nut!
Hulk, no!!!
Bring it on!
RAHRRR!
The riverbank's collapsing!
Oh, you big, green pain in the--
SPLOOOSH

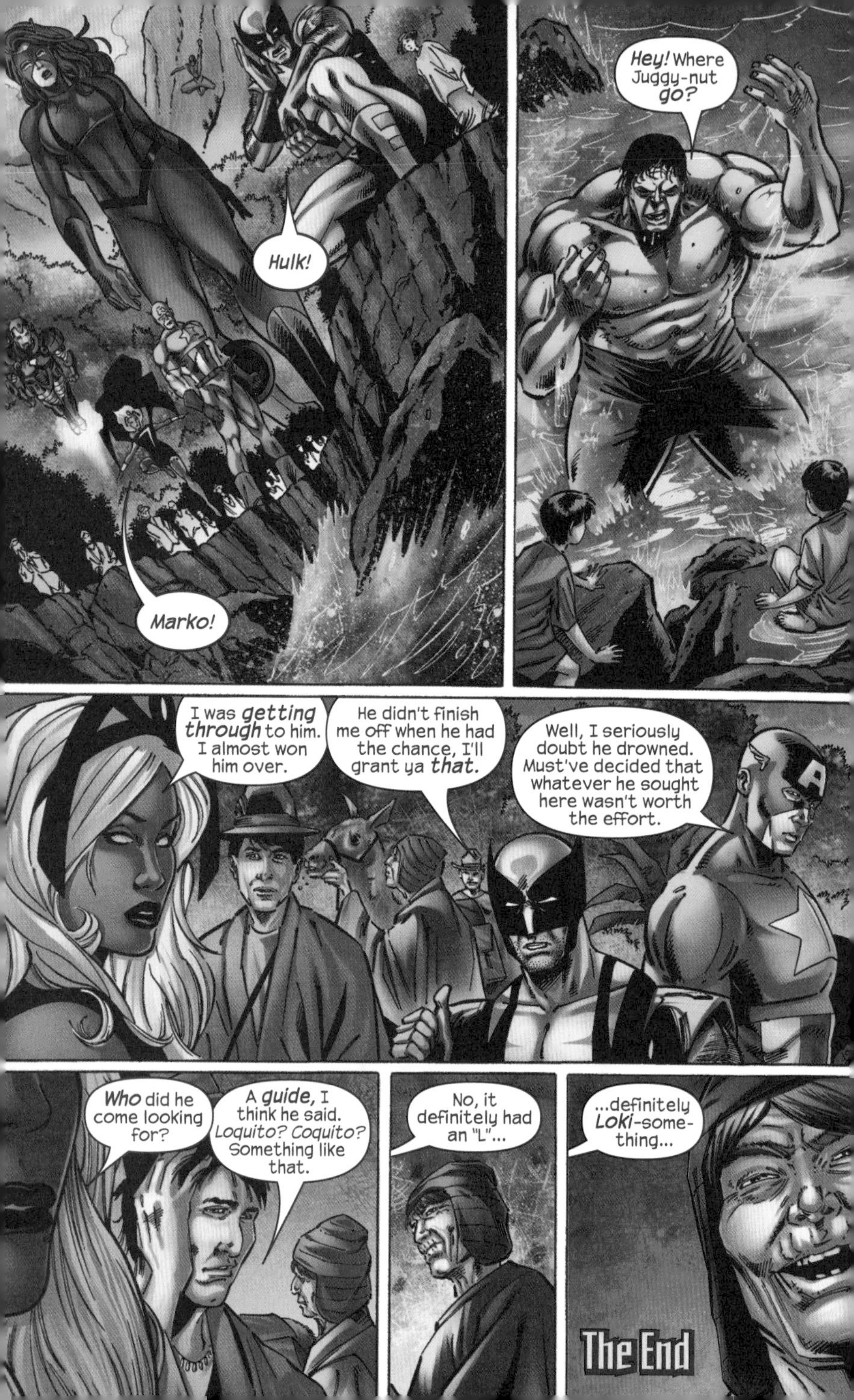
Hulk!
Marko!
Hey! Where Juggy-nut go?
I was getting through to him. I almost won him over.
He didn't finish me off when he had the chance, I'll grant ya that.
Well, I seriously doubt he drowned. Must've decided that whatever he sought here wasn't worth the effort.
Who did he come looking for?
A guide, I think he said. Loquito? Coquito? Something like that.
No, it definitely had an "L"...
...definitely Loki-something...
The End

#8

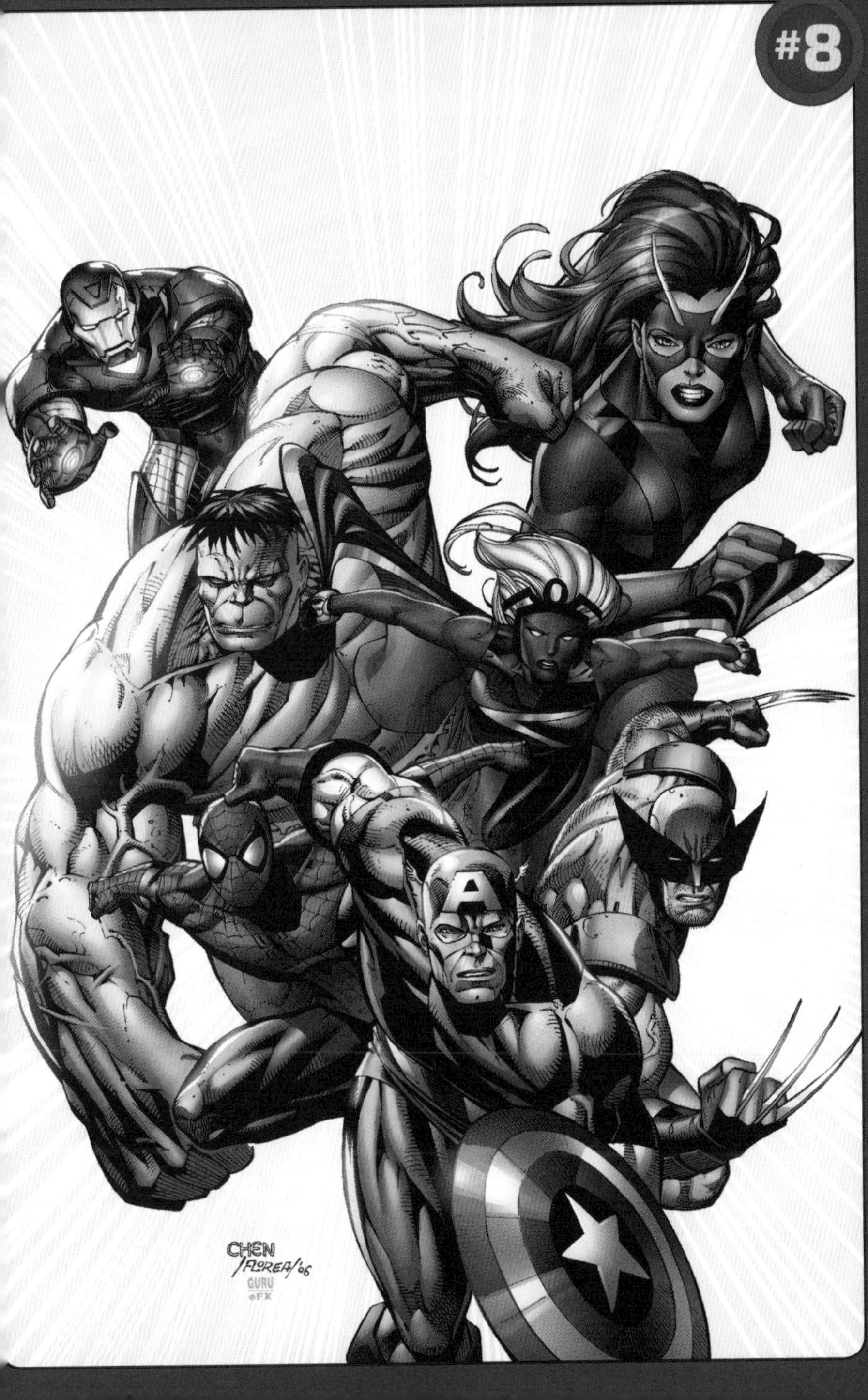
CHEN
/FLOREA/'06
GURU
eFX

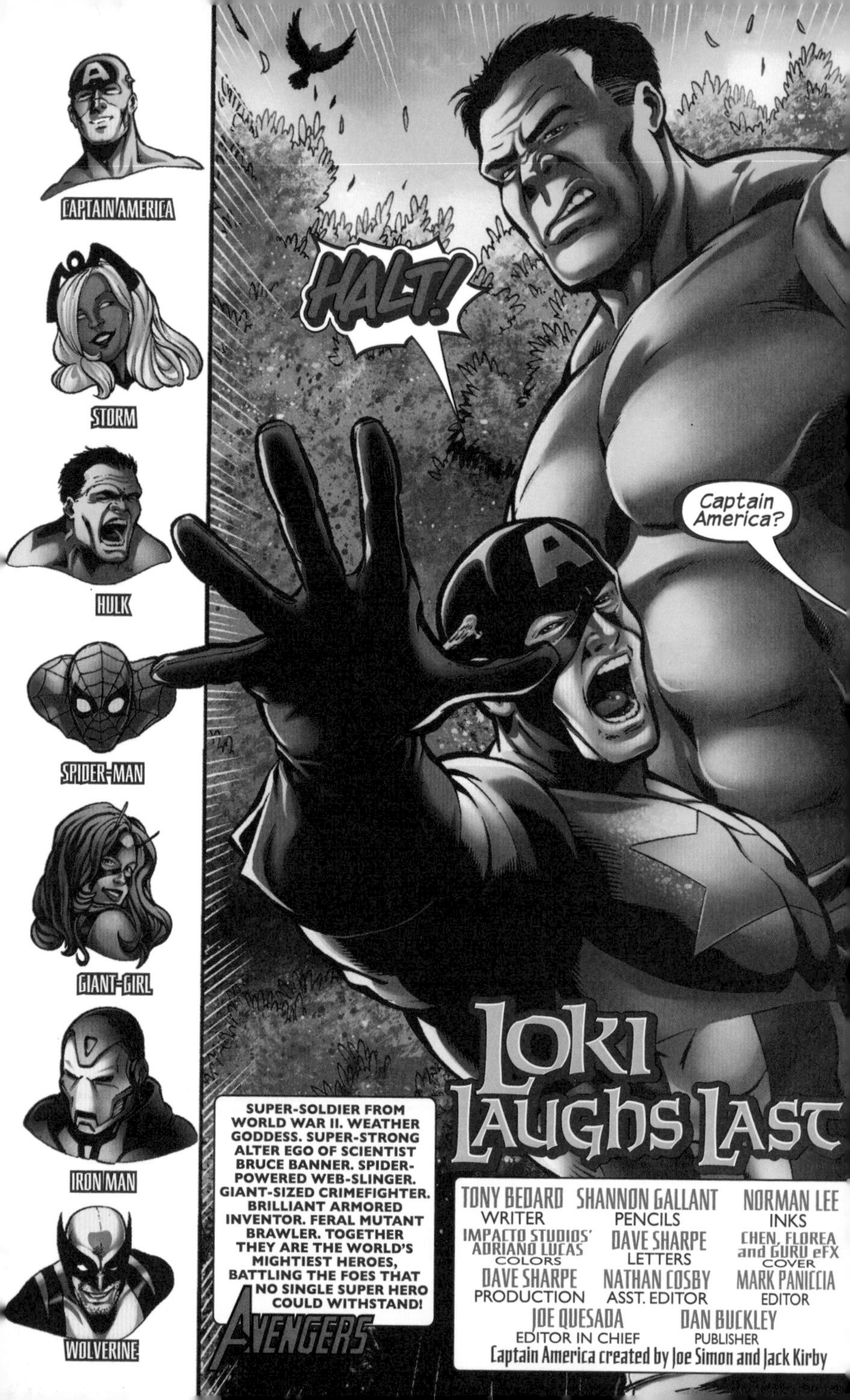
CAPTAIN AMERICA
STORM
HULK
SPIDER-MAN
GIANT-GIRL
IRON MAN
WOLVERINE
HALT!
Captain America?
LOKI LAUGHS LAST
SUPER-SOLDIER FROM WORLD WAR II. WEATHER GODDESS. SUPER-STRONG ALTER EGO OF SCIENTIST BRUCE BANNER. SPIDER-POWERED WEB-SLINGER. GIANT-SIZED CRIMEFIGHTER. BRILLIANT ARMORED INVENTOR. FERAL MUTANT BRAWLER. TOGETHER THEY ARE THE WORLD'S MIGHTIEST HEROES, BATTLING THE FOES THAT NO SINGLE SUPER HERO COULD WITHSTAND!
AVENGERS
TONY BEDARD WRITER
SHANNON GALLANT PENCILS
NORMAN LEE INKS
IMPACTO STUDIOS' ADRIANO LUCAS COLORS
DAVE SHARPE LETTERS
CHEN, FLOREA and GURU eFX COVER
DAVE SHARPE PRODUCTION
NATHAN COSBY ASST. EDITOR
MARK PANICCIA EDITOR
JOE QUESADA EDITOR IN CHIEF
DAN BUCKLEY PUBLISHER
Captain America created by Joe Simon and Jack Kirby

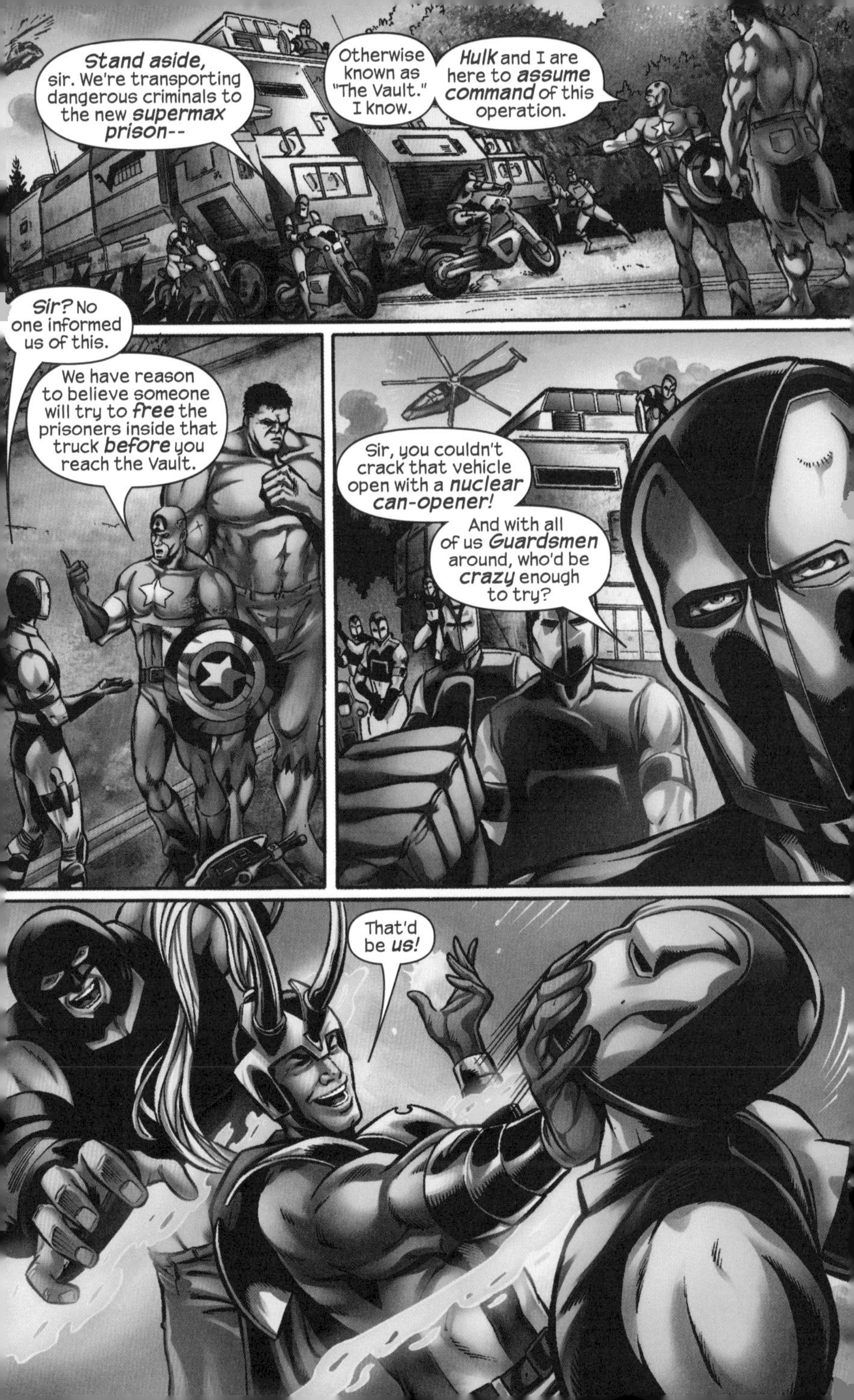
Stand aside, sir. We're transporting dangerous criminals to the new supermax prison--
Otherwise known as "The Vault." I know.
Hulk and I are here to assume command of this operation.
Sir? No one informed us of this.
We have reason to believe someone will try to free the prisoners inside that truck before you reach the Vault.
Sir, you couldn't crack that vehicle open with a nuclear can-opener!
And with all of us Guardsmen around, who'd be crazy enough to try?
That'd be us!

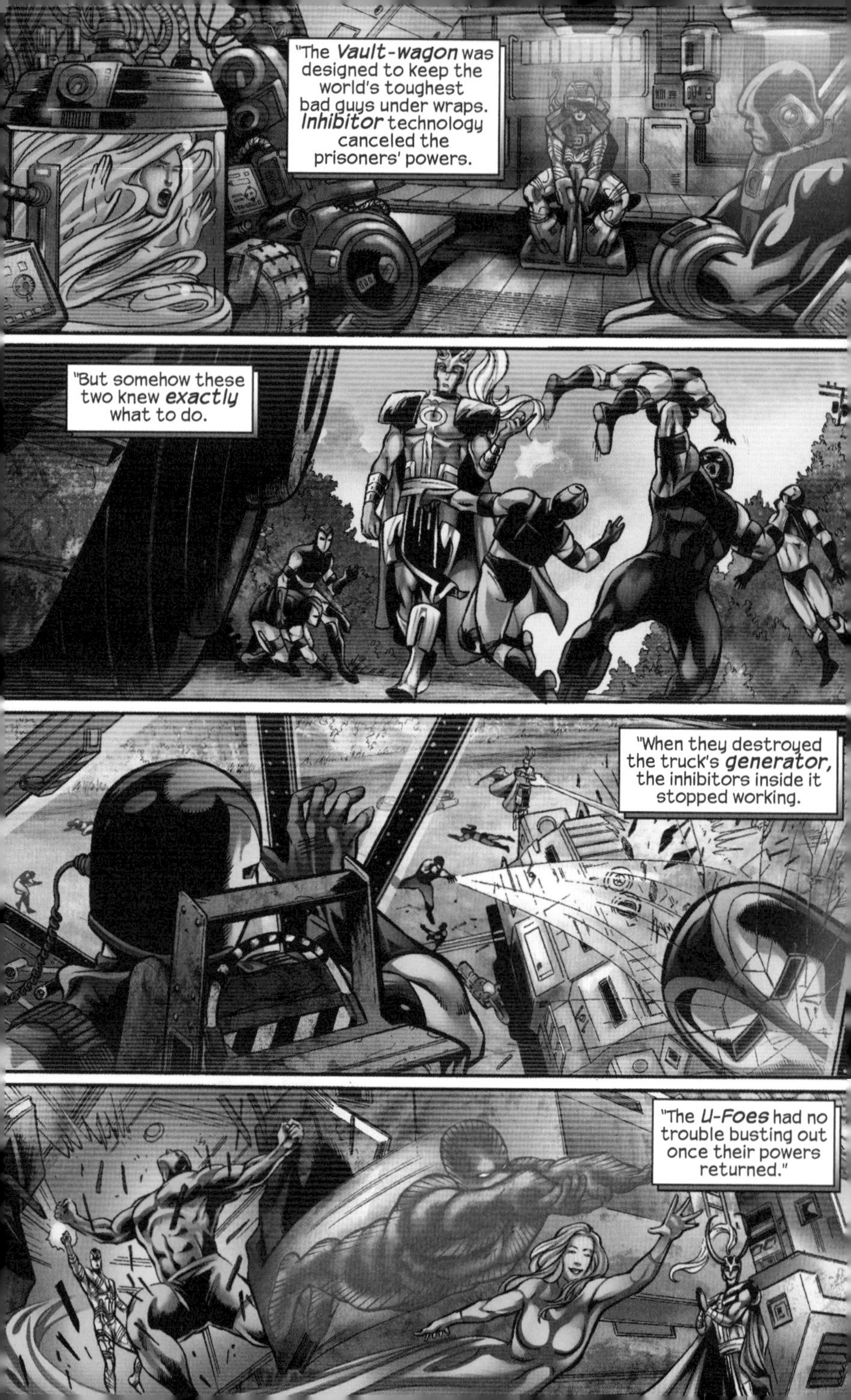
"The *Vault-wagon* was designed to keep the world's toughest bad guys under wraps. *Inhibitor* technology canceled the prisoners' powers.
"But somehow these two knew *exactly* what to do.
"When they destroyed the truck's *generator*, the inhibitors inside it stopped working.
"The *U-Foes* had no trouble busting out once their powers returned."

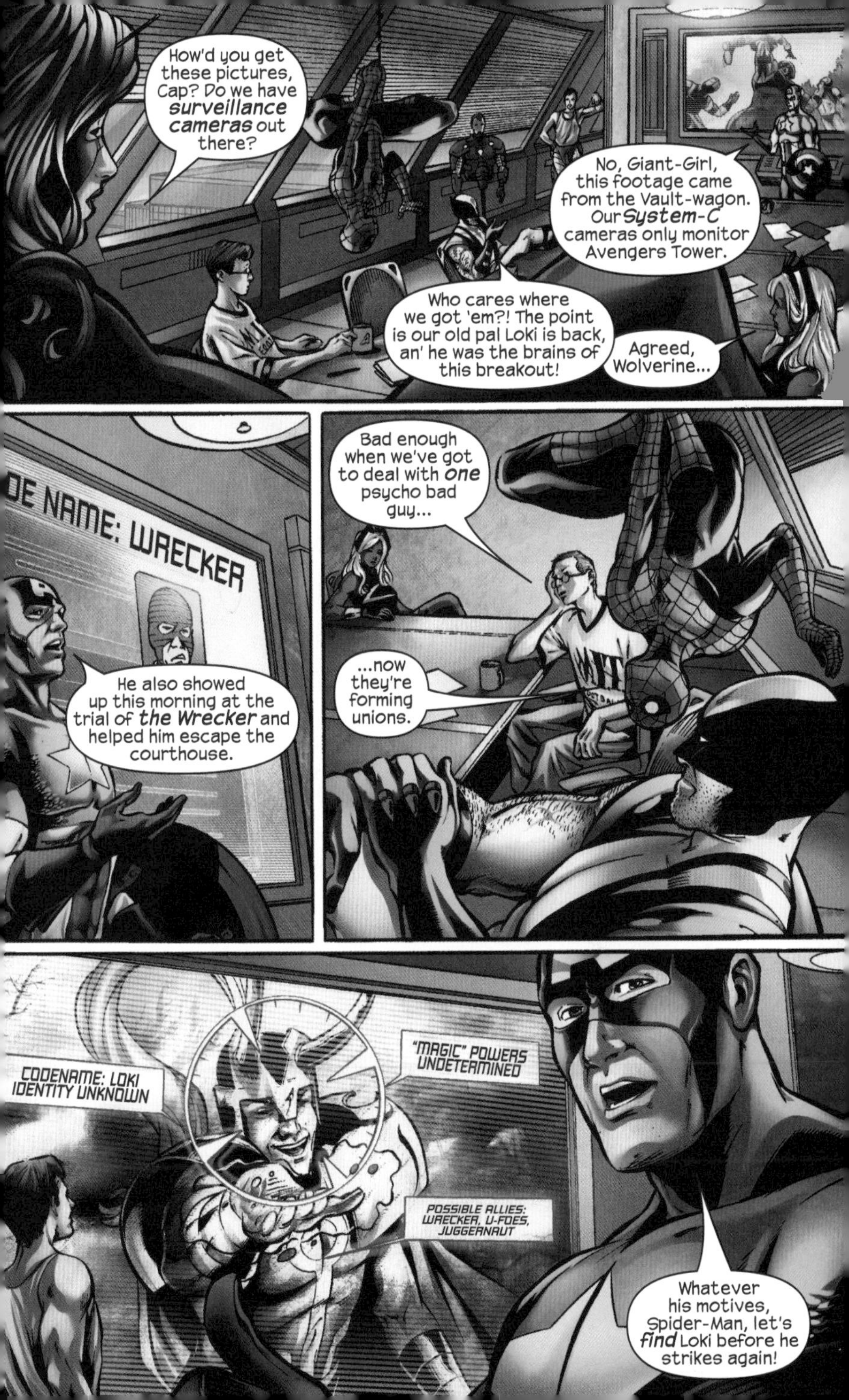
How'd you get these pictures, Cap? Do we have *surveillance cameras* out there?
No, Giant-Girl, this footage came from the Vault-wagon. Our *System-C* cameras only monitor Avengers Tower.
Who cares where we got 'em?! The point is our old pal Loki is back, an' he was the brains of this breakout!
Agreed, Wolverine...
DE NAME: WRECKER
He also showed up this morning at the trial of *the Wrecker* and helped him escape the courthouse.
Bad enough when we've got to deal with *one* psycho bad guy...
...now they're forming unions.
CODENAME: LOKI
IDENTITY UNKNOWN
"MAGIC" POWERS UNDETERMINED
POSSIBLE ALLIES: WRECKER, U-FOES, JUGGERNAUT
Whatever his motives, Spider-Man, let's *find* Loki before he strikes again!

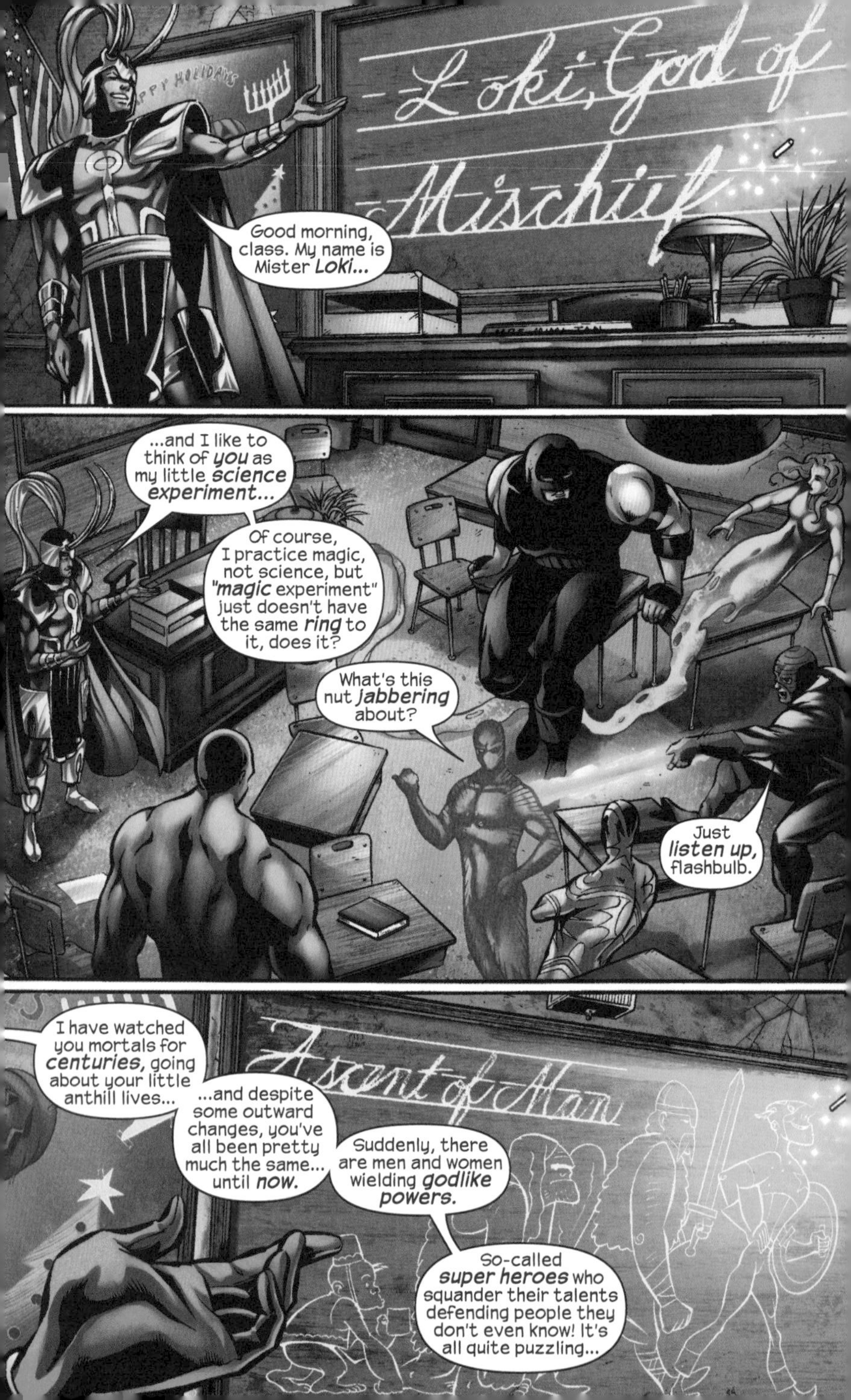

HAPPY HOLIDAYS
Loki, God of Mischief
Good morning, class. My name is Mister Loki...
...and I like to think of you as my little science experiment...
Of course, I practice magic, not science, but "magic experiment" just doesn't have the same ring to it, does it?
What's this nut jabbering about?
Just listen up, flashbulb.
Ascent of Man
I have watched you mortals for centuries, going about your little anthill lives...
...and despite some outward changes, you've all been pretty much the same... until now.
Suddenly, there are men and women wielding godlike powers.
So-called super heroes who squander their talents defending people they don't even know! It's all quite puzzling...

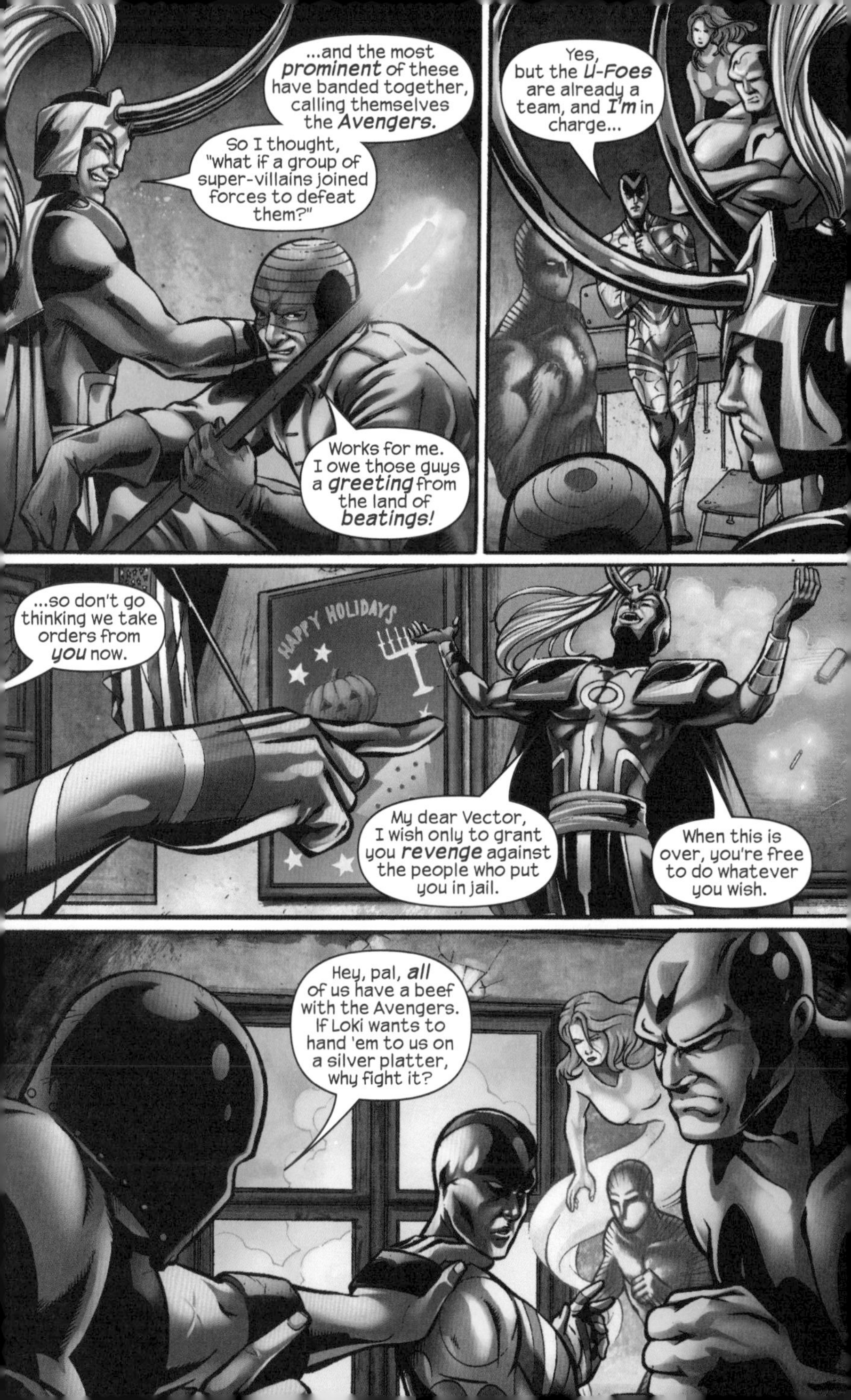
...and the most prominent of these have banded together, calling themselves the Avengers.
So I thought, "what if a group of super-villains joined forces to defeat them?"
Works for me. I owe those guys a greeting from the land of beatings!
Yes, but the U-Foes are already a team, and I'm in charge...
...so don't go thinking we take orders from you now.
HAPPY HOLIDAYS
My dear Vector, I wish only to grant you revenge against the people who put you in jail.
When this is over, you're free to do whatever you wish.
Hey, pal, all of us have a beef with the Avengers. If Loki wants to hand 'em to us on a silver platter, why fight it?

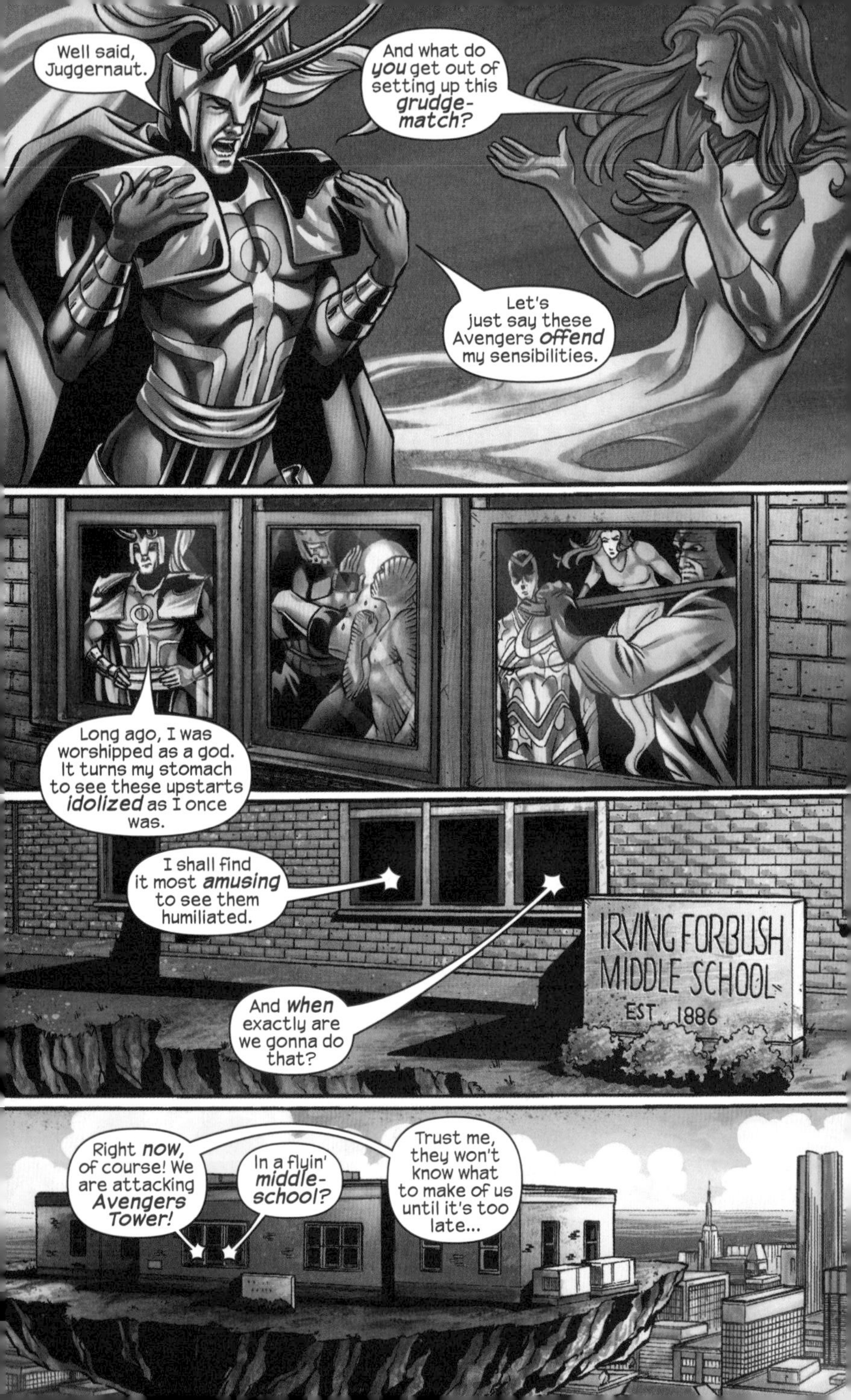
Well said, Juggernaut.
And what do you get out of setting up this grudge-match?
Let's just say these Avengers offend my sensibilities.
Long ago, I was worshipped as a god. It turns my stomach to see these upstarts idolized as I once was.
I shall find it most amusing to see them humiliated.
And when exactly are we gonna do that?
IRVING FORBUSH MIDDLE SCHOOL EST 1886
Right now, of course! We are attacking Avengers Tower!
In a flyin' middle-school?
Trust me, they won't know what to make of us until it's too late...

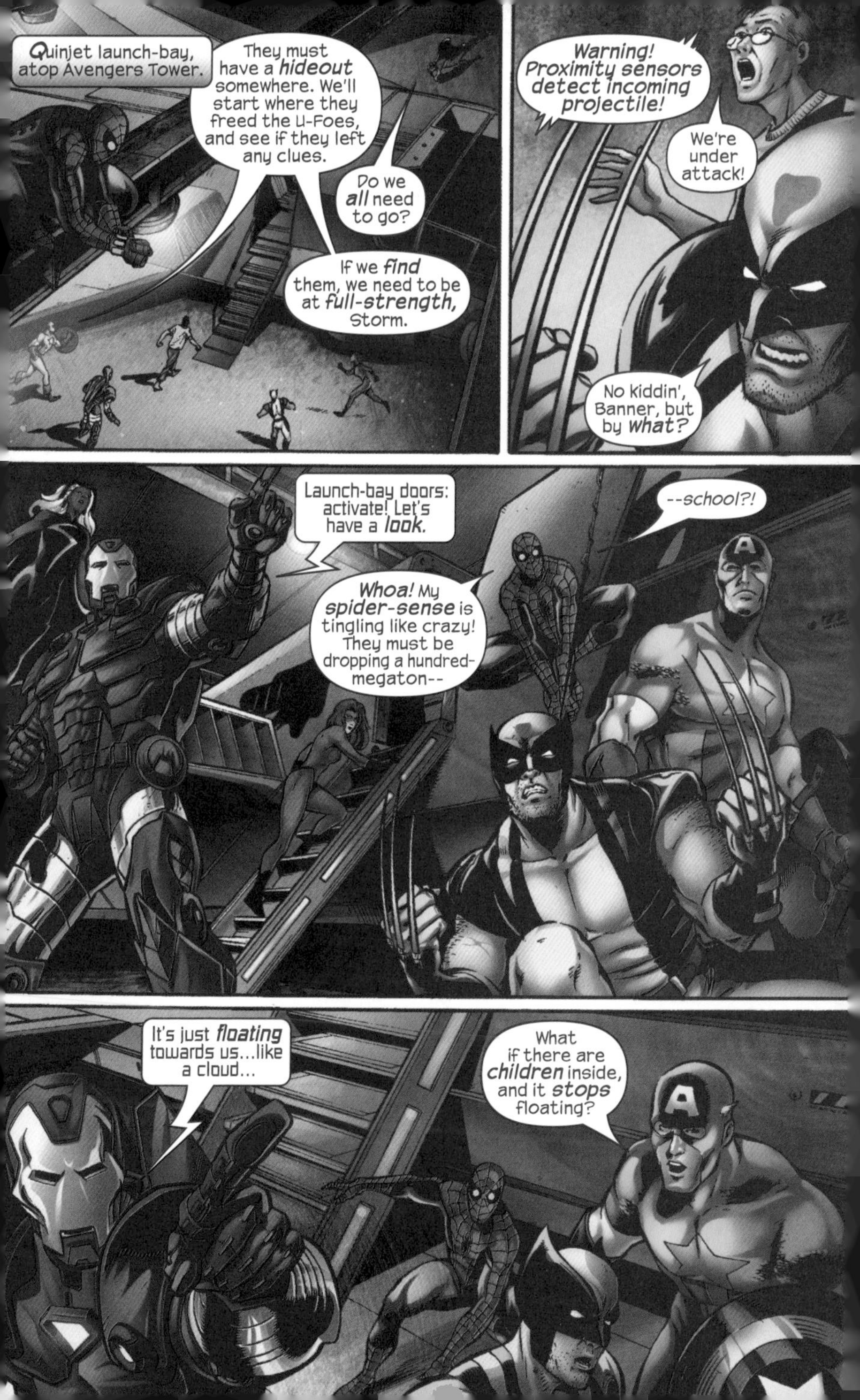
Quinjet launch-bay, atop Avengers Tower.
They must have a hideout somewhere. We'll start where they freed the U-Foes, and see if they left any clues.
Do we all need to go?
If we find them, we need to be at full-strength, Storm.
Warning! Proximity sensors detect incoming projectile!
We're under attack!
No kiddin', Banner, but by what?
Launch-bay doors: activate! Let's have a look.
Whoa! My spider-sense is tingling like crazy! They must be dropping a hundred-megaton--
--school?!
It's just floating towards us...like a cloud...
What if there are children inside, and it stops floating?

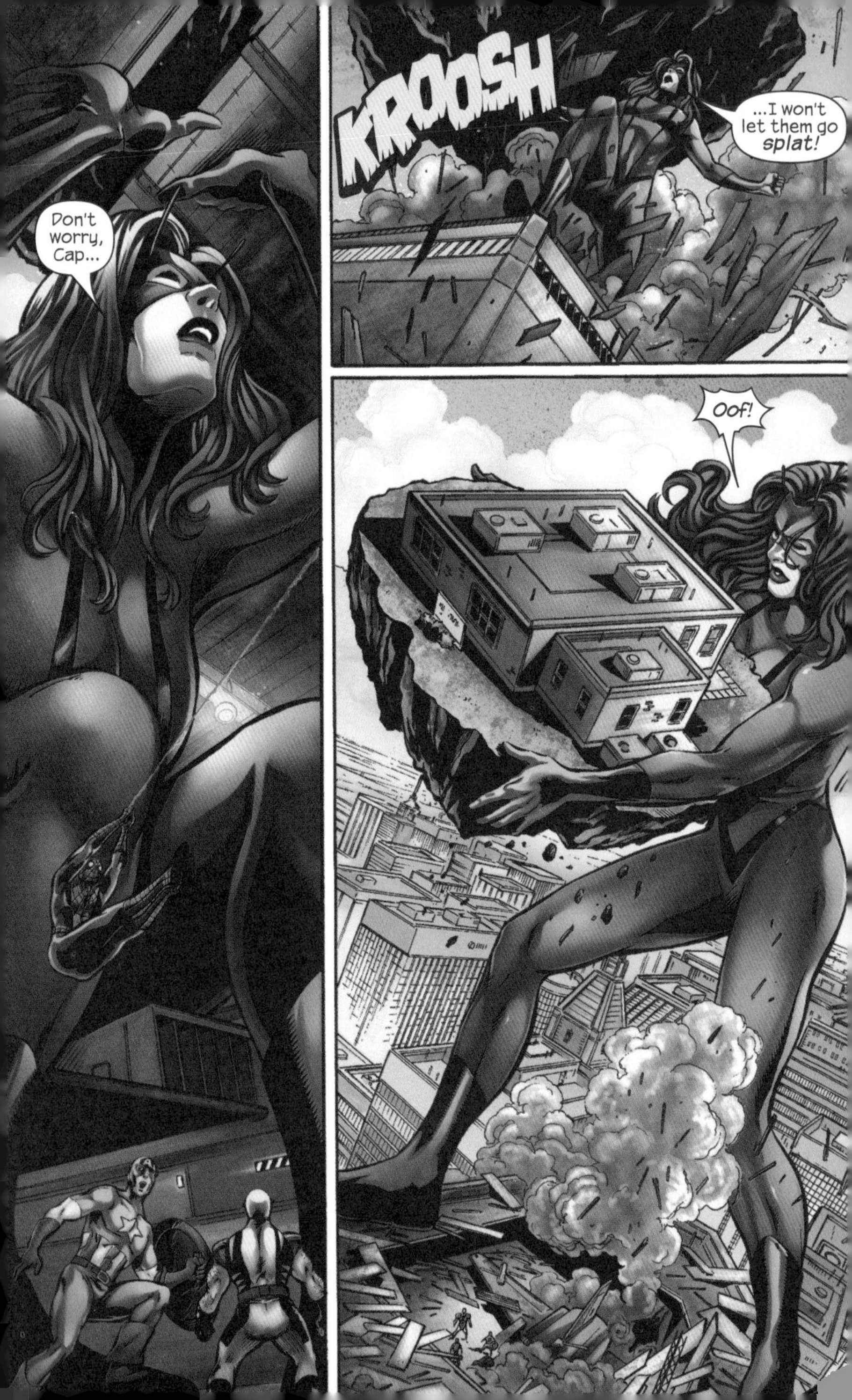
Don't worry, Cap...
KROOSH
...I won't let them go *splat!*
Oof!

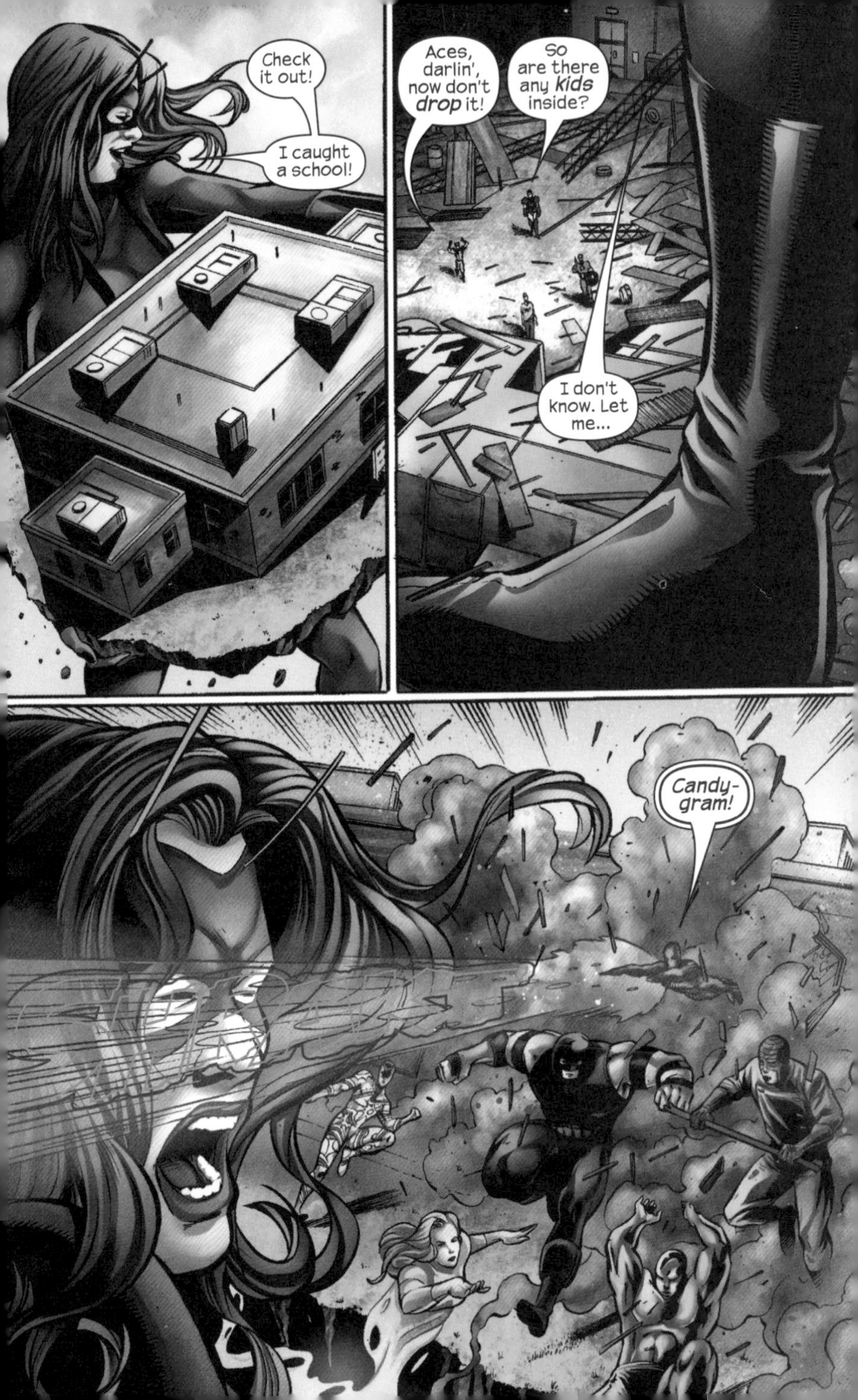
Check it out!
I caught a school!
Aces, darlin', now don't *drop* it!
So are there any *kids* inside?
I don't know. Let me...
Candy-gram!

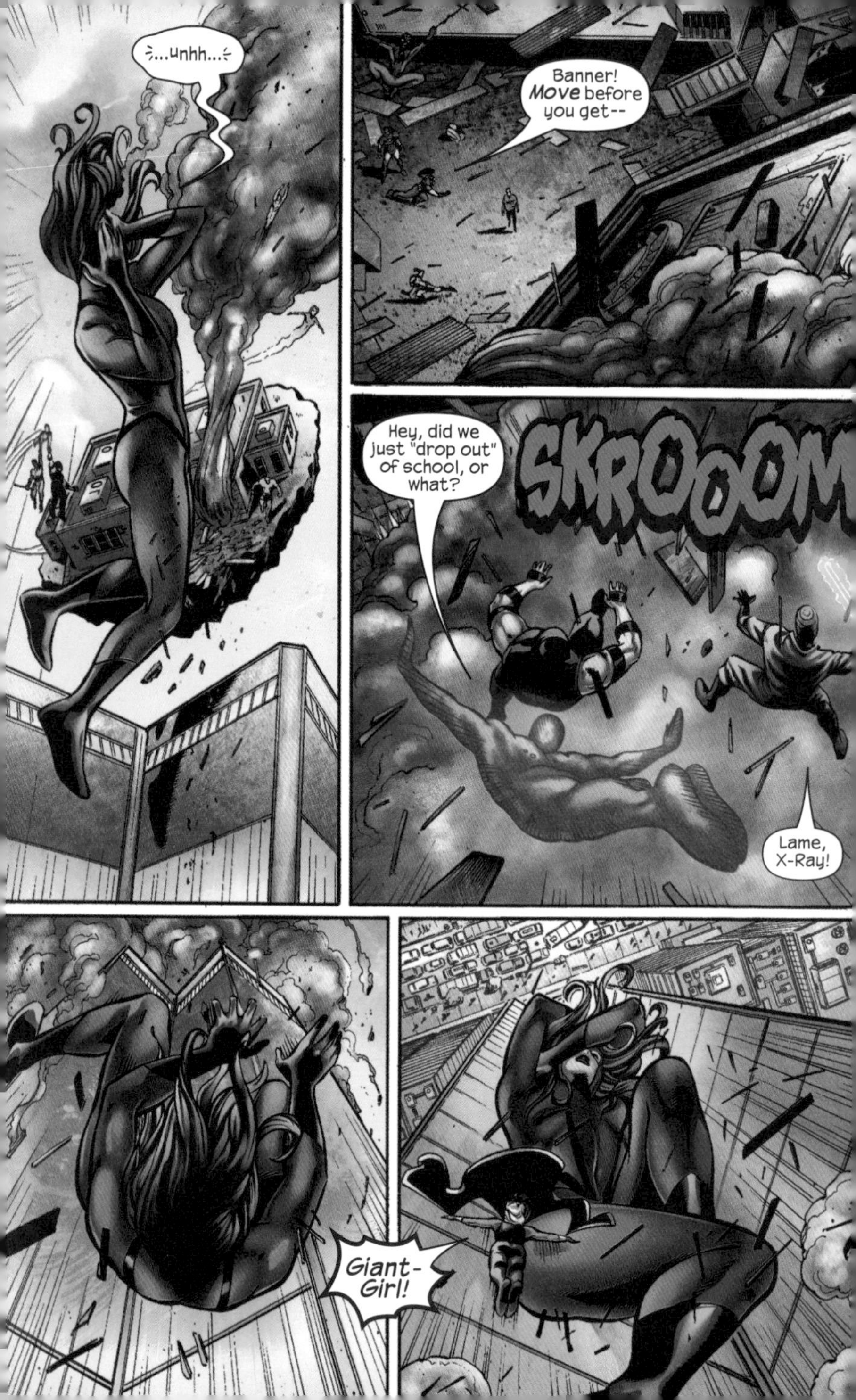
...unhh...
Banner! Move before you get--
Hey, did we just "drop out" of school, or what?
SKROOOOM
Lame, X-Ray!
Giant-Girl!

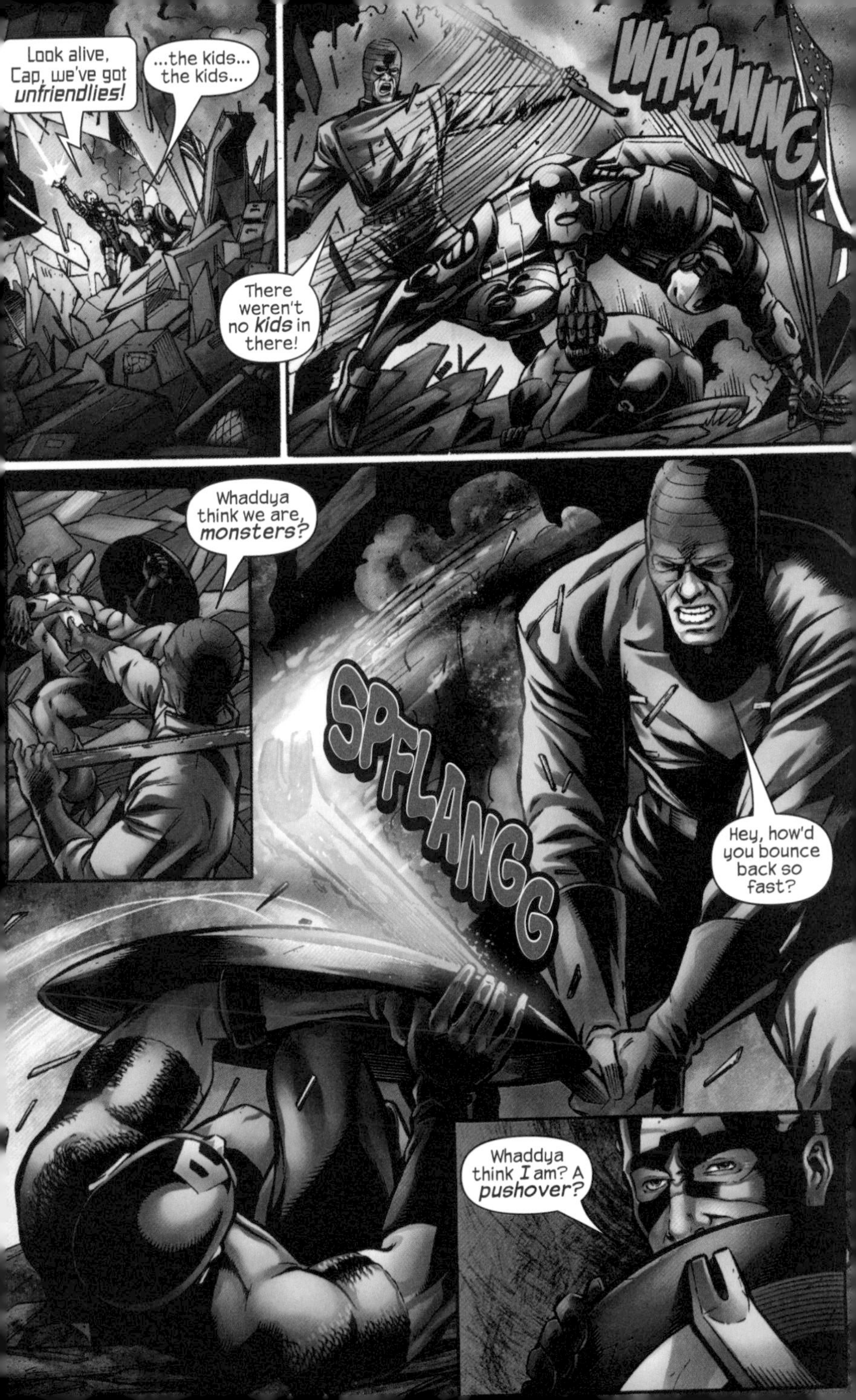
Look alive, Cap, we've got *unfriendlies!*
...the kids... the kids...
WHRANNG
There weren't no *kids* in there!
Whaddya think we are, *monsters?*
SPFLANGG
Hey, how'd you bounce back so fast?
Whaddya think *I* am? A *pushover?*

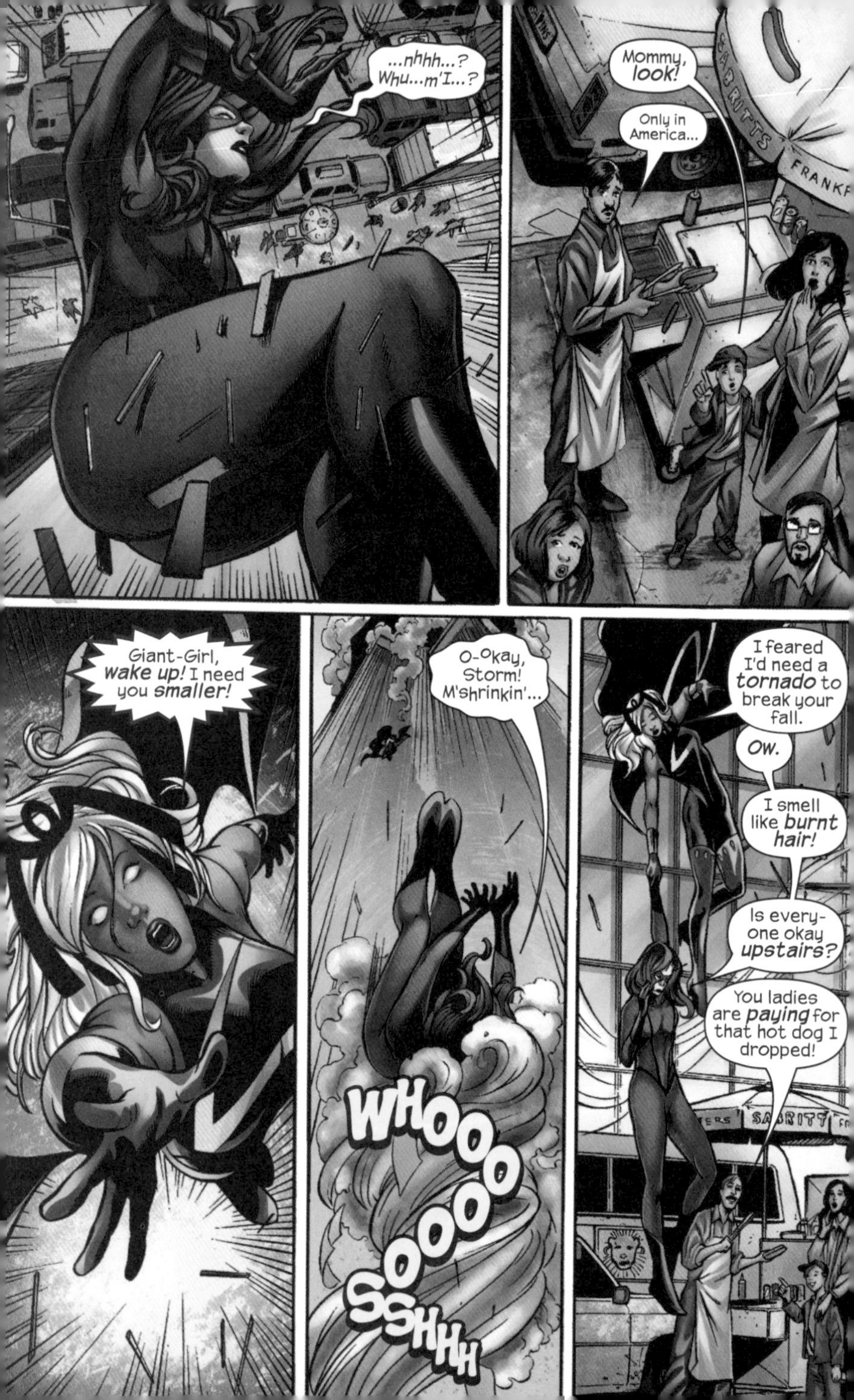
...nhhh...?
Whu...m'I...?
Mommy, look!
Only in America...
Giant-Girl, wake up! I need you smaller!
O-Okay, Storm! M'shrinkin'...
WHOOOOSOOOOSSHHHH
I feared I'd need a tornado to break your fall.
Ow.
I smell like burnt hair!
Is every-one okay upstairs?
You ladies are paying for that hot dog I dropped!

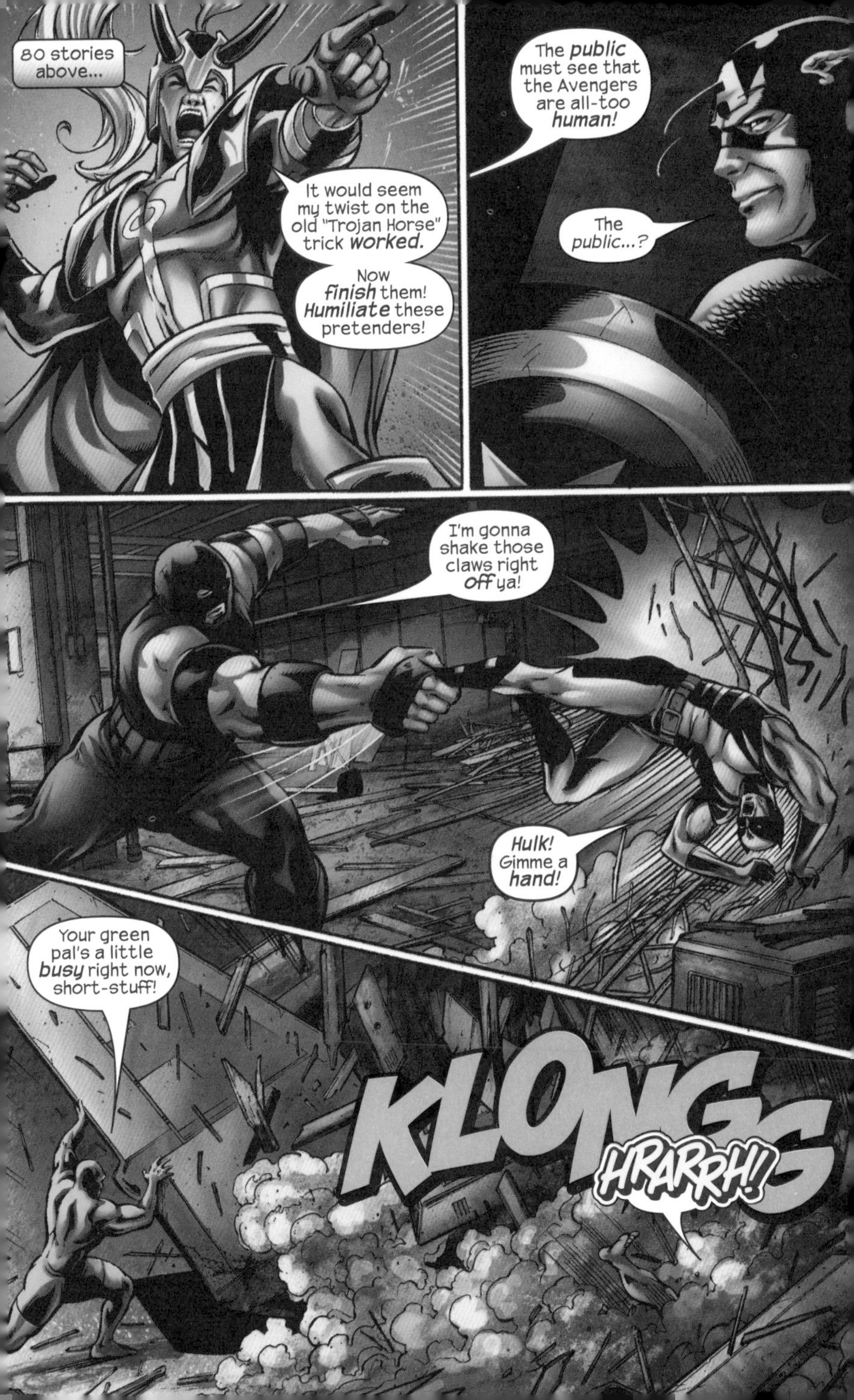
80 stories above...
It would seem my twist on the old "Trojan Horse" trick *worked.*
Now *finish* them! *Humiliate* these pretenders!
The *public* must see that the Avengers are all-too *human!*
The public...?
I'm gonna shake those claws right *off* ya!
Hulk! Gimme a *hand!*
Your green pal's a little *busy* right now, short-stuff!
KLONG
HRARRH!!

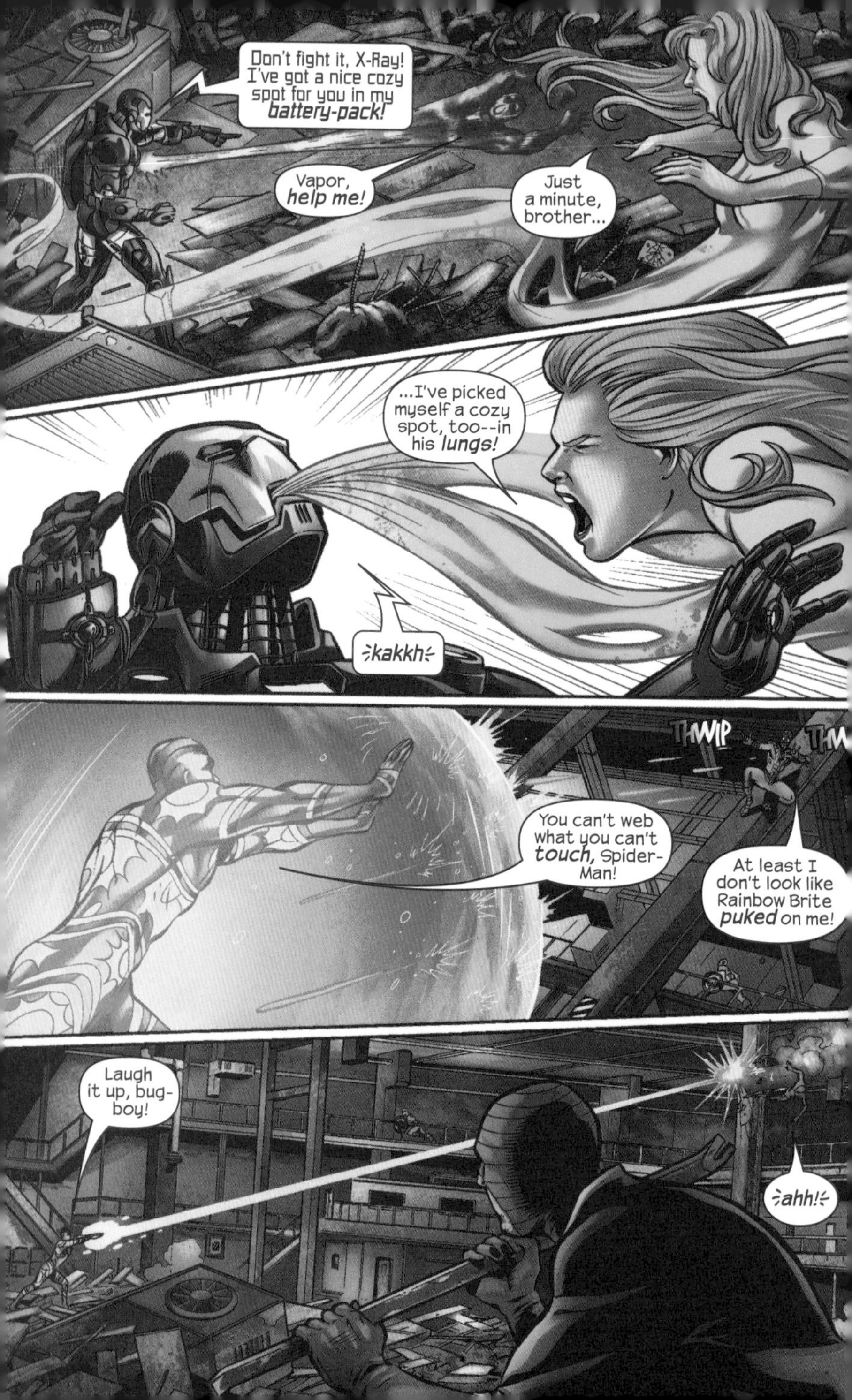
Don't fight it, X-Ray! I've got a nice cozy spot for you in my battery-pack!
Vapor, help me!
Just a minute, brother...
...I've picked myself a cozy spot, too--in his lungs!
kakkh
THWIP
You can't web what you can't touch, Spider-Man!
At least I don't look like Rainbow Brite puked on me!
Laugh it up, bug-boy!
ahh!

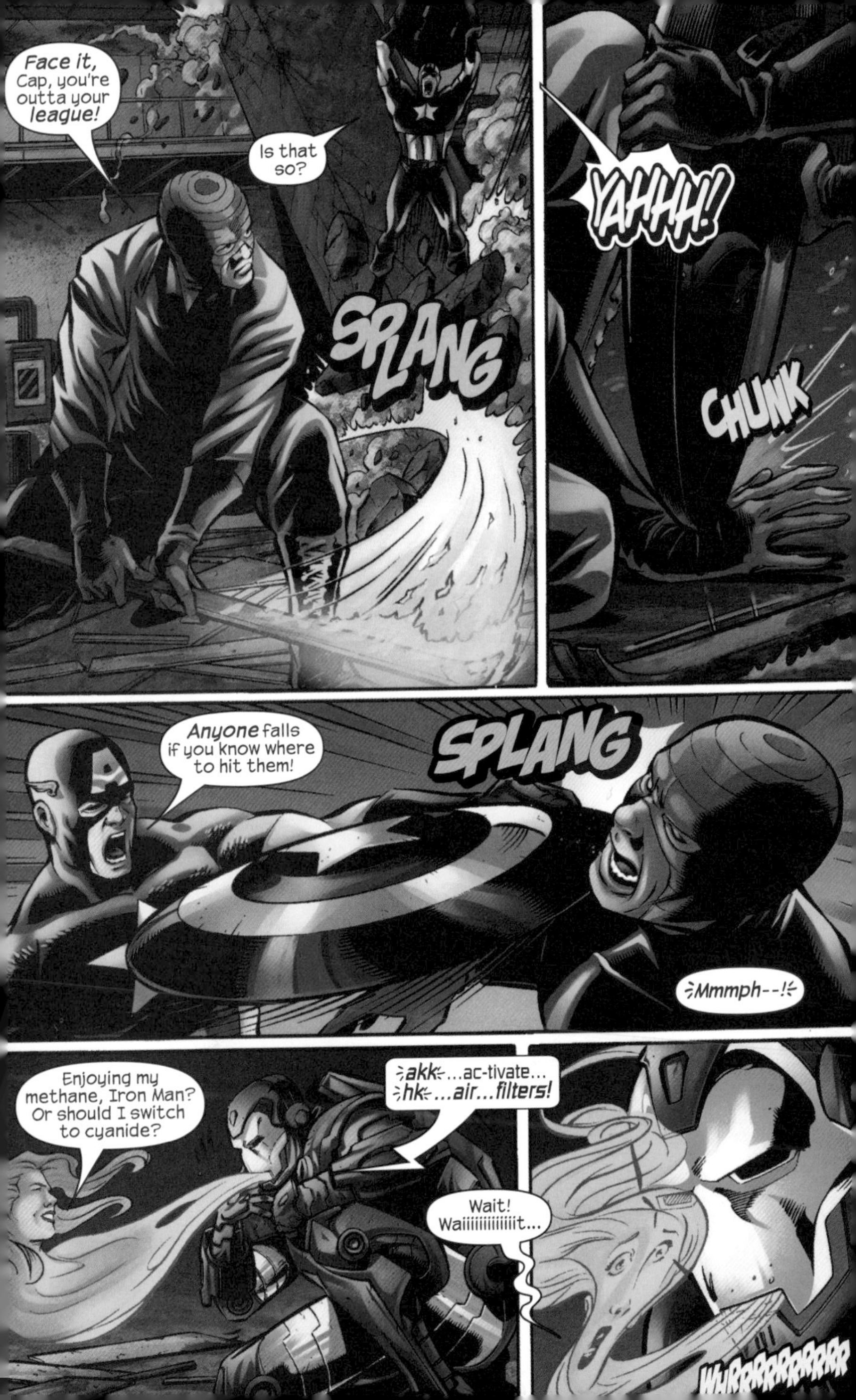
Face it, Cap, you're outta your league!
Is that so?
SPLANG
YAHHH!
CHUNK
Anyone falls if you know where to hit them!
SPLANG
Mmmph--!
Enjoying my methane, Iron Man? Or should I switch to cyanide?
akk...ac-tivate... hk...air...filters!
Wait! Waiiiiiiiiiiit...
WHRRRRRRRRR

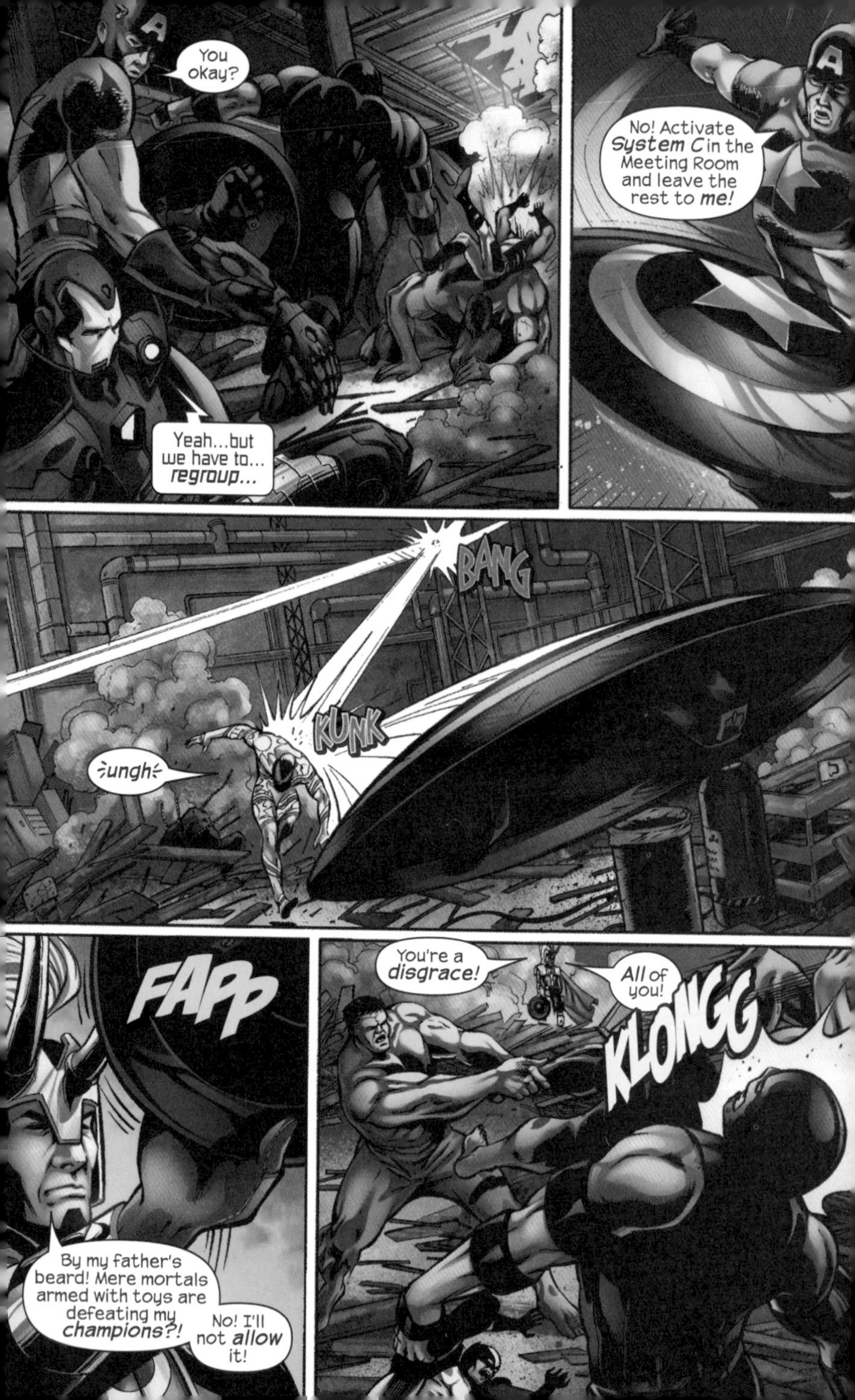
You okay?
Yeah...but we have to... regroup...
No! Activate System C in the Meeting Room and leave the rest to me!
BANG
KUNK
ungh
FAPP
By my father's beard! Mere mortals armed with toys are defeating my champions?!
No! I'll not allow it!
You're a disgrace!
All of you!
KLONGG

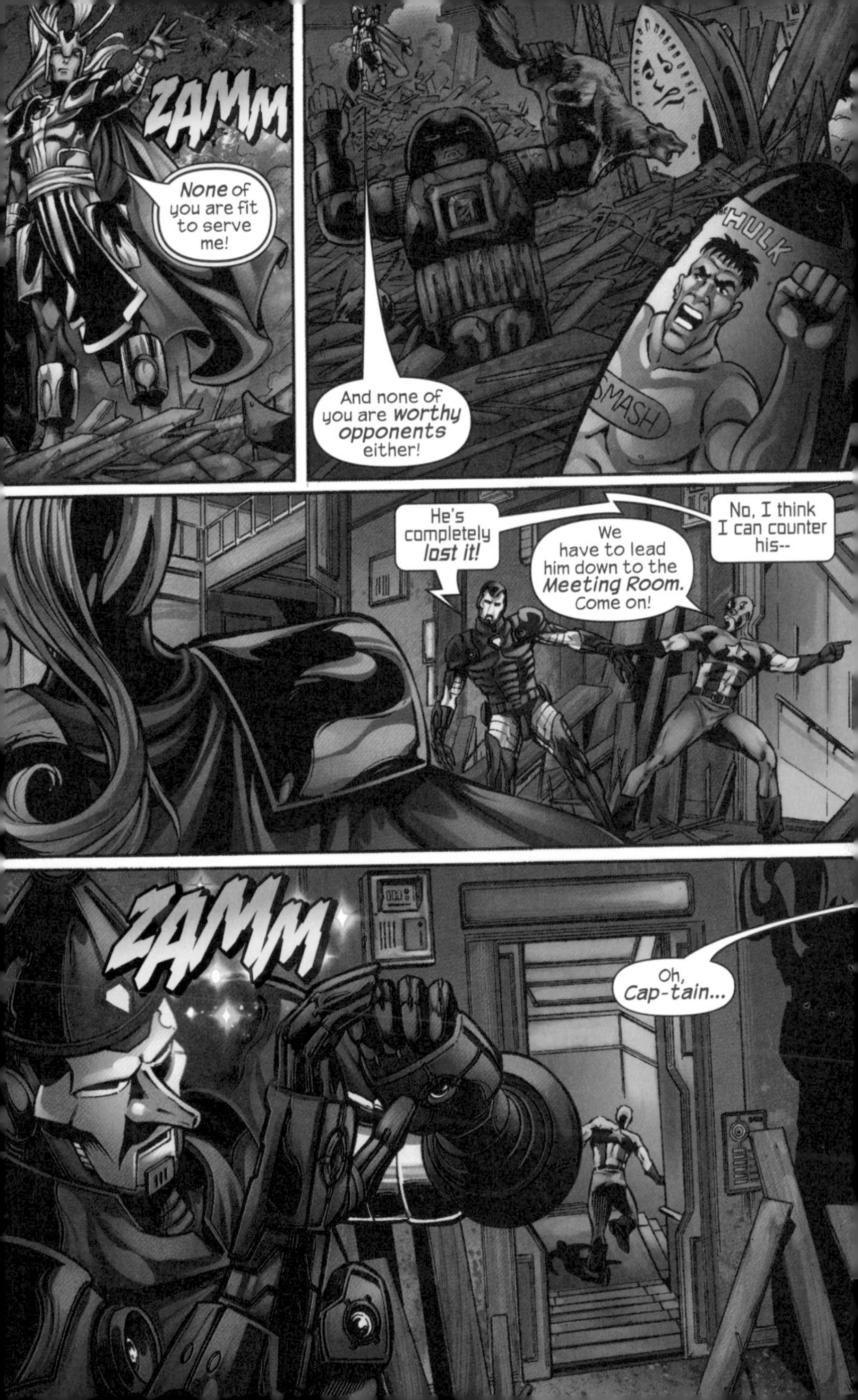
ZAMM
None of you are fit to serve me!
And none of you are worthy opponents either!
HULK
SMASH
He's completely lost it!
No, I think I can counter his--
We have to lead him down to the Meeting Room. Come on!
ZAMM
Oh, Cap-tain...

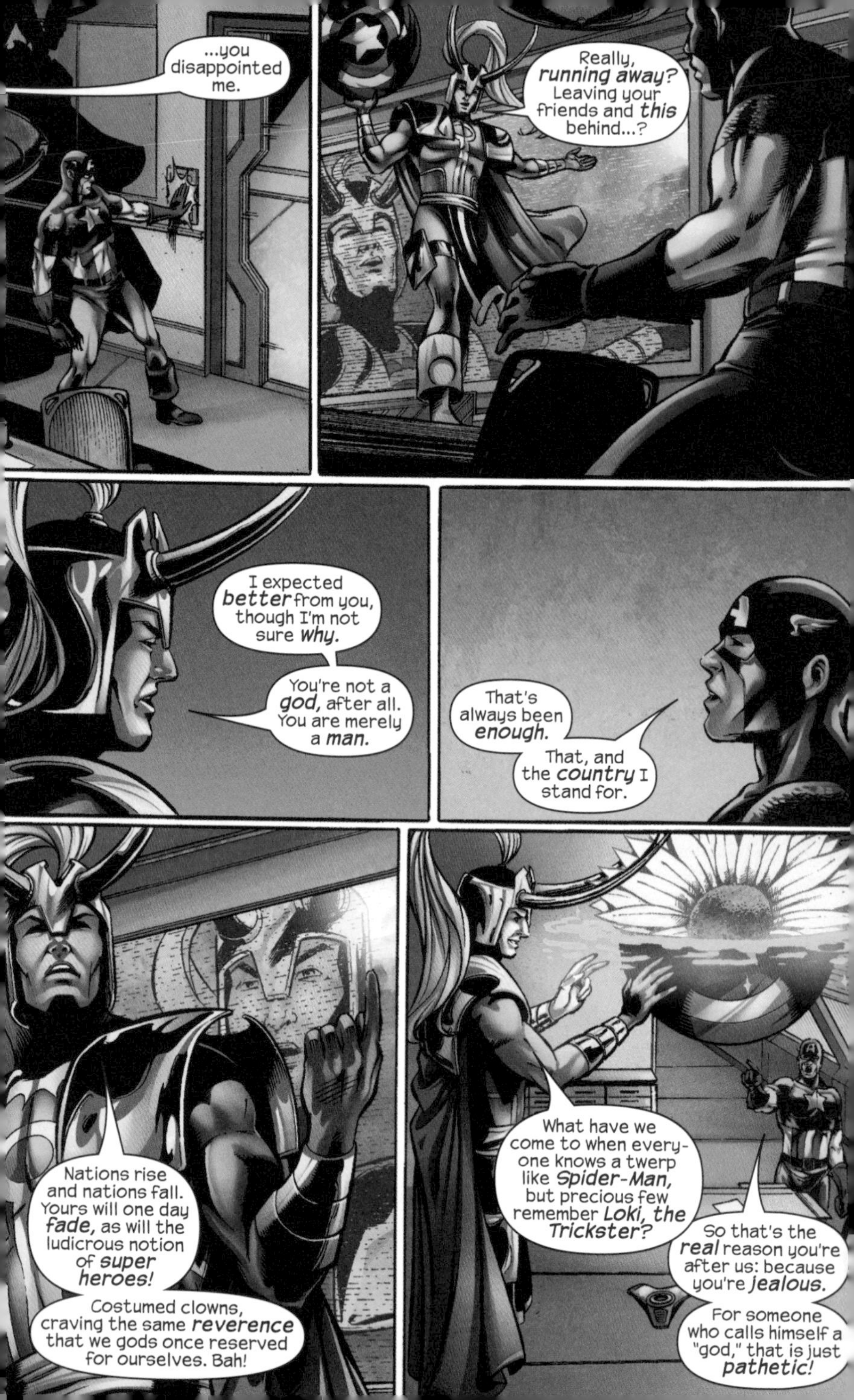
...you disappointed me.
Really, running away? Leaving your friends and this behind...?
I expected better from you, though I'm not sure why.
You're not a god, after all. You are merely a man.
That's always been enough.
That, and the country I stand for.
Nations rise and nations fall. Yours will one day fade, as will the ludicrous notion of super heroes!
Costumed clowns, craving the same reverence that we gods once reserved for ourselves. Bah!
What have we come to when every-one knows a twerp like Spider-Man, but precious few remember Loki, the Trickster?
So that's the real reason you're after us: because you're jealous.
For someone who calls himself a "god," that is just pathetic!

Perhaps I *am* a bit petty, but that is a secret you will take to your *grave*.

No, Loki. Take a real good look around you. Your secret is *out*.

Eh? What is that contraption?

It's a *camera*, Loki...

...*several* cameras, actually...

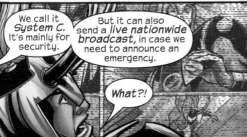

We call it *System C.* It's mainly for security.

But it can also send a *live nationwide broadcast,* in case we need to announce an emergency.

What?!

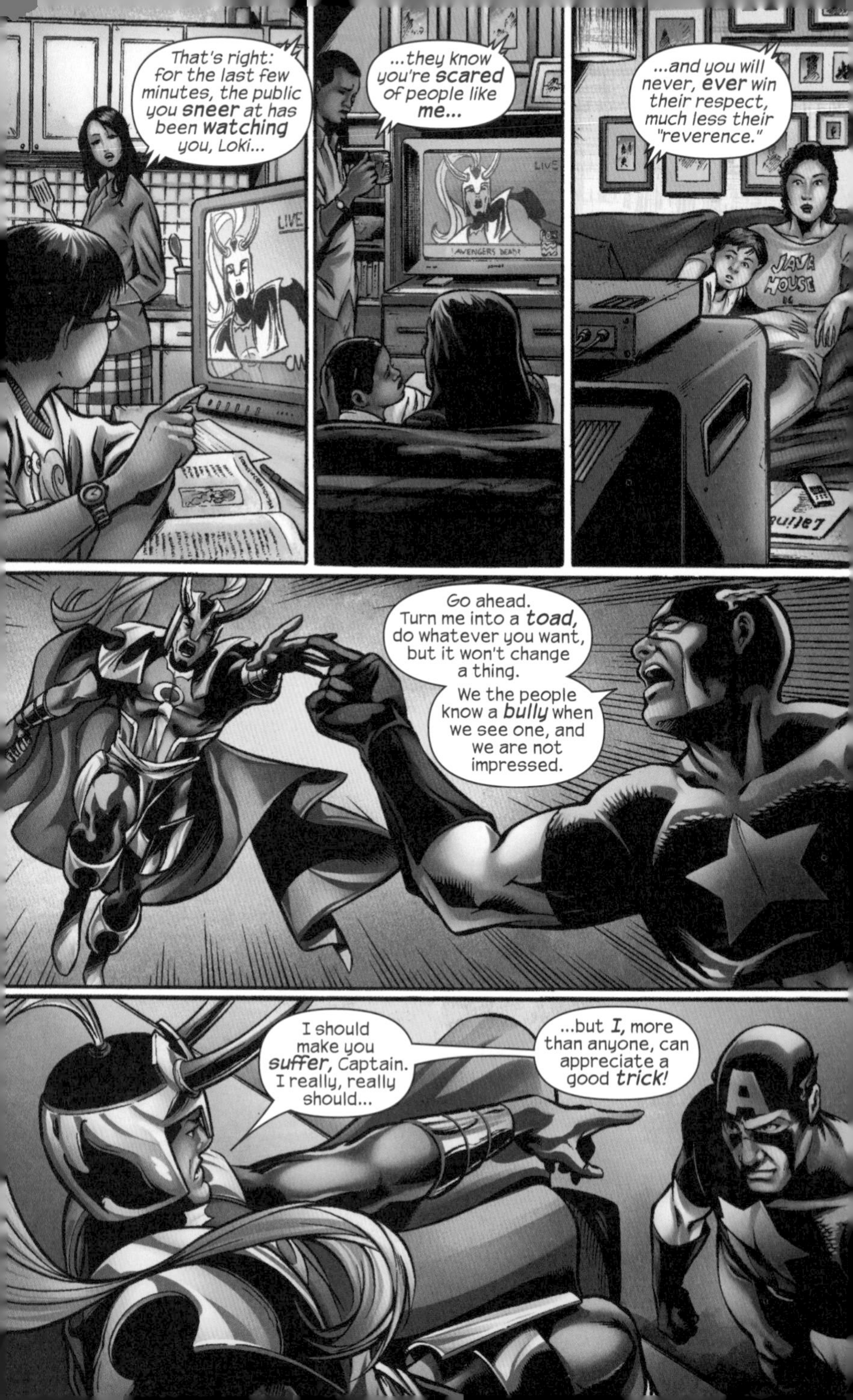
That's right: for the last few minutes, the public you sneer at has been watching you, Loki...
LIVE
...they know you're scared of people like me...
LIVE
AVENGERS DEAD?
...and you will never, ever win their respect, much less their "reverence."
JAVA HOUSE
Go ahead. Turn me into a toad, do whatever you want, but it won't change a thing.
We the people know a bully when we see one, and we are not impressed.
I should make you suffer, Captain. I really, really should...
...but I, more than anyone, can appreciate a good trick!

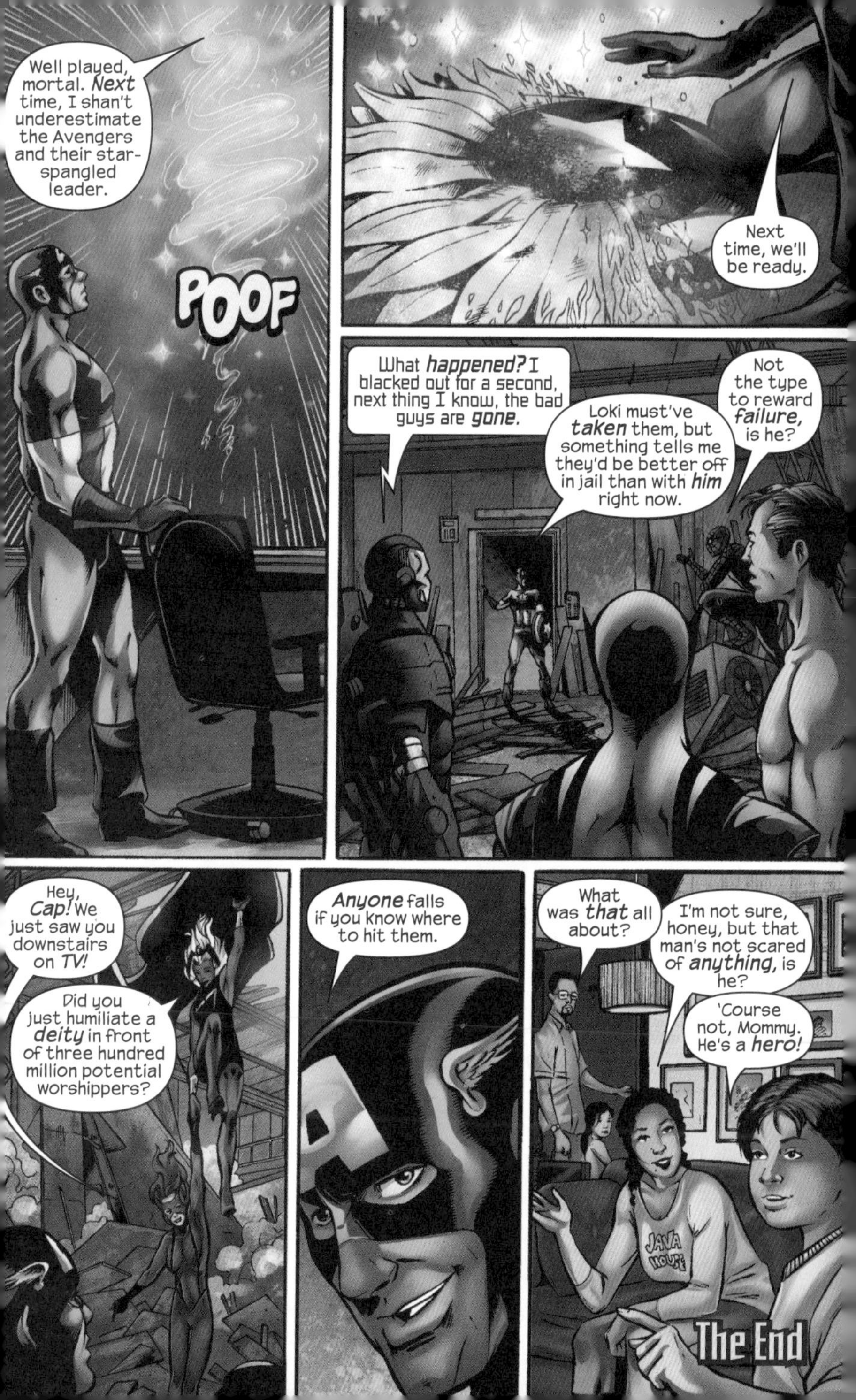
Well played, mortal. Next time, I shan't underestimate the Avengers and their star-spangled leader.
POOF
Next time, we'll be ready.
What happened? I blacked out for a second, next thing I know, the bad guys are gone.
Loki must've taken them, but something tells me they'd be better off in jail than with him right now.
Not the type to reward failure, is he?
Hey, Cap! We just saw you downstairs on TV!
Did you just humiliate a deity in front of three hundred million potential worshippers?
Anyone falls if you know where to hit them.
What was that all about?
I'm not sure, honey, but that man's not scared of anything, is he?
'Course not, Mommy. He's a hero!
JAVA HOUSE
The End